A BOAT
NAMED
BLIND FAITH

Norman Philip Jeddeloh

Printed in the United States of America
Hardcover ISBN: 978-1-959096-44-3
Paperback ISBN: 978-1-959096-45-0
Ebook ISBN: 978-1-959096-46-7

Canoe Tree Press

4697 Main Street
Manchester Center, VT 05255
Canoe Tree Press is a division of DartFrog Books

"Give me a spirit that on this life's rough sea
Loves t' have his sails filled with a listy wind
Even till his sail-yards tremble, his masts crack
And his rapt ship run on her side so low
That she drinks water, and her keel plows air."

—George Chapman,
The Conspiracy of Charles, Duke of Byron, *III, 1*

"One ship drives east and another drives west
With the selfsame winds that blow
'Tis the set of sails and not the gales
Which tells us the way to go."

— *Ella Wheeler Wilcox,*
The Winds of Fate

"If the Devil doesn't exist, but man has created him,
he has created him in his own image and likeness."

— *Fedor Dostoevski,*
The Brothers Karamazov, *V, 4*

Acknowledgements

I GRATEFULLY ACKNOWLEDGE THE wonderful advice and assistance of many friends in creating this work, especially my mentor, Duncan, my dear friends Larry, Mazen, Fran and Sue, Giancarlo, and others so ably serving as beta reviewers. My special thanks to my editor Natalie Tighman, who, through this work and her insightful, incisive critique, has taught me the craft. Finally, a tip of the hat to my crew the day that *Regalito* really did encounter *Blind Faith*.

NPJ

I

AT FIRST LIGHT ON the day they encountered *Blind Faith*, Lake Michigan was dark and troubled, the air clammy and inhospitable, the sky gray and foreboding. Despite these conditions, Frank and his crew were standing on the dock deciding whether to venture out for a sail.

"It's too risky," Frank said.

Marco shrugged, likely irritated by Frank's cautiousness. "It's gonna be fine."

"Fine? The marine forecast said high winds and fifty percent chance of rain by noon." A stiff gust blew in; Frank zipped up his windbreaker. It displayed the Harvard Sailing Club logo.

"It's already starting," Frank said. "This spells trouble."

"Oh come on, Frank. Don't be such a killjoy. Okay? That was just a little zephyr." Marco frowned. "Yesterday, you said it was going to be a perfect day for a sail. Those marine forecasts are worthless." Dressed only in a tee shirt and shorts, Marco propelled his six-foot-four frame into Frank's boat as if he had already decided to go out.

"That was yesterday. Remember, this is Lake Michigan, not a pond in your backyard." Frank did not move from the dock.

"Frank's got a point," Jeannie said. "When I was at Stanford, I went sailing a couple of times in the Pacific. It got very bumpy. We almost tipped over." Her long blond hair peaked out from her wool scarf.

"Well, we would be…" Frank began.

Marco interrupted. "No different from a ride at an amusement park. Come on. Don't worry. We won't go out for long."

Famous last words, Frank thought. Marco looked at Frank.

"Besides, what's a little wind?" Marco said. He smiled broadly. "Makes for a thrill, not like one of your boring excursions on a sunny, breezeless afternoon." He took the blue cover off the oversized wheel and sat down behind it.

"Can your boat take it, Frank?" Chris asked. "What's it called, *Provocateur?* Right?" *Provocateur* was Frank's thirty-five-foot sloop, a classic, trimmed in well-polished teak and mahogany, but Frank had it fitted with new mylar sails and state-of-the-art electronics.

"*Provocateur*'s made for a day like this. It's heavy and stable," Marco said. "And he keeps it in perfect condition," pointing to Frank "He's out here all of the time, polishing, painting, and fixing. Sort of obsessed."

"Something could always go wrong," Frank said.

"What for heaven's sake?" Marco put on his green and gold stocking cap and pulled it down over his head as another gust howled around his ears.

"Well, you never know…"

"Please Frank, I am so anxious to get back on the water I can taste it, what with my miserable year in New Mexico. Let's do it, what you say?"

"It's really up to Chris and Jeannie," Frank said. "This is supposed to be a reward for their hard work, not a gauntlet for the unwary." Chris and Jeannie were junior associates in Frank's law firm.

"They don't need to worry," Marco said. "I'll play captain. The boat'll dance through the waves. You'll see. All you guys need to do is sit there and savor the power of nature. Drink it in."

Marco crawled up from the cockpit to the deck and began to take the deep navy-blue sail cover off the boom. He looked down at the three others, still standing on the dock.

"Besides, I'm bored. Bored to the core. Really. I'm craving a little adventure before going back to my grind at the lab. Don't deprive me. You know what I mean?"

The sun emerged from between the clouds and briefly illuminated his face. The wind subsided a bit.

"See, there's a sign. Things are gonna be great." Marco grabbed the bag of provisions Frank had brought and extracted a bottle of champagne. Frank always made sure that there was a good bottle of wine or two to go along with a sail, and Marco knew it. Holding the bottle high in the air, he said, "Good stuff. Better open 'em now. Who knows what could happen later." He winked and gave a hearty laugh.

Frank frowned, seized the bottle from Marco's hand, and took the provisions below.

"So, I've never done this and I would love to try…" Chris said, staring intently at Marco, A little of his stomach protruded out where his 'Princeton Law' sweatshirt met his work-out shorts. "As long as you say it will be okay, Professor." His eyelashes fluttered. Chris seemed quite impressed by Marco and the idea of being on the same boat with a theoretical physicist. "Besides, it's okay right now." He climbed onboard.

"We're here, we might as well see what happens. Hopefully, the weather will improve," Jeannie said as she too climbed into the cockpit.

Frank found it hard to say 'no' to Marco when Marco wanted something badly enough. He had been like Marco's favorite older brother ever since Frank was a graduate assistant coach for Marco's high school softball team and became a regular at Marco's family gatherings. And he loved the debates on religion and philosophy they had every so often over a bottle of wine.

But he wondered if Chris and Jeannie really knew just how nasty and rough Lake Michigan could be. Their reactions were too blasé. Still, outnumbered and resigned to a miserable day on the lake, he disconnected the shore power cord, untied dock lines, and gave the boat a push out of the berth. As the boat powered out of the harbor, he had his fingers crossed.

★   ★   ★

As SOON AS THEY GOT a few miles off-shore, Frank's fears were realized. The wind kicked up and began blowing hard out of the northeast to thirty-five knots. Pretty soon, they were bouncing through six- to seven-foot waves. Frank trimmed the sails down to the minimum needed to keep moving forward, but the boat heeled over at about thirty degrees anyway. Everyone had to sit on the windward side of the boat to balance the power of the wind against the sails. And the brief moments of sunshine from when they left were replaced by a seamless cover of gray, ominous-looking clouds, darker than at daybreak.

Provocateur hit every wave hard, each time threatening to throw the crew around the cockpit like ragdolls and dousing them over and over with chilly spray. It gyrated violently, as the crest of each wave first lifted it up, then dropped it down, testing the capacity of the boat's deep keel to keep everything upright and moving. The sails flapped turbulently as they struggled to keep their shape while being cast about by the wind and jerked around by the rocking of the boat.

"This is way too brutal," Frank said. "Time to go back."

Marco ignored Frank's direction. Frank did not insist because he could see how happy Marco was. He was reluctant to deprive Marco of this potent antidote to his disappointing time in New Mexico. They sailed on.

"Awesome...don't you all agree?" Marco yelled from his stance behind the wheel, which he gripped with both hands and turned forcefully as he wrestled with the elements. Now wearing stained, well-used, foul weather gear complete with a musty old-fashioned southeaster' rain hat, he looked like crusty old Captain Ahab of *Moby Dick* fame.

"Couldn't wait to get out here. This is exactly what I wanted," Marco continued. "Hope you like this as much as I do, Chris? How about you, Jeannie? You like the ride?"

Jeannie labored to stay in her place on the cockpit bench as the boat jumped around.

"Well, this is worse than the Pacific but...well...well, it's, it's interesting." She shivered a little. "Tell me, Professor, is it always like this on Lake Michigan?"

"No, Jeannie, it is not," Frank interjected with pique in his voice. He kept himself from moving around by holding both his arms stretched out on the lifeline surrounding the cockpit. "This is anything but a typical day. Usually, when I come out, it is pleasant and peaceful. Blame Marco if you get seasick."

"Cummon, Frank, don't be an old fuddy-duddy. This sort of day is unique," Marco responded. "Navigating in conditions like this is just plain titillating. No other way to describe it. I love the sensation of staying one step ahead of disaster. Love it." Marco's knees flexed like shock absorbers to compensate for the violent motion of the boat.

"Maybe we should go in, Professor? This is getting scary," Chris said as he wiped the spray off his glasses. "The waves and the water look mean." Chris' face had turned ashen and his lips white.

"Nothing to be afraid of, Chris, but call me Marco. Don't want to toot my own horn, but as each wave hits, I instantly sense my next move just in time to keep good ol' *Provocateur* going forward and more or less stable. It's like a sixth sense."

"Well, okay, Professor, I mean Marco," Chris said. He sat, not moving, firmly lodged into the corner where the cabin bulkhead met the cockpit bench. There, he was relatively protected by the dodger awning covering the entrance to the cabin.

Marco turned the wheel hard over to prepare for the approach of a large wave.

"When did you learn to sail?" Jeannie asked.

"Learned right here on this boat when I was in college, right after Frank bought it. We both love the water." The boat hit the trough of a wave extra hard with an unnerving thump, making the dishes below shake.

"Whew, how can you like that, Marco?" Jeannie asked. "It's like the boat is going to break apart."

Marco spotted a monster wave headed directly for *Provocateur*.

"Hang on," he yelled as a wall of water engulfed the bow and charged back to the cockpit. Chris and Jeannie were more or less protected by the dodger, but the full force hit Frank and Marco, momentarily dousing them. As the water dripped from his nose, Marco yelled an emphatic "Yes!" as if he had just rolled the winning dice in a game of craps. He emitted a hearty laugh and kept steering the boat right into the waves, hoping for more.

"Enough," Frank said. "Head back, Marco. Jeannie and Chris are miserable." Frank had run out of patience to feed Marco's craving for danger and challenge.

FOR AS LONG AS Frank had known Marco, he had been this way, lusting after risk, speed, and peril. In high school and college, he had been a star football quarterback bringing finesse and intellect to the violent sport. In the off-season, he was an avid softball player and had gone to the state championship. He gave up competitive sports to focus on his first loves, physics and mathematics, as graduate school and its demands overtook him and deprived him of time to pursue non-essential pastimes. In school he also did well, earning his PhD from MIT and going on to a junior faculty research position at the Fermilab National Accelerator facility west of Chicago.

Marco often talked about his love for work in the lab, focusing on quantum physics and studying the properties of a ubiquitous subatomic particle called the neutrino using the large particle accelerator there. That device caused particles to collide at ultra-high-speed, breaking them up into their component parts so that they could be analyzed. All this had led him to a visiting professorship at the University of New Mexico in Santa Fe to collaborate with the theoretical physicists working there. Hence his year-long exile from the water and the waves and his insistence on taking *Provocateur* for a spin immediately upon his return, regardless of the conditions.

Frank also knew that Marco's life was unsettled as he approached his fortieth birthday. During their call the night before, Frank had asked Marco how his year in New Mexico had come out.

"Not well, not well at all," Marco had said. "My collaborations there were supposed to lead to data backing up my theories. Instead, all I got was more inconclusive results. Sad to say. I'd hoped to be able to publish a paper in a major journal. That would have gotten me on the road to tenure and promotion. Now I do not see that happening."

"Doesn't sound good."

"Yeah, nobody is going to think of me as a true theoretical physicist unless my ideas bear out in the real world. That means data."

"Are you sure you're not blowing this out of proportion?"

"No question my career is on the line. Without a good publication or two in my back pocket, I'm headed for the garbage heap of physicists. No options for employment, except maybe as a lab rat, carrying out experiments dreamed up by others…maybe teaching science to business majors at some junior college in Nowhereville, USA. God, what a miserable thought."

Marco paused as if he was considering what to say next. Then he gave out a slow, dolorous sigh. "All my year in New Mexico did was take me away from the city I love, no new data, no new ideas. Not a happy picture. Nope."

"Sounds like it's only a setback, not the ballgame," Frank responded. "I still have great confidence in your mind. You'll come through, I'm sure. What do they say at Fermilab?"

"Radio silence so far, but they can't be pleased. It's unclear what they will do, you know."

"Well, at least we can have a nice sail tomorrow and forget about the cares of the world," Frank replied, trying to end the conversation and get off the phone.

"Actually, Frank, I would say that the year was a total disaster," Marco continued. "Completely. New Mexico is a social wasteland and the women dull. Dull beyond measure. Really. I didn't meet a single interesting, sexy woman. None to be had. Right. Not one fun date. As for getting laid, forget it."

Again Marco paused. "You know, sometimes I wonder if there is something wrong with me. Just can't seem to find the right woman anywhere. Kind of a bummer. Could be I'm destined to live alone. Now there's a thought that really pains me."

Frank had heard Marco say something like that many times before. They talked about Marco's frustrations with his personal life every so often. Frank served as sort of Marco's father confessor in affairs of the heart. It had been a very long time since Marco was in love, real love, not just a passing fling.

On the surface, Frank found it hard to understand why Marco had not gotten what he was looking for. He was a swarthy Greek American with thick, curly, dark brown hair, a classic Mediterranean nose, and high gothic cheeks. He was tall with a muscular, well-proportioned body. He looked like a living version of one of those Greek god statues in a museum. Women flocked to him, but each time when a relationship would begin to turn serious, he ended it. He said there was no spark.

NOW THOUGH, MARCO MADE no mention of his troubles as he happily navigated the rough seas. He could have stayed out all day. "Oh, come on, Frank, just a couple of minutes more," Marco said in response to Frank's strong injunction to turn around. He continued to sail.

They were about seven miles offshore, heading further out, when, virtually out of nowhere, another sailboat appeared and approached, coming from the opposite direction but on the same tack. It was an older boat, not in terrible shape, but clearly past its prime. Its hull was painted a baby blue, now scratched, chalky, and faded. Its sails were yellow and stained, patched many times, barely serviceable. The boat's crew in all likelihood did not see *Provocateur* until they were very close since its approach would have been hidden by their fully extended sails, and it was plenty hazy and foggy to boot.

When *Provocateur* got even with them, about fifty feet distant, Frank, Marco, and the crew got a good look at the people on the other boat. There were three of them. Two were men dressed in what appeared to be flowing black robes. They wore pointed black hats with wide floppy brims, secured tightly to their heads with straps under their chins. The taller of the two, standing with the boat's tiller in one hand and holding on to the railing with the other, had a long scraggly beard, which had been shaped into two cones below the chin. A beer gut made a bump in the front of his robe. His face was ill-formed. He looked rough, unkempt, and crude. The other man, seated, had his back to *Provocateur* but was clearly hefty.

The third person was a beautiful twenty-something woman dressed only in a white bikini. On her head, she wore an object like a bridal crown with a veil extending to her shoulders. She was blond and trim, with a shapely body. Her angular visage was at once innocent and intelligent. Dimples graced her face on both sides of her mouth.

As *Provocateur* passed, Frank waved and yelled: "Ahoy, mates. Crazy to be out here today, don't you think?"

Frank's friendly gesture was not returned. The two men kept their eyes on the horizon as if *Provocateur* did not exist, although the pilot was scowling, perhaps unhappy to have come so close to another boat so far out at sea.

The girl reacted quite differently. From the instant she saw Marco, she fixated on him and froze, like in a trance. He was mesmerized as well. He thought, *Melissa,* as a sense of loss welled up inside him. He smiled, and she smiled in response. To Marco, it was a smile imbued with sadness, like she had just suffered a great tragedy.

As *Provocateur* passed, Frank saw the name of the boat, *Blind Faith,* with no port of call identified. These words were formed with individual, stick-on letters like ones from a hardware store, and they were not carefully applied. *Blind Faith* quickly faded from view and became almost like a ghost ship before it disappeared entirely in the waves and fog.

★   ★   ★

BACK ON PROVOCATEUR, MARCO'S mind went flying. *Oh my God. So much like Melissa. Her shape; her flowing blond hair; the provocative, slightly quirky way she was dressed; the lines and contour of her face; the whiteness of her skin. Even the dimples. Especially the dimples.* He couldn't believe what he had just seen. But it was not the right time to share that story with the rest of the crew.

"My God, what a knockout," he said instead. "What's she doing on that dump of a boat with those lowlifes? And the way they were dressed. Good Lord. She must have been freezing in that bikini. Weird. Gotta be a story there. Right."

Marco gave a sigh. "I'm going to turn around and catch up to them. Gotta find out what this is all about."

That idea did not sit well with the others. Jeannie, obviously still trying hard to sound upbeat and polite despite the conditions, said, "Gosh, I'm having a good time out here, but I really do need to get back for a very hot date tonight if you don't mind." She forced a tight-lipped smile.

Chris cringed. "Yeah, I need to get home too." By now he was sitting in the cockpit with an eye for how he could heave over the side if he had to.

Frank shook his head. "Marco, we all have better things to do than chase after some strange people in a beat-up old boat. We need to go in... not later, now." His eyes sent a dagger aimed at Marco. "No more excuses."

"Okay, okay. Got the message." Marco was more than a little annoyed with the prospect of returning to the harbor and letting the girl get away, but Frank's face told Marco he had made up his mind. There was no use quarreling. He looked down at the instruments to get a reading for the return.

"Oh my God, our instruments have gone out. That seals it. We've got to go back. No chasing after our dazzling beauty. I hope she'll be okay."

Marco turned the wheel sharply over, yelling as if he was a crusty old salt, "Helm's a lee."

The boat reversed course, and the sails flapped leeward with a snap as the crew moved to the other side of the cockpit. Frank suggested that they douse the sails and motor back, arguing it would be faster. He said it was past time to get back and uncork the champagne. Marco would not hear of it.

"No, Frank, you can't deprive me of my sailing time. Nope, not on a great day like today. Anyway, we are going at a pretty good clip with only the sails. Motor's not going to be any faster. To boot, it's noisy. It will drown out the sweet music of the wind and the waves, so beautiful to hear."

Marco continued to sail.

It took more than two hours to get back because they were so far offshore. But back they went, bouncing and chucking in the waves and the wind.

★   ★   ★

As THEY BEGAN TO approach the mouth of the harbor, even Marco anxiously anticipated the calm and peace awaiting them there. He pointed the boat into the wind so the sails would slide easily down the mast and the forward shroud with no resistance from the wind. Then, on Marco's command, Frank released the lines holding up the sails. But as it settled toward the deck, the forward sail and its raising line got all tangled up by the action of the wind and the motion of the boat. Worse, the line for the mainsail was yanked off its winch in the cockpit, then wrapped itself loosely around the mast.

Not a big deal, Marco thought. They were going to motor into the harbor anyway now that they were so close. No need for the sails.

Marco switched on the ignition as he pushed the start button. Dead silence. He pushed the button again and then again. Still nothing. The starter did not engage and the motor would not turn over. This left *Provocateur* powerless in heavy seas, being thrust leeward by a gale force breeze, catapulting it directly toward the massive, craggy rocks lining Chicago's coastline. There was nary another boat in sight to help. The shoreline loomed larger and larger as they were being blown toward it, appearing increasingly ominous in the gray, dreary, late-afternoon light. Marco's estimate placed the boat only about three to five minutes away from being tossed on those rocks and turned into so many fiberglass toothpicks, leaving them thrashing around in the water like helpless sea urchins.

"Holy shit, we're in trouble," Frank yelled. "We've got to get the sails back up. What happened to the mainsail raising line? It's not on its winch."

Marco responded calmly as if he was having a chat with a neighbor about a good book. "Relax, Frank, just relax, okay? The line flew off when the sails came down, and now it got itself fouled around the foot of the mast. No big deal. I'll go up and get it. Here, come and drive."

Frank quickly grabbed the wheel. Marco was sure that Frank was happy to stay in the cockpit and steer. Considering how the boat was bouncing and wheeling around, it was quite risky to leave the relative safety of the cockpit and go to the mast. Marco trusted his own natural strength and agility much more than Frank's, and Frank's associates, by then, were useless. They sat there petrified, silent, incapable of anything but hanging on for dear life.

As soon as Frank was behind the wheel, Marco headed toward the mast. Frank exhorted him to get a life vest or tie-line before he left the cockpit.

"Out of time for that," Marco said. "We're too close to the rocks to dally. Just need to be very careful. Wish me luck." Secretly, Marco was excited to confront the danger unrestrained by safety equipment.

Frank and the crew kept their eyes glued on Marco as he climbed out on the gyrating upper deck and began to crawl on all fours toward the mast. Mindful of the peril, Marco steadied himself by very consciously grabbing rigging and rails as he went. Still, it was like riding an angry, bucking bull. The wrong bounce and Marco would be thrown into the swirling water with no hope of rescue.

"Watch out, Marco, here comes another killer wave," Frank yelled when Marco was halfway to the mast. It hit Marco directly and caused him to lose his grip. He began to slide over the side headed for the water.

"God no," Jeannie screamed.

But a second before he went overboard, he was able to grab one of the guard poles along the deck rail and then slowly pull himself back to the deck. He sat down briefly to steady himself. Looking back at the crew, he flashed a toothy smile that said, "No big deal."

Marco continued his crawl to the mast. When he got there, he hollered at Frank, straining to make himself heard over the din generated by the bellowing wind and crushing waves.

"Point 'er into the wind, Frank; I'll raise the main here by hand."

"Can't..." Frank replied, also yelling at the top of his lungs. "the boat's sliding sideways, not moving forward. It's stalled in the water. Can't do anything. Wheel's useless."

Oh God, Marco thought, *It'll be a fight to get the sail back up. Hope I can do this.*

Marco grabbed the mainsail line and began to pull. At first, he got part of the sail back up the mast, but the wind held it hard and firm, jamming against the rigging so that it could not be raised more than a few feet. That was not enough to give any forward momentum to the heavy boat. Marco had no choice but to keep trying. Each time the wind subsided a touch, he was able to pull up a little more of the sail, still not enough. At the same time, from the corner of his eye, he watched the rocks grow larger and larger as the boat catapulted toward them. Finally, as they came perilously close to destruction, the wind relented long enough for one last monumental pull. Energized by nothing but the strength of his will, Marco got enough of the sail in the air to give the boat at least some power and forward momentum.

"We're moving," Frank yelled. "I can steer."

As soon as the boat got a little speed, he pointed the boat away from the rocks and into the wind. Then, freed from entrapment in the rigging, the rest of the mainsail easily finished its crawl to the top of the mast. Sail power restored, they were underway, moving slowly, but out into the lake and away from the rocks.

Marco returned to the cockpit as carefully and deliberately as he had crawled to the mast and took the wheel from Frank. "Whew. That was close. For a second, ya know, I was a little scared."

Frank furrowed his brow. "We're not out of the woods yet," he said. "We've got to get in somehow. I don't want to be out here at night with no motor and no lights. Maybe I can get the motor started."

Frank went below and threw open the engine room door. Nothing seemed out of order, no loose wires, no smoke, no belts off, just a motor that would not start. *No easy fix to get this tub back in the harbor and tied down. Time to call for help,* so he went over to the marine radio and switched it on. It was dead. He ran back up on deck. Marco was managing to keep the boat more or less under control, but they were now way downwind from the safety and calm of the harbor with no chance of getting back without tacking for hours in dark and stormy seas. And then, once they could get back to the harbor, there would be no good way to get the disabled vessel to its spot.

Jeannie, having recovered some of her composure, asked, "Anyone got a cell phone? Unfortunately, I left mine at home."

"I never bring those nasty things out here," Marco said. "They are way too much of an intrusion into the beauty of nature."

"Same with me," Frank added. "The boat's got a radio, that's usually enough. What about you, Chris?"

"My roommate told me not to bring anything I didn't want to lose."

Just at that moment, they heard the radio crackle as it sprang back to life. Marco yelled that the instruments had powered up. He pushed the engine start button again, and it fired up like the dependable iron beast it had always been. Frank released the mainsail, and they bounced back into the harbor under motor power. They got to Frank's mooring, tied up the boat, and drank the champagne followed by several chasers of Green Spot Irish whiskey. They recounted the events of the harrowing and freakish afternoon, now that they were safe and basking in the warm glow of a friendly alcohol buzz.

"I WANT TO PROPOSE a toast," Chris said as he smiled and eyed Marco. Although he had thick black hair and stylish close-trimmed beard, he was not a good-looking young man, His talent was words.

"To our professor and captain. He saved our lives. Our hero. Today, we witnessed a dazzling display of physical prowess, mental discipline, and calm determination. I speak for each of us when I say that we are all deeply and profoundly indebted to you for what you did, Professor. Raise your glasses in toast."

Everyone said, "Here, here," touched their plastic glasses together, and took a sip of the fine French wine Frank brought.

Marco cleared his throat, getting ready to make a little speech himself, when Jeannie interrupted him. Her urgency to get home, apparently invented for the moment, was no more, probably forgotten once she heard the pop of the champagne cork.

"It was a remarkable day; but the motor…it acted so strangely, first refusing to start, then easily turning over as if nothing was wrong. What in heaven's name caused that?"

"Good question," Frank said. "With all of that bouncing around, some connection may have gotten loose somewhere in the main electrical circuit but jolted back. Could be it was a loose clamp on the cable from the battery. Who knows. It could have been anything."

"Sounds complicated," Chris said.

"Sounds mysterious," Jeannie said.

"It's both," Frank said. "Older boats like this are quirky. They're like a classic British sports car, stylish but prone to breakdown, usually at the wrong time. And there are more things to go wrong on a boat like this than protons in the universe."

That bad reference to the quantum particles he studied seemed designed to please Marco, but he managed nothing more than a thin, indifferent smile. He was preoccupied by the girl in the white bikini, not by the motor's quirky behavior. She was all he could think about.

"Talk about mysterious, Marco. We saw how you reacted to that woman," Jeannie said, scratching her head and staring at Marco as if confused.

Marco's voice became soft and sweet. He smiled just a little. "You know, she was so different from the other two. Didn't seem to belong, oh no. She was elegant, innocent, and pure, almost virginal. Maybe she was trapped on that boat, held prisoner by those perverts. God. Horrible thought, really horrible."

By now, Marco was a little high from the drinks. He was almost slurring his words. Frank started to speak, maybe to change the subject and get Marco's mind off the subject of this woman. Before he could, Marco continued.

"When I saw her, I felt a bolt of energy surge through me. It was like a shiver but warm and pleasant. Powerful, right. I couldn't take my eyes off her. No way. Almost like I could peer inside her through her sweet eyes."

Marco sighed, then paused and looked away, as he dwelt upon the encounter in his thoughts.

"When the boats started to move apart, our eyes remained fixed. Like a scene from one of those old, World War II tearjerkers. You've seen them. One with the pretty girl standing on the platform, gazing longingly at her handsome soldier boy, you know. While he's peering at her sadly from the window of the train taking him off to war."

Marco could hardly stay in his skin. "God, she was so incredibly beautiful."

Frank and the two associates sat silent, unmoving, as if stunned by the intensity of Marco's unexpected, evocative, personal declaration.

"Sorry, guys," Marco added. "I guess I got carried away, ya know. Forgive me." Another awkward silence followed.

"Professor," Jeannie began, "I mean Marco, it sounds almost like something I saw on a PBS documentary the other day about quantum entanglement."

Chris asked what quantum entanglement is, giving Marco the opening to lecture and to get the conversation back to neutral territory.

"Careful, Marco, please, no lectures today," Frank joked before Marco could speak.

"As I recall," Jeannie said, "Subatomic particles, things called quarks and protons, somehow interact despite being great distances apart. Supposedly, they do it instantly, communicating at many times the speed of light. They said on the program that Einstein called it 'spooky action at a distance.'"

"Astounding," Chris said.

"What is incredible is that this occurrence has been confirmed over and over in experiments," Jeannie continued. "Originally, scientists thought that this phenomenon only applied to the smallest of subatomic particles, but now they think it can occur in larger structures like bacteria. So the idea is that a collection of particles in several different objects can become interconnected--hence the word 'entanglement.'"

"Did I get that right, Professor?" Jeannie looked intently at Marco with her bright green eyes.

Again, before Marco could answer, she went on. "I thought about that TV show when I heard you speak. It sounds like you are saying that something like action at a distance happened when you saw that woman."

"Well, Jeannie," Marco replied, "as a physicist myself, I would not draw that analogy, right, although I have seen books in the popular press, which talk about quantum entanglement in the context of human physical attraction..."

"Maybe what happened is something like mental telepathy," Chris interjected before Marco could finish. "I read an article in *Psychology Today* about that, some sort of direct brain-to-brain communication. Experiments indicate that can occur over very great distances. And what about dogs who find their masters despite them moving thousands of miles away? That's got to be telepathic. How else can it be explained?"

This comment peeved Marco, still basking in the afterglow of what had been for him an otherworldly, mystical experience. He felt put down by these two brash junior attorneys who, in his mind, were being insensitive to the beauty of what he had just experienced. He especially didn't like being compared with a dog. He felt compelled to put these two youngsters in their place. To him it was quite irrelevant that he had just met them.

"Hey folks, what's going on?" He raised his hands as if to emphasize his irritation. "When I told you about the connection I felt with that woman, you know, I really didn't expect to be analyzed as if I am a lab animal. Come on now. Trying to squeeze my experience into some scientific pigeon-hole robs it of all of its beauty. Don't do that."

Marco realized that he had again said too much too brusquely. When he continued, it was in a much softer tone. "Sorry, I don't know what just got into me, especially in front of you, Chris and Jeannie."

"Maybe the alcohol at work, " Frank said.

"No, it's not the alcohol." Marco shook his head. "I don't appreciate analyzing my feelings out of existence. What happened to me was profound, like, uh, magic. Sometimes there are no explanations for things like this. Could we please leave it at that?"

With these words, the party broke up and everyone went their separate ways, relieved that a disaster on the water had been averted and happy to disengage from what had become an uncomfortable exchange in the harbor. The encounter with *Blind Faith* had given the crew that day a great story for cocktail party conversations. That was the extent of the experience for everyone, except for Marco.

II

Marco was exhausted emotionally and physically by the time he got back to his car. The excitement of the day combined with the alcohol had worn him out. He was astonished to find Jeannie standing by his car, waiting for him.

"Professor, I'm sorry, Marco, uh, I waited to apologize for upsetting you. So I want to see if I can, kind of, make amends by asking you over to my apartment for a glass of wine. I live pretty close by."

Marco studied her for a second and considered the invitation. *No 'very hot date,' I guess.* As a shapely, tall blond, Jeannie was Marco's type. *She is pretty sexy and good looking,* he thought. Having some wine with her could be fun, and, besides, he hated the idea of going back to his house all alone that early in the evening. He agreed.

Before long they were sitting on the couch in Jeannie's upscale but sparsely furnished apartment, drinking cheap Chianti. As the evening progressed, Jeannie inched closer and closer to Marco, eventually almost touching his leg with her hand. There was no question in Marco's mind that Jeannie wanted to connect more intimately, and, after his year in New Mexico, he was ready. As she steered the conversation towards more personal subjects, her voice became sweeter, softer, and her frequent smiles more seductive.

Jeannie told Marco about her unremarkable, sheltered childhood growing up in rural Vermont. Her parents were professors at a small liberal arts college and valued intellectual prowess over money and possessions. She spent her high school years dreaming of a career as a swashbuckling trial lawyer, trying big cases, but married to a handsome professor at a big-time university.

Marco thought, *Okay, so that's why I'm here.*

"Marco," Jeannie said after they had talked for a while, "I really do hope you don't mind, but I have a bit of a personal question. You don't need to answer, but I hope you will." She looked him squarely in the eye and held her gaze like she was sizing up a witness at a deposition.

"Tell me, why aren't you married?"

Jeannie's bluntness and audacity startled Marco. The question was so direct and lawyerly like, much different from her tone a minute before. *Frank has taught her well,* he thought.

But then Jeannie slipped back into her coquettish voice. "You are, uh, handsome, brave, and, for sure, really smart. You know, it was incredibly amazing how relaxed you were when we were going to crash into the rocks. You acted as if it was nothing more than a walk in the park. I can't believe that some woman hasn't already grabbed you up. You're a great catch."

God, spoken like a starry-eyed schoolgirl nurturing a crush, Marco thought.

"Jeannie, to answer your question, I am pretty picky about women. I remember what Frank said to me one day."

"'Marco,' Frank said, 'what you need is someone who is smart enough to match your wit but sexy enough to scratch your itch.'" Marco stopped speaking for a minute, recollecting the conversation.

"These words stuck in my mind. They are catchy and describe me to a *T*. Frank has a way of saying things, don't you think?"

"I see him in action every day." Jeannie smiled like she knew.

"But he's usually also right. No doubt about it. I love beautiful women, but they must also be very intelligent, right? No reason to mince words. A clingy, dependent woman without a brain is an immense turn off. Immense. Doesn't matter how beautiful she is."

"Oh," Jeannie said with a noticeable lift of her left eyebrow.

"You are also right about something else, Jeannie. Women are attracted to me, ya know. No use to deny it. Not everyone, I've had some disappointments, but also opportunities aplenty." Marco grinned a little as images of his past affairs flashed in his mind. "Maybe too many. But so far, I've been in love only once."

"That definitely surprises me, Marco. What about her?"

Marco was always willing to talk about his love for Melissa, particularly today because the woman on the boat looked so much like her. She was fresh in his mind.

Marco looked past Jeanie as he spoke. "Yup, I was in desperate love with my high school sweetheart. She was blond and beautiful, an all-state gymnast and national merit finalist. Blue eyes, a terrific body, and knew how to use it. Get the drift? Totally perfect as far as I was concerned. Really. I was ready to tie the knot, ready as anyone could be." Marco's eyes teared up.

"What about her, did she feel the same?"

Marco was silent for a moment as if trying to compose himself. "That was a bit of a problem, you know," he said, shaking his head. "No question she liked spending time with me, but I was always unsure about how deeply she cared. Never would tell me she loved me. Well, only once she said that. I wasn't sure she meant it or was only trying to be nice."

"What happened to her?"

"She decided to go after her first desire, a career in South America. I was devastated. Not only did I love her a lot, but I had a hard time handling the rejection. I couldn't understand how a thoughtful, good-looking woman could turn me over to go and work in some god-awful third world country. No woman had ever told me 'no' before."

The corners of Marco's lips turned down and his head dropped.

"I got pretty depressed. Didn't want to see anyone, talk with anybody. I spent years longing for her, writing to her, pleading with her to return. Then her letters became less frequent. Eventually we lost touch. I think it was her who just didn't answer my last letter. But I remembered her passionately for a long time."

"Past tense? Is she finally out of your mind?" Jeannie asked.

"Tried to contact her about a year ago. You know, after I came across some of our old letters. I discovered that she had been killed in a crossfire between street gangs in El Salvador. She was there on some kind of UN peacekeeping mission or something. I cried for an hour after I read the newspaper clip I found. I still miss her so." A tear ran down Marco's cheek. He brushed it away.

"Sad story, Marco." Jeannie put her hand gently on his knee.

"Yes, but today it was like she had, uh, well, I guess you would say, returned. The woman on the boat looked like her in so many ways, right down to her dimples. Seeing her rekindled feelings I thought were long gone, you know. Today, I fell in love with Melissa all over again."

"No wonder you were all worked up over that woman. I couldn't figure out what got you so excited. Didn't make sense."

"Yeah, it's not since Melissa that I have connected with a woman with the right combination of intellect and sex appeal Frank was referring to. I've found no one even close. That's why I'm still not married. Yep, definitely looking for the new Melissa, but so far no luck."

Jeannie took her hand off Marco's knee and edged away. A matter-of-fact tone returned to her voice. She sounded a little irritated and definitely disappointed.

"Hard to compete with a fantasy, Marco."

"Come on, Jeannie, that's harsh. You asked a question and I answered it." Now Marco was upset, and, as usual, when he was angry, he got very blunt very fast. "Maybe you're angry because I threw cold water on your little fantasy. What gives? When I came over, I knew you were interested, but this is no way to show it."

Jeannie furrowed her brow. "Hey, Marco, you are the one being unfair," she said, not looking at him. "You make it sound like I'm trying to chase after you. Just so you know, that's not going to happen. You can put that in the bank."

Marco saw the situation going from bad to worse, and he did not want to further offend one of Frank's star associates. *Time to beat a hasty retreat,* he thought.

"Jeannie, You are a very nice person," he said. "You really are. It's been good getting to know you. I mean that. And to boot, I appreciate your compliments. Don't doubt that. But I'm in a strange place right now."

"No kidding."

"It's probably best if I leave. Hopefully, I will see you on Frank's boat again."

"Maybe," Jeannie said coldly as she stood up to escort Marco to the apartment door.

As Marco drove home, all the way he longed for Melissa. He thought back over all those good times he had with her. The night they spent at Great America with the senior class, so what if it was rainy and cold. *I was with her.* The picnics on the beach. Senior prom. She was so beautiful in her low-cut blue silk formal. Her eyes gleamed and, goodness, those dimples. His body still throbbed when he thought of those dimples. *My God, so intoxicating. Like no others.* He loved to brush his cheeks against them, to kiss them with his tongue. *Why did she go, why?*

From that moment, Marco knew he had to meet the woman from *Blind Faith.* It was almost as if Melissa really had returned. He decided he would contact Frank to strategize. Frank was very good at finding solutions to difficult problems.

III

WHEN MARCO CAME TO visit the next afternoon, Frank was at the harbor on *Provocateur*. The weather had cleared, and it was a warm, sunny day, typical of Chicago summers and ideal for spending time on a boat. When Frank had free time, he was usually out there. Today, he was installing a new Bimini awning over the cockpit and using the cloudless day to catch some sun. He had his shirt off, showing his well-developed chest and abs. Although he spent most of his time in the office or in court, he was in great shape for a guy in his later forties. His thick salt and pepper hair was combed back, giving him a dashing, Roaring Twenties look.

As soon as Marco got to the dock, Frank put down his tools, smiled, and waved Marco on board.

"Busy, Frank?" Marco asked.

"Nope, just finishing. Perfect timing, my friend. Come on board and sit down," Frank said. "Let me pour you a cup of coffee. I've got some home brew here in my thermos."

"That was quite an experience yesterday," Marco said.

Frank smiled. "Good to be alive after that."

Marco nodded in agreement.

"What really bothers me most is what happened with the motor," Frank said. "I checked out everything earlier today, every system, every cable, every fitting. I couldn't find anything wrong. Nothing."

"Curious," Marco said. "Sure was a problem yesterday."

"Yeah, and it could do the same thing again, again at the wrong time. That's the real worry. I even had Chip come by. You know, that marine electrician I use sometimes."

"You introduced me to him once. Seems like a very thorough guy."

"Here's what has me flummoxed. He said that the electronics on *Provocateur* were actually in far better condition than most boats its age, as good as much newer vessels. Absolutely no problems." Frank grimaced. "He ended up charging me five hundred dollars and for that I got nothing."

"Ooooh, that hurts."

"Here's the bottom line. It appears there is no physical cause for what happened yesterday."

Frank took a large swig of coffee as he thought. "Maybe those lowlifes put a hex on us. Maybe they were some sort of Devil worshipers or witches."

"Oh good Lord..." Marco began.

But Frank continued. "I can't imagine why. Maybe we got too close, invaded their space or something like that. They sure did look pretty angry about something."

Marco shook his head. "That's crazy talk, plain crazy. You don't actually believe that, do you?"

"Come on Marco, it's not at all crazy. There doesn't seem to be any other way to explain it. I'm sure you have read stories about people who claim to be witches. I certainly have. Some of them are pretty grizzly and a few quite believable." There was annoyance in Frank's voice.

"Well, maybe, but these people do not have any kind of extraordinary power. Hexes and curses are the stuff of dark fairy tales, not the real world." Marco took off his shirt to get some sun himself. It was beginning to get hot, and no wind.

"I know, I know, but still..."

"Anyway, I doubt those people were warlocks or witches. Didn't fit the stereotype. What would they be doing in a sailboat on Lake

Michigan in the middle of the afternoon? Witches set around black pots at midnight chanting, at least that's the image. Remember *Macbeth*?"

"What about the way they were dressed?"

"Maybe they like to dress up like that to rattle people like us." Marco took another sip of coffee, wanting to end the conversation. "Obviously they succeeded."

"So, explain to me why the electronics stopped functioning and then came back to life?"

It seemed like a rhetorical question, but Marco answered anyway.

"No doubt that was out of the ordinary. Still, I am sure, if we dig into it deeply enough, we would find some physical cause. Know what I am saying? It would not be the first time in recorded history…"

Frank gestured "stop" with the palm of his hand. "Please, not another lecture about the mystery of gravity or the actions of subatomic particles." He moved under the brand-new Bimini to get away from the sun which, by now, was burning him a little.

"Okay, but here's my point: Magic…no. Facts hidden from our understanding…definitely. For everything, there's a rational explanation." Marco moved his hands like an umpire calling "safe." "Everything," he said emphatically.

"Marco, I don't see how you could say this after our discussion yesterday about your attraction to that woman. All you could talk about is how otherworldly it was. You wouldn't hear about logic then. It sounded like you were saying that some things can't be reduced to an equation."

"You must have misunderstood me, Frank. Clinically that woman and I communicated with our eyes and our bodies over a distance, utilizing ancient, likely primordial, forms of ordinary expression. No magic there. Only science." Marco finished his coffee, then looked out into the harbor, again wanting to find a way to end the conversation.

"Then why did you get so upset with Chris and Jeannie? You rattled them. I could tell."

"What annoyed me was that your still wet-behind-the-ears associates ignored, discounted is a better word, the magnificent beauty of my romantic interlude. They wanted to reduce it to some sort of scientific phenomenon. Very exasperating." Marco ran his hand through his hair.

"Okay, but your oversized reaction ended up unnecessarily causing an awkward scene."

"Sorry, Frank, I really do apologize. I concede I shouldn't have blurted out what I did. I also shouldn't have gotten so testy. Understand what you are saying. I do."

Frank started to speak, "Well…"

"On the other hand," Marco said, "Once I crossed that threshold, they should have kept their mouths shut and respected what I had expressed for the beauty of it. To me, they were the ones out of line. Don't you agree?"

Frank looked at Marco for a moment. "So no otherworldly experience yesterday?"

"Call it what you want. I am not sure what you mean when you use the word 'otherworldly.' This I will say." Marco smiled a Devilish smile. "There was a haunting out there yesterday, no question. That woman haunted me."

"Sounds otherworldly to me." Frank shrugged as if confused.

"Not otherworldly but still a haunting. Since I saw her, I cannot stop thinking about her, so innocent, so beautiful. She was the first thing on my mind when I woke up and the last when I fell asleep. I fear that she is in danger, maybe mortal danger. I've got to find her. Help her if I can. You with me, Frank?"

The thought that she may be in trouble and in need of him excited Marco.

Then Marco added, somewhat sheepishly, "And she reminds me so much of Melissa I wanted to cry. All I could think about was Melissa and her tragic death."

"Oh, so that's it. Now I got it." Frank screwed the cap on the now-empty thermos and threw it into his duffle bag. He was silent for a moment.

"Here's some free advice. Don't let that coincidence get you carried away. I wouldn't go fooling around with those people."

"Yes, but…"

"You saw them. They were pretty outrageous looking and who knows what they were about. You could get yourself right in the middle of a very touchy situation. Don't go chasing after her. Need I say it? She is not Melissa. For Christ's sake, get that woman out of your head. Don't feed your fantasy with an illusion."

Marco frowned and put his shirt back on, ready to leave. "Oh, come on now, Frank. As always, I appreciate your concern, but what could these people possibly do? Right. Can't imagine why they would be that upset because I wanted to meet the woman. That's no big deal, you know."

"Even then, Marco, how do you plan on finding her?"

Marco stood up and peered down at Frank still sitting in the cockpit.

"Easy. All I need to do is locate the boat. If I can do that, chances are I can find her."

"Maybe true. But that doesn't come close to answering my question. Lake Michigan is immense with so many nooks and crannies where you could stick a small boat like that. It could have gone anywhere."

Frank too stood up.

"And you don't have much to go on." Frank shook his head as he spoke. "All you know is the name of the boat. My intuition says there are more boats named '*Blind Faith*' floating around. You don't know its home port, either. We didn't even notice the direction they headed after we saw them."

"Don't know how I will find her, but I've got nothing better to do until school starts in September and a very big itch to scratch. Investigating curious forces and hidden phenomena is what I do for a living, don't you know? If that boat is out there, I will find it. Wait and see." Marco turned to jump off the boat.

"Well, good luck... I guess. I think you are embarking on a fool's errand; but I'm done trying to save you from your obsession."

★   ★   ★

THE NEXT DAY, MARCO began his quest for *Blind Faith*. It was organized and systematic. First he checked boat registration information in the states of Illinois, Wisconsin, and Michigan. No luck. Then he called harbormasters and marinas in each harbor all around the lower part of the lake, starting in Wisconsin. He told the people he talked to that he was looking for the owner of a Gucci windbreaker he had retrieved in bad weather, and he was sure the owner would want it back. Still nothing.

With each call, he became more depressed and desperate. *Maybe Blind Faith was just a phantom,* he thought. Marco began to think that he was not chasing a real live person, but a specter, his own self-created fantasy of a sublime damsel in distress. He knew himself well enough to realize that his desires could play games on his mind. In this case, the lust was definitely there.

But he plugged along, making his calls, until he got to St Joseph, Michigan, where the St. Joseph River is broad and deep, emptying into the lake. He called the harbor master there and repeated his speech about the windbreaker.

"I do remember seeing a boat like that once or twice as it headed out on the lake from upstream," the master responded. "It was an older boat with a blue hull, I think. Odd because the crew was always dressed sort of bizarre as if they were going to a funeral or some such. I could never figure it out, but around here there's a lot of strange people and stranger habits. The only time they ever seemed to go out was when the sky was gray and a north or northeast wind was blowing hard, whipping up the waves. They always seemed to come back just fine, though, even after being out all day, so I think they was very good sailors."

On hearing this, Marco was ecstatic. He was sure that now he could locate *Blind Faith* and, with any luck, from there connect with the woman. His body quivered with the thought of meeting her in person and bedding her down, maybe getting to know her and make real love. Once again Marco's fantasies took over. Even though he was now approaching midlife, his libido still ruled over his reason more often than not.

"How can I find that boat?" Marco asked the harbormaster, trying hard not to sound giddy.

"I don't know if I can tell you. I don't want to invade nobody's privacy nor nothin' like that."

"Oh come on, sir. I only want to return this windbreaker to them. Nothing more." Marco knew that was a little fib, but so what if it meant getting to the woman?

"Well, okay. It's sort of obvious anyway. Rent a powerboat and drive it up the river. There are only two more bridges after the harbor swinging bridge, which can open to allow a boat with a mast to pass by, an' it's far too big of a boat to haul out of the water each time it's used. So must be floating not far away. You can rent my boat. It's a little old, but it should work fine."

Marco immediately began making plans to drive to St. Joe, expecting to bring his quest to a happy conclusion. First, he did an Internet search to find out as much as he could about where he was going, and then he looked at Google maps to see what he could spot from the air. He discovered that St. Joe was a rust-belt town in slow decay. It lay between upscale areas to the north and south but remained depressed after much of its manufacturing moved to the far east.

From what he could see on the maps, the resulting blight had seeped into the surrounding area of small, poor farms, each on a couple of acres of land, remote houses surrounded by overgrowth and dilapidated out buildings. Marco speculated that the area was probably populated with plenty of hillbillies and white trash, all toting rifles. Likely, the landscape was dotted with lots of old rusty pickup trucks missing hubcaps but adorned with Confederate flags and skull and crossbones bumper stickers.

Digging deeper, Marco found more disturbing information. Newspaper articles he unearthed talked about hate group activities in the area. The KKK had just conducted a big recruitment campaign in neighboring Benton Harbor. In the past, it had been the center for a right-wing religious cult called the "Israelite House of David," and there were still remnants of it in town. Marco guessed that there must be plenty of MAGA signs and paraphernalia all around.

Marco was not deterred by the information he uncovered. All he was going for was to meet the girl. He couldn't see how that would be very controversial, even in that world. He thought, *I can leave my politics in Chicago. Besides, the owners of Blind Faith are sailors, so how bad could they be.*

The day after he completed his research, Marco drove up from Chicago and rented the harbormaster's boat, a sixteen-foot turquoise and white runabout left over from the 1960s with an old Johnson 40-horse gasoline engine. It was a little hard to start, but eventually it kicked in. *I hope it works when I need it*, Marco thought. *These old engines are notoriously finicky.*

Marco ignored the risk and ventured out. As he traveled up the river, he passed by upscale houses and fancy boats. The landscape quickly changed. The river narrowed, and the houses became shabby and more spread out. Row boats, some overturned on the shore, replaced the larger yachts. Creaky, misshapen wooden docks, many missing planks here and there, jutted out from the land. There were occasional willow trees growing along the shore with one or two rubber tires on ropes hanging from their branches. Every so often, fenced-in fields with grazing cattle or horses butted up against the riverbank. He was in the county.

This is getting a little creepy, Marco thought. And it did not feel quite right. It seemed unlikely that a sailboat would be this far up river away from everything, especially a sailboat operated by people dressed in black with pointed hats. But he was driven by his single-minded quest for the elusive damsel, not by objective rationality.

So he continued, going about two miles further upriver and passing under the second opening bridge. If he was to find *Blind Faith*, it needed to be soon. Already the river along the shore was too shallow to accommodate a boat with a deep keel like the one under *Blind Faith*. Finally, he rounded a bend in the river and saw the first low highway fixed bridge. The tall mast on *Blind Faith* would not let it go further than this. He had come as far as he could and had not located the boat.

Marco felt instant, grave disappointment when he realized that what had seemed like such a good lead had come to nothing. Worse, he could think of no other steps he could take to find the boat. His effort to find *Blind Faith* appeared doomed. He began aimlessly circling around in the runabout, following the wake made by the boat. *Another fantasy bites the dust*, he thought. *Oh Lord. Like my career. There, no data, no promotion, and no future. Here, no Blind Faith, no dazzling beauty, and no romance. Very depressing.* He shook his head. *Why, oh why, can't I meet the person of my dreams?*

From the vantage point of this reversal, Marco's life seemed to be fizzling out before his eyes. He saw no possibilities on the horizon. Would he end up unemployed and, worse, alone? *God*, he mused. *Who would know or care if I never return from this rathole?* He remembered the time that he and Melissa had their only fight and she walked out. From the second she slammed the door, he had felt desperate, alone, drained, sensations which now returned in spades.

He turned the boat around to return it and get on the road back to Chicago. Regardless of how disconsolate he was at the moment he knew he had no choice but to carry on with his life as best he could. Jeannie came to mind as he proceeded downriver. He had sort of squandered that opportunity, but, he thought, with a little sweet-talking and attention, maybe he could rekindle her interest. He could turn on the charm when he needed to. And Jeannie wasn't so bad.

Her eyes were uniquely tempting, and he was quite impressed that she had learned about quantum entanglement. *Not as sexy as I would like,* he thought. *Don't like attorneys either, but maybe I could grow to appreciate her.*

But then, when Marco was about to pass through the railroad swing bridge next to the harbormaster's office, he saw a boat far off in the lake heading in. All of his attention riveted on it. It looked to be about the size and sail configuration of *Blind Faith. Could it be?* he asked himself, hoping against hope it was. He watched it carefully as it got closer. Finally, he could make out the pasty blue hull and the old yellowish sails. It definitely was *Blind Faith* coming back to port. Marco was flabbergasted with his good luck. His timing couldn't have been better. Another thirty minutes and he would have been back on the road to Chicago. *This is glorious,* he thought. His feelings of despair melted away, replaced with renewed happy anticipation. Romancing Jeannie was off the table. His fantasy damsel was again who he craved.

Marco drove the boat over to an unused dock and tied up while he waited for *Blind Faith.* He decided to let it go by and then give the crew some time to get it home and settle in before he made his move.

In a few minutes, it passed. There were only two men on the boat, the same two from the week before, no lovely woman. They were dressed exactly like they had been, and, as on the lake, they seemed preoccupied with their own thoughts, paying no attention to him. The boat progressed up river and disappeared around a bend. A bit later, Marco decided he had given them enough time to get to their destination and tie up the boat. He began his second trip up river.

This time he found *Blind Faith* neatly tied up at the end of a fairly long dock into deeper water, just downstream from the first low bridge. It was where, moments before, he had despaired of ever locating the object of his search. The dock led to the yard of a wooden house, which fit right in with *Blind Faith.* It was two stories, of wood, in need of a coat of paint, with scraggly unkempt shrubs growing randomly in front. Over the years it must have settled unevenly so it tilted to the side a little. Aluminum storm windows had been added as an afterthought. By now, many of the screens were out of alignment or torn. The yard's beaten-down grass was littered with random trash here and there. A couple of faded metal lawn chairs sat side by side near a broken-down bike lying flat, with grass growing through the spokes, and an old, rusted push lawn mower leaned against the side of the house. A small porch led to the front door. While there were definite signs of life, it was obvious that the occupants were uninterested in their surroundings or in what others might think about their home.

It was not as if there were neighbors who would care. The house sat at the edge of a river backwater with brush and woods on both sides, far away from any other house or peering neighbors. Marco speculated that a house so unkempt and isolated could only be occupied by eccentrics or kooks. Still, there was nothing particularly sinister looking about it.

Now Marco had located *Blind Faith* but what to do? *You don't just park the boat next to Blind Faith, walk up to the door, knock, and say, 'Hello, I am here to bed down your daughter.' Not a good idea.* Marco recalled Frank's warning and how outlandish these people looked both times he saw them. *Better be a little careful,* he thought. Still Marco was fairly confident of his ability to handle anything and the feeling of impending danger arising within him sort of excited him, in a way egged him on. He felt ready for a little challenge and definitely some passion. Besides, he did not see that he had anything to lose.

IV

───══───

MARCO DECIDED TO SEE if he could find someone who might know about the girl. It was a little past noon and the sun was beating down, so plenty of time to say hello and make his inquiries before it got dark. To be on the safe side, he drove the boat a little up river from where *Blind Faith* was moored and secured it in some weeds along the shore. He made his way through light brush back to the house and walked up to the door. It had an aluminum screen like one of those popular in the 1960s with the owner's initial in the center. The letter *L* on a piece of cardboard was taped over whatever letter had been built in when it was installed. He knocked.

Even though the wooden door behind the screen was closed, he could hear a mean-sounding dog let out a bark, then come scurrying up to the other side of the door, and snarl. He waited and then knocked again. Still no one came. *Good Lord,* Marco thought. *I have come all of this distance and they have already left.* He was irritated with himself for waiting too long before coming back up river.

Since it seemed that no one was home, he decided to look around a little. He was curious about what these people were all about. He walked to the side of the house, then to the back. It was set about 500 feet from the road, with a long dirt and gravel lane leading to it. Thick overgrown vegetation lined both sides of the lane, which, along with the dense, overhanging trees, made it dark and a little foreboding. Almost like the entrance to an old tomb.

Next to the house there was a small barn in about the same shape as the house. It had a wooden swing door which was open. He could see very little of what was inside of the barn, only what looked to be long black velvet drapes hanging on the inside walls. *Peculiar,* he thought. Next to the barn there was an animal pen, and in the pen, three black goats grazed on the meager pickings of weeds and grass.

As he walked closer to the pen, he saw that a pentagram had been branded on each of their rumps. That stopped him cold. Goosebumps ran down his back. These were not just quirky people who liked to dress up and go sailing. Marco's previous incredulity was instantly transformed into fear as he put the pieces together, a boat named *Blind Faith,* people dressed in black with pointed hats, a supposed hex on *Provocateur,* an isolated barn with black drapes hanging inside, and now black goats branded with a sign of the Devil. Frank's intuition had been right. Marco had landed himself in the middle of a coven of Satan worshipers, Satan worshipers who liked sailing but witches no less.

Holy Jesus, this is no joke, Marco thought. It was high time to lay aside his wild fantasies about the beautiful siren and beat a hasty retreat to the boat. But as he started to turn toward the river, Marco was rocked by the blast from a rifle as a bullet whizzed not far above his head. When he turned around, he saw the man who had been steering *Blind Faith.* He couldn't be more than twenty-five feet away. The two-coned beard was unmistakable. The man's penetrating eyes fixed on Marco.

"What the fuck you thin' you're doin'?" he snarled. "We folks likes our privacy here and we's don't like folks a comin' snoopin' round, 'specially city people like you."

Marco saw he was in real trouble. It was not far to the river. He could probably outrun and out dodge this freak but not the bullets from his gun. *Besides, who or what else was in the house to back him up?* he wondered. At the very least, a mean dog was in the picture. Anyway, if he could get back to the boat, there was a question as to whether that clunky old engine would start right away. Marco had some talking to do.

"Oh sir, I'm sorry. I was the guy driving the boat you passed last week. Something--I have no idea what-- made me come here." Now was not the time to mention his lust for the girl.

"My name is 'Marco;' what's your name, sir?" Marco asked, trying to find a way to appear friendly. He held out his hand, offering to shake.

"Tha's fur ya to find out."

By then the man had walked up to Marco and stuck the barrel of the rifle right into his gut, forcing the hard, cold steel against his stomach. He gave it a couple lunges for emphasis as Marco instinctively raised his arms. His hair stood on end and a quiver ran through his muscles. He felt frozen in place, unable to move.

The lunatic cocked the trigger as if he was about to shoot. One impulsive twitch of this man's finger could send Marco to oblivion. Marco had never felt so powerless, impotent, or horror stricken.

"Git yurself inside."

Marco moved. It did not occur to him that, by going into the house, he would get that much more deeply in trouble, trouble from which he might never emerge. All that was on his mind was the terrible, unthinkable damage this man could do if he pulled the trigger. He opened the squeaky screen door and entered. The dog barked again and lunged toward Marco.

"Zano, yous be still now," the man hollered.

The dog stopped but his flashing teeth and continued low growl signaled that he remained ready to attack.

Marco's head was in a spin as he was pushed by the barrel into a sort of living room. It was furnished with a couple of moth-eaten couches, a stuffed chair, and a water-stained coffee table. A few beer cans and an ashtray filled with cigarette and cigar butts sat on it. A musty, fetid smell, something between vomit and rotting food, filled the room. Marco hardly noticed.

The man called out, "Hey, Saul, I think we got ourselfs a live one." Within seconds the other man from the boat encounter appeared, the one who had his back to Marco as they passed on the lake. The two men looked like brothers, equally rough, equally sleazy, and equally dense. For the first time, Marco saw Saul close up. He had a large protruding forehead and a recessed chin, making his pockmarked face and head something like an inverted pear. Long black sideburns framed his face, and a pitch black, scraggly goatee grew from the bottom of his chin. His eyes were also black, small, and far apart, set deeply above two lumps for cheeks. He had not shaved for several days. His stubble was uneven and rough.

"Well, Clem, we sure do and he's a purdy boy on top of it." Saul moved close to Marco and looked him over as if he was inspecting a side of beef.

"Found 'im prowling roun' the house," Clem said. "He was jes gettin' around to lookin' in the sanctuary. Got 'im jes' in time. So, what we's gonna to do wit 'im, Saul? Don't want him interruptin' us gettin' ready for our mass tonight, what now we's a remembering our dear departed Pappie. We's got a lot to do."

"Not sure," Saul said. "We can't just let him go. What ya think, Clem?"

"Could be we use 'im as part of the mass? Ya know what I mean, don't ya?

"Somethin' to think 'bout, Clem."

Clem nodded and then said, "Well, Sister Semantha's on her way. I'm sure she'll want to talk about tha' when she comes."

Saul turned to Marco. "So yous been standing there without sayin' nothing. Let's git you tied down for righ' now while we figgers what to do wit ya."

Clem grabbed Marco's arms from behind, jerking them backwards, and pushed him with his knee into the kitchen, a dark and dirty room with a single naked lightbulb hanging overhead. There they threw him on a straight-back chair and tied him up, hands and feet, with thick rope. For extra measure they took an old belt and put it around Marco's chest, pulling it tight to the chair and eliminating any room to maneuver. They got some duct tape, pulled a strip off the roll, and were about to use it to seal Marco's mouth.

Marco saw he better say something while he still could. Maybe this would be his one and only chance to talk himself out of this mess. What could he say? He didn't want to make things worse, but then again, they were already about as bad as they could be. In the split second he had, he considered how to approach these crazies. Should he threaten them by saying people will miss him and come looking, apologize and beg for mercy, say who he is in the hope they will be impressed and change their tactic? None of these alternatives seemed right.

"Hey, what the Sam hell are you doing treating me like this?" he said finally, trying hard to sound indignant. "I told you I was drawn to you when we passed by on the boat last week. Can't explain why. All I know is that I felt your power and your energy." He strategized that, if these folks thought he came to find out about joining their group, they might lighten up and he would get a chance to escape.

Clem and Saul stood there with blank expressions on their faces, staring at him, saying nothing, but not moving. Marco thought they were listening. He was encouraged.

"I want to learn more about what you do, what you believe," he continued. "Don't understand why you are treating me like dirt. Shooting at me and tying me up. Come on."

"How'd ya get here?" Saul snarled.

Apparently, they had not heard the boat approach. Marco decided that it was better not to mention the boat. It could be his way out of this lunatic asylum.

"That's the strange part," Marco said. "Can't explain how I got here, ya see. Got on the train in Chicago, got off at St. Joe, and walked out here. It's only about four miles. Felt like I was in a trance, pulled along by some power. Never had that happen before."

As soon as he said that, Marco realized that he may have made a big mistake. Maybe he had burned his bridges. If they went out and found the boat, they would know he was up to something and things would not go well. But it was already early afternoon, and it sounded like they had other things on their minds besides checking out his story. Now he had to get out of the place before daybreak when they might find the boat.

"You a churchgoer?" Saul asked.

Marco was surprised by that question. *Why does that make a difference?* he wondered. He hoped that maybe the question showed that his pitch had gotten through. *Simpletons like this are so gullible,* he thought with disdain. They reminded him of most believers he had ever met. No objectivity, just looking for confirmation of what they already take to be gospel, regardless of how ridiculous. Marco continued the ruse.

"No, right now, I don't believe in much but am interested in learning. I've been looking for something to believe in for a while. Some sort of dynamic spiritual power. Could be that's why I was drawn here." Marco decided he would push his line to the limit. "I think the dark force wants me to join up with you, ya see."

Marco thought that, at the very least, this exchange would bring him a little time, valuable time to figure out how to get out of there. He complimented himself on the strategy.

"How's we know if you's tellin' the truth?" Saul asked. "Maybe you's just tryin' to git outta here and you's sayin' this to git us to untie you. Maybe yous just came searchin' for the girl. Clem tol' me how you looked at her on the lake."

At first Marco was stumped by Saul's question. How could he convince these lowlifes that he really wanted to believe and that he had been steered to them by the Devil?

"Whoa, you guys," Marco said after he had thought for a minute. "Stop right there. Tell me how I would ever show up way over here, up river in the middle of nowhere, unless there was some force directing me? And I'm guessing from what you said that today is a special day for you. Think about it. That all by itself makes me showing up here mysterious."

★   ★   ★

UPON HEARING MARCO SAY that, Saul told Clem to stuff a rag in Marco's mouth to keep him quiet. He went outside. Astounded that this man was talking about some sort of mystical force as if it was real, he needed a little time alone to think. He walked down the dark, overgrown lane toward the road. The stones crinkled under his feet

...till now never did believe Pappie...none of that crap, dark forces an' what have you...cummon...I hain't no fool... thought I had it all figgered out...this Devil thing...gotta see more than jes Pappie sayin' it's so with all them big words...gotta see more than jes some incense smoke Pappie said looked like Lucifer...that don't prove nothin'...

Saul picked up a rock and threw it hard into the brush, hitting something hidden there. Whatever it was scurried away. The leaves rustled where it had been.

...went along with all them fancy ideas jes so I could stay in the Circle and do a few nasty tricks on folks...well, that hain't worked out so good so far...

Saul brushed aside a thistle, which had overgrown the lane. He continued to walk.

...hey, wait jes a minute...wha' this man jes said, now there's sumpin' to think 'bout...wha' Pappie always say...over an' over an' over...never forget them words...there's Pappie a sayin' them again...

"Remember, Saul, the mystical dark force and its wondrous capacity to work its eternal will in all sorts of divergent circumstances and situations. This glorious force uses all things and everyone to its advantage to accomplish its grand end on the Earth, Lucifer's final, decisive triumph."

Saul's heart began beating faster as he heard a gust of wind howl through the tops of the trees.

...maybe Lucifer did get this faggot to come alla way over here...maybe its like Pappie said...Lucifer got a plan to win...could be this man's a comin's part of it...no explainin' his comin' otherwise...he's right...alla the way from Chicagoia...to here...way up river, way hard to get to...can't explain what this man jes said no other way...nope...no other way...

Saul stopped walking. Everything around him was now silent.

...holy shit, maybe this is good ol' Lucifer tryin' to show me his way... must be he wants me to believe...me, imagine that...me...

Saul didn't notice the possum that lumbered into the pathway right ahead of him. The animal stopped, gave him a look, and then disappeared into the heavy brush.

...fuckin' shit...Lucifer really exists... sent this man directly to me...to me of all folks...guess all them big words a-flowin' from Pappie's mouth... they's all true... Saul's body quivered all over. His spine tingled. ... *hain't never felt like this...shit...*

Saul thought he heard a voice whisper his name. He dropped to his knees.

...Lucifer, I believe...I'm wit ya...feelin' ya rit' here, rit' now...evil... hate...pain, bring it... aggg.

Saul stayed on his knees for a few minutes as these words reverberated in his head. Then he got up and looked back at the old house and barn.

...whoa, wait jes one minute...now gotta figger out what Lucifer wants me to do with 'im...must be sumpin' big...not jes try to convert him...not jes beat 'im up a little...scare 'im to death...no, no, no...big...whoa...hol' yer horses, Saul... what ya thinkin'...wha's wrong wit ya...you's been sayin' for as long as can think, use a human durin' mass...felt it righ' in my balls...felt it righ' there fer so long...

Saul's heart was racing.

...must be this man showin' up means Lucifer wants that too...that's it... Lucifer wants me to use this man inna mass tonight...holy shit...damn... holy shit...

Saul began walking back, his steps coming faster and faster. ... *some folks not gonna like that...well, Lucifer's backin' me up, it's gonna happen...now I'm sure...no stupid rabbit, a real human...fuckin' shit, a real human...part of Lucifer's gran' plan...we's gonna do it, right here, right now, tonight...gotta be...been wantin' fo' so long...*

...gonna be purdy...knife going in him all over...firs' time righ' in his balls...twist a little so he's gonna feel it real good...then eyes...gut...blood flowin'...screamin' in pain...holy shit...squirmin' roun'..last inna heart... Saul's body shook to the soul. He screamed at the top of his voice. "FREEDOM."

Saul stopped in front of the pen with the black goats and looked at them. *I'm ready...I knows what to do...Lucifer, yous here an' wit me... gonna be great, you jes see.*

NOW ALONE IN THE kitchen, Marco quickly concluded that his ploy to escape had not worked and that he remained in terrible danger. He struggled with all of his considerable muscle power against the ropes binding him to the chair, but he could not loosen them. Clem and Saul knew how to tie somebody up.

And what were they talking about? What did they do with people who accidentally showed up on their property? What did they mean when they talked about being of "use" in their ceremony? *Sounds horrific,* he thought. *Am I going to end up being a sacrifice to the Devil? Is that what he means?* He wondered about the purpose for *Blind Faith,* whether they used it to dispose of the remains of their sacrifices. Marco recalled seeing them on the lake that day. They sure didn't fit his image of sailors out to commune with nature on a warm summer afternoon. The day fit their beliefs perfectly, dark, cold, unforgiving.

What in God's sake am I going to do? Marco thought, as the desperateness of his situation overtook him. Here he was, a young physicist looking to solve important scientific problems, now helpless, bound, and gagged, held captive by these vicious animals, and, from all appearances, on his way to a tortuous death.

What a fool I am, unbelievable fool. I ignored all of the warning signs and got myself right in the middle of a very crazy situation with Devil worshipers and for what? For a woman I have never actually talked to. No doubt, a dark force pulled me here… nothing mystical, just my own foolhardy, fantasy-driven carnal lust. And there was no sight of the woman. From the looks of the place she did not live here anyway. The place was way too run-down and ratty for that. Frank was right. This had been a disastrous fool's errand.

God help me, please, he pleaded. *God come, if I ever needed you, I need you now. In the name of the Blessed ever Virgin Mary and all the angels and saints, come, please come. I don't want to die, please, I don't want to die,* he thought over and over. *Especially not offered up to the Devil like some animal. No, no, no.* Tears poured out from his eyes and wetted the old rag stuffed in his mouth. He tried to scream through the rag, but could not, emitting instead indiscriminate but loud moans of anguish. He wanted to cry out "help me" but the words were blocked and, at any rate, would have gone unanswered even if he could have uttered them. Grunting and twisting, he continued to fight against the ropes until he was wet with sweat and his muscles ached. Then, he gave up the struggle, exhausted and emotionally spent. He began to moan uncontrollably.

SAUL AND CLEM HEARD Marco's wailing in the barn as they were preparing for the mass.

"This ain't gonna be no good at all, what with him groaning like that. Folks gonna start comin' soon and some of them not gonna like to hear him makin' so much noise," Saul said. "All his groans might get 'im some sympathy. I'm gonna stop this right now." He went back to the kitchen and grabbed Marco by the neck, pushing his long, dirty fingernails against Marco's throat.

"Look ya fucker, you gonna shut up," he said. "No more moaning or I'm gonna out you right here and right now on the spot, ya hear. Now shut the fuck up." Saul squeezed his neck tightly for a minute, causing Marco to gag, then slapped him hard across the face with the back of his hand. Marco's groans turned to quiet sobs.

Once Saul rejoined Clem outside the kitchen, he looked at Clem with a mean smile. "We've got ourselfs quite a golden chance here. This queer shows up from Chicago and nobody knows he's here. An' it's perfect on the night of the mass to honor Pappie."

Clem's eyes bulged out. "Wha's ya got in mind, Saul?"

"Like you say, we's gonna use this man in our mass tonight. We's been talkin' about taking the sacrifice part of the mass to the next level for a long time. This be our chance. Lucifer done sent us this man to use. I believe that, gotta tell ya. Everybody's gonna believe that. It's gonna be so purdy, yous gonna see."

"Weren't Pappie against this? And wha's Sister Semantha gonna say when she gits here? Ain't she gonna be the new high priest now that Pappie's done gone?"

Saul scowled.

"Fuck Pappie and his goddammed sailboat. He's gone to Lucifer and not any time too soon. He was gettin' pretty feeble, always talkin' and never doin'. Never wanted to do nothin' nasty or evil. You ask me, he was foolin' around with Semantha some way or the other, and she made him weak. Too bad he got kilt, but he had to go. That stake in his heart. Not purdy but real sure. I say good riddance."

Clem nodded as if to approve.

"An' for Semantha..." Saul spat on the ground and mashed his spittle into the soil with the heel of his boot. "She's jes interested in fuckin' every man she sees. Over my dead body, she's gonna be the new high priest. As far as that goes, if there's gonna be any dead bodies aroun' here, it's gonna be hers, but only after it's nice 'n cut up. One way or the other, I'm gonna have her.

"Fuck Pappie......fuck Semantha," he hollered. "This Circle is mine now. Nobody gonna stop me; we're gonna do what I say. You with me, Clem?"

Clem nodded again. They were ready.

V

```
|——— ═══ ———|
```

"HEY SAUL," CLEM SAID, "Now's that we've got that settled, let's us have a littl' drink, sorta a cele-bration, ya know I's got a flask of good shit righ' here in my pocket." Clem motioned to Saul to go outside. Going over to the big oak at the end of the lane, they sat down on the cool moss around its roots. Even in the shade, the air was hot and heavy. Clem handed the flask to Saul and he took a long swig.

"He ho, that is good shit," Saul said. "Down some yerself. Hain't no good to drink alone, ya know." Saul was in an agreeable mood. Thinking about the man in the kitchen, he was as close to happy as he ever had been.

Clem took a drink. "Saul, I got a question, sorta burnin' in my mind. Been thinkin' bout it for a while. Now that Pappie's gone and you's gonna be in charge, kin I ask ya?"

"Okay. We's got time…ask away." Saul knew he had to be nice to Clem. He needed Clem's help to make the Circle what he wanted… and no one was better at sneakin' up on someone from behind…

"What's ya know 'bout how all this got started, I mean, with Pappie and Semantha. I know she hain't his natural kid."

Saul grabbed the flask and downed the rest of the hooch.

"Ahhh…" He belched.

"Mostly, all Pappie wanted to talk 'bout was the big war inna sky, ya know 'tween God and the Devil."

51

Clem frowned and shook his head.

"But now and then, when Pappie got a little drunk, he'd tell me this or that 'bout how he got into the Lucifer thing, 'bout Sister Semantha too. Also some folks in the Circle got big ol' motor mouths. Quite a story, gotta tell ya, quite some story."

Saul paused. He looked toward the barn, then toward the old house and kitchen door. Saul fidgeted some as he thought about the man tied up there. It had become oppressively hot. He was not good at waiting patiently especially in the heat. He grabbed a twig and began picking his teeth.

"So here goes, Clem. Folks say it all commenced at the will readin', nigh on to eighteen years ago when Pappie's ma and pa was kilt in a car wreck."

VI

———══———

"'I SEBASTIANUS PAPADIAMANTOPOULOS, BEING of sound mind and memory, hereby bequeath my entire estate to my faithful wife Aphrodite Thailia, if she survives me, and if she does not, to my two obedient Christian children, Sebastianus Theodoros, Jr, 'Pappie,' and Calissa Aphrodite, in equal sums, share and share alike, except for our home at 1326 West Wigmore Street, Benton Harbor, which I bequeath to them jointly for their lives, the remainder interest to my beloved faith congregation, the Israelite House of David.

'To my third child, Ajax Jason, I bequeath the sum of one dollar, it being my intention to otherwise disinherit and hold him anathema, with the hope that this chastisement will speed his repentance from his profligate ways.'"

With the reading of these words, the family attorney, Bradley Craword, took off his glasses and placed them on the table in front of him. He looked off in the distance.

"There you have it, your father's wishes for his estate," he said. Do you have any questions?"

Calissa, Pappie, and Ajax looked back and forth at each other, waiting for reactions. They had assembled in the dining room at the house on Wigmore Street for the reading of their parents' wills. It was a grand room, fitting for such a solemn occasion, filled with antique oriental vases, carved, stained teakwood furniture, and other classical accent pieces.

Pappie and Calissa had dressed formally as they had been required to for family dinners during their upbringing, every night at 8:00 p.m. to be precise. Calissa had chosen a low-cut beige gown, which accented her matronly but still shapely body, and matched well with her brown eyes and brunette hair. Pappie was in a three-piece, somewhat dated, tweed suit with British-style leather elbow guards. With his horn-rimmed glasses and slicked down, thick black hair, he looked a little like an itinerant nineteenth century tent-crusade preacher, either that or a traveling snake oil salesman, one or the other. Ajax wore sweatpants and an old polo shirt with a hole under the armpit.

"What about Mother?" Ajax asked. "Maybe she wasn't such a low-life prick."

Pappie winced. "Please do not use such a disgusting street term in connection with our dear departed father, Ajax," he said. "I beg you. For once, show just a little respect. The accident was just a week ago, and we sent them to their eternal rest only yesterday. Please."

"Oh, shut up you, Theo-doros," Ajax sneered. "You hated him just as much as I did. Don't play all self-righteous." Turning to Craword, he asked, "What about Ma's will?"

Craword shuffled apprehensively through some papers as if he was trying to find it and then cleared his throat. Looking down at the table, he appeared afraid to tell them what he already knew. "Uh um, her will mirrored your father's, so she disinherited you too," he said. "She also cut you off from getting any of her trust fund."

"Trust fund, to what does that refer?" Pappie asked.

"Aphrodite was the beneficiary of a trust fund from her father. She had the right to pass that on to her children as she wished,"

Craword responded with a nervous half laugh. He started to throw his papers into his leather briefcase.

"Yeah," Calissa said. "I knew about that because Mother threatened to cut me off when I married Jake. She told me that he did not meet the Papadiamantopoulos standard. Apparently she never got around to changing her…"

"Craword, this is shit after all my years putting up with their rules," Ajax said. "Rules rules, rules. That's all I got. And their arrogance. Where does this leave me? You better figure out how I get my share."

"Leave the poor man alone," Calissa said. "It's not his fault you defied Mother and Father at every turn and treated them like swine. You know what they say about what goes around…"

"You shut up too, Miss Calissa," Ajax said. "You were like Pappie, playing the game to keep them off your back. We all hated them." His face began to turn red.

"You were both such suck-ups. Playing them for everything you could get."

"That is so unfair," Pappie said.

"Unfair? Shit. How about that fancy Ivy League education they gave you? They told me I was on my own if I wanted to go to college."

"Makes sense to me," Calissa said, shaking her head. "You barely got through high school."

Craword stood up abruptly, accidentally hitting the ornate crystal chandelier with his head. He grabbed it to keep it from shaking.

"Not staying for lunch, Mr. Craword?" Calissa asked.

Without answering, Craword picked up his briefcase and began to walk toward the door.

"Hey man, wait a minute. Aren't you going to answer my question?" Ajax said.

Craword stopped, turned around, and stood under the arches leading to the foyer. "Please, please sir. I just helped your parents with their wills. I don't want to get into the middle of a civil war."

"Oh, Mr. Craword, before you go, I do have one small question," Pappie said. Craword waited. "Please, kind sir, tell us what these words about the house mean, you know…for our lives…?"

"You can have use of it for as long as either of you live, but then it goes to Sebastianus's church. Practically speaking, it means you can't sell it, but you must keep it up. He told me when we did his will that he and the other leading officers of his church made a pact to give their homes to the church when they died." Craword scurried to the door.

"One more intrusion by that stupid religion into our lives," Calissa said as she knotted her brow.

The three sat quietly for a minute, looking at each other blankly.

By now Ajax's face was bright red and his eyes were bulging. All of his 235 pounds began to shake.

"I want my share. I have it coming," he yelled.

"So you can waste it on drugs and that slut wife of yours?" Calissa said. "No way."

"Better than your weak, milk toast husband you treat like a slave."

Again Pappie frowned. "How dare you, Ajax. You are talking to your sister. She has always treated you like royalty, even though you never deserved it." Pappie was very protective of Calissa. They were bonded together with a tie that only a joint experience of parental oppression could forge.

Ajax ignored Pappie's words. "What do you say, Pappie?" Ajax glared at him. "Are you gonna be my brother or an asshole like Calissa? If you don't want to help me, what about poor little Semantha. She could use a few things." Semantha was Ajax's four-year-old daughter.

"My Lord, Ajax, you have never treated me like your brother, why should I do that now, tell me? As to Semantha, she is your child, not mine. And I agree with Calissa. I would not want to see one penny going to Penelope."

"That's rich. How could I be a brother to you? With your nose always buried in those silly science fiction books. As far as I was concerned, you were AWOL from the family from the instant you could read."

Ajax stood up and glowered at his brother and sister. "I've had it with both of you."

He headed for the door. Looking back, he raised his fist and shook it hard. "You'll be sorry," he said. "This family gonna pay big time, one way or the other." He exited, slamming the door so violently its inlaid stained glass shook.

Pappie and Calissa sat silently for a minute, amazed by Ajax's performance. "What do you think Ajax meant by that?" Calissa eventually asked.

"Just blowing off steam, I am sure. He will consume a few pills and settle down."

"Hopefully nothing more. I worry that he will go off the deep end one of these days and make real trouble."

PAPPIE DID NOT WANT to think about that possibility. His head dropped as he recalled his childhood. Ajax was right. He had spent all the time he could reading science fiction novels, mostly about dark and mysterious forces waging a life and death struggle for some planet or taking over the Earth. In the books, good usually won out. In his fantasy, the dark force conquered and converted humankind into something less loving, less human, many times into mindless slaves. He spent hours imagining what it would have been like to be a warrior fighting for the dark side. There he felt free, free to do what he wanted, free from the taunts of his classmates, and free from the tight controls of his parents and their fanatical religion.

"Theo, wake up," Calissa said. "What's you thinking?" Calissa used the shortened form of Pappie's formal name. She made no secret of her dislike for his nickname.

Pappie's head jerked back to attention. "Sorry, Calissa, what Ajax said took me back to when I was an innocent." Pappie had picked up a rather stilted manner of speaking from his Shakespeare professor at Dartmouth.

"You mean child?" Calissa said with a smile. By then, Hattie the housekeeper had put out a luncheon spread on the buffet: prime rib, mashed potatoes, and fried green beans. Calissa went to the buffet and filled her plate.

"Yeah, well, that science fiction stuff you used to read always worried me," she continued after she sat back down. "I thought your obsession with these books was taking you to a very strange place." She shook her finger at Pappie like a schoolmarm. "You know what they say, 'The brain of an adult is formed by the fantasies of the child.'"

"Interesting quote, Calissa. But I don't think that my youthful escape has affected me as an adult." Pappie also filled his plate and sat down.

They continued to eat in silence for a few minutes. Calissa took a sip of cabernet from her crystal wine glass.

"So, Theo, you've gotta figure out what to do with your life now, what with this big house and half the trust fund income. Do you have anything in mind?" Calissa cut a bite of meat.

"What do you mean? This house, as we just heard, belongs to both of us for as long as we live."

"Jake and I have our house together, and I don't want to move. You might as well live here. I don't need it and I really don't want to deal with renters."

"I do not see that as being just to you, Calissa." Pappie ate some green beans.

"Don't worry. It's fine. Frankly, I don't want to have anything to do with this old hulk, other than to come and visit you every so often." She smiled a wide, warm smile.

"I will always be delighted and overjoyed to see you, my sweet, darling little sister. I will welcome you with great pleasure." Pappie extended his arms as if for a hug.

A look of disquietude then spread over his face. For some time, he had felt he must tell Calissa about the direction he was headed in his life but had not been quite able to summon the courage. Her question about his future plans brought the issue to a head. Especially if he was to live in the family house so close by, he could not hide what he was doing from his sister. He adjusted his tie and squirmed in his seat. He cleared his throat and squirmed some more. He took off his glasses and cleaned them. Finally, Pappie carefully laid down his knife and fork on the edge of the bone-white china plate.

"Before we go any further, Calissa," he said. "There is something you should know. It strikes me that it is high time to tell you about my new interest in life."

"No more science fiction fantasies, I hope."

"No, I made a conscious decision to abandon reading them a long while ago. Now, my new pathway consumes me. I am sure you will find it to be quite a digression from what you might expect. I warn you. You, most likely, will not sanction or approve of it."

"Try me, Theo." She too had stopped eating. She was staring at her brother and sitting on the edge of her chair. For a minute neither of them spoke as Pappie searched for words.

"All right. Since the time I have been living independently from those dominating parents of ours, I have been seeking to define my own purposes and interests, plotting my own little rebellion against the values Mother and Father forced on us so oppressively. I have been exploring a number of different ways to do that."

"Okay, so out with it, Theo."

Pappie hesitated some more, audibly sighed, and cleared his throat again. He placed his hands on the table and looked down. "I have been studying about the dark force and the power of Lucifer." He lifted his water glass to take a sip. The ice tinkled against the crystal as his shaky hand raised it to his lips.

Calissa's jaw dropped open; she raised her eyebrows. "Oh good Lord, Theo," she said after a pause. "That's bizarre. Pa will spin in his grave."

"It happened entirely and totally by accident. One day while I was perusing volumes in a used bookstore, one grabbed my attention. It is called *The Satanic Bible*. I picked it up and started to read right there. I could not believe what I was reading."

"I thought you said no more bizarre fantasies."

"It's nothing like what I used to read. *The Satanic Bible* is a modern book devoted to the worship of Lucifer. It has all the satanic rituals and black masses currently practiced, essays on the beliefs of satanic groups, and one on how satanism is in conformance with current scientific thought. I was mesmerized and bought it instantly. I studied it from its first powerful page to its last compelling word."

Pappie looked away as if contemplating his own words.

"What about everything we were taught in church about the Devil and his cabal?" Calissa asked. "You forget all that?"

"I am surprised you ask that question, Calissa. You and I always agreed about the idiocy of Father's religion."

"I know, I know, but worshiping evil, that's another matter," Calissa said, shaking her head. "That goes beyond the silliness of the teachings of Father's church. " Calissa pushed her plate away.

"Calissa, in digesting and absorbing this book I realized that what I have always wanted is a mystical force to believe in, despite the painful experience we both had when we were youth. To me, that is the meaning of life, to find the true spirit."

"So, you are just like your old man after all. He always talked about spirituality."

"Maybe to that extent, dear sister, I am like Father. That doesn't matter now. What I am quite assured of is that, in that book, I found what I was looking for. The ideas expressed there were so powerful, so logical, and so engrossing." Pappie looked up at the ceiling.

"But evil? You're not an evil man, Theo. You're actually quite tame."

"It's not about evil in the commonly accepted understanding of that word, Calissa. It's about the compelling power of human avarice as the driving force in the universe. I am convinced deeply and profoundly that the power of evil is the most sublime force in the universe, much more powerful than the force of good. Lucifer is the manifestation of that evil."

Pappie held out his hands as if asking for a response.

"Calissa, hear me. The only way to live a full human life is through bowing down to worship him. Join me."

"God, no, Theo. This whole thing disgusts me. And you had better be careful. Something tells me this will not end well."

Pappie and Calissa finished eating in icy silence. Then they both got up, gave each other an automatic, perfunctory hug, and left the house. Calissa would return only once more. Pappie continued his journey into the world of the occult. He devoted all of his time to immersion study, freed from the necessity of holding down a job by his mother's annuity and the small sum he inherited from his father.

As his faith strengthened and deepened, Pappie's passion became a true religion, complete with moral values and a theology of sorts, a unique set of beliefs he dreamed up as he went along. He dropped out of a coven he joined in Chicago, for example, when their practices shifted away from worship of the Devil and turned into thinly-disguised orgies. He did not understand melding satanism and sexual promiscuity. They were such different things. Worship of Satan or Lucifer was cosmic, in its own way pure and ethereal, a means to commune with the grand force of the universe. He saw it as transcendent and very spiritual. Sex was carnal, nothing more. To him, like to some of the ancient Christian church fathers, carnal desire distracted people and pulled them away from a full experience of spirituality.

Finally, after several years of studying, dreaming, and theorizing, already at age forty-five, Pappie was ready to make his mark. He felt prepared to pursue what had become his aim, proselytizing in the name of Lucifer and forming his own coven where he could preside as high priest at black masses. This alone drove his passion, not cars, boats, or material things.

One Saturday night at midnight, he addressed a group responding to a flier he had distributed earlier in the week. The meeting was outside, way out in the country, near an abandoned limestone quarry. With a bonfire raging behind him and standing on a make-shift stage, he spoke in a deep resonant voice, drawing his words out one by one and gesturing wildly.

"Ohhh, my dear friends, we are indeed soooo everrrlastingly fortunate, because we live in the end times, a time monuuuuumentally critical to the future of mankind and this our home, our planet, our place in the cosmos."

Walking to the edge of the stage, and with outstretched arms, Pappie continued.

"Yes, you must surely believvvve me when I say that this is the time when we will have the great privilege and singularrrr honor to see the auspicious grand arrival of the mighty, mighty prince of darkness and the underworld. He will come to Earth driving a splendid, fiery chariot, drawn by eight dazzzzzling steeds of the apocalypse, surrounded on all sides by his valiant angels each dressed in glowing, silver-plated armor. He will dispatch them along with hisssss legions with the call of a thousand trumpets to collect his faithhhhful followers to hisss bosom, those who truly believe and who have done his will on Earth."

Pappie returned to the center of the stage and crossed his arms in front of his chest as if in judgment. He scowled. "Those who do not believe, he will vanquish with a rod of iron to unending, excruciatinggggg punishment too awful for us lowly humans to imagine. Their pain will be everlasting."

Again he stopped, let his arms fall to his sides, and smiled. "Once he has dispatched these, the infidel, he will establish a new timeless dominion, his dominium, conferrrring vast, inexhaustible power and uncountable, dazzling riches on thoseeee who have acknowledged hissss absolute supremacy on the Earth."

Pappie extended his arms in front of him, made a fist with his right hand, and pounded it against his left emphasizing each point he made.

"This is my prophecy. This is my expectation. This is my solemn promise to you. Lucifer will not be mocked."

Then he opened his hands and held them out to his audience as if welcoming them. He continued, now in a quiet voice, almost a whisper, forcing the audience to strain to hear.

"Oh, my very dearrrr friends, I exhort you in the strongest of all possible words to prepare yourselves to rise to the occasion and be rrrready to greet him with passion, love, and spirittt." Slowly raising his voice toward a crescendo, he continued, "Your rewards will be immeasurable!"

Pappie then extended his arms high above his head, looked toward the pitch-black sky, and boomed out, "Great Lucifer, come to us."

That night eight people joined with Pappie.

Over time, using his powerful voice, dynamic style, and forceful personality, Pappie attracted over 100 members to his coven. It was an eclectic group of people, each with a different story to tell about life far from the mainstream. Like the Pied Piper with his flute, Pappie held them together with little else but his fire and enthusiasm. He called his group the "Circle." He divided them into ten cells, sort of like Sunday school classes.

Pappie was quite sure that Lucifer was pleased with his work and would reward him for what he had done. He anticipated more power, more glory, many more followers. Pappie was not prepared for what life actually sent his way.

VII

———

SAUL AND CLEM WERE still under the big oak, enervated by the heat and with not much to do until it was time to complete preparations for the mass. Saul got up and started pacing. He began chain smoking his cigarillos.

"What's wrong, Saul? You's seems a littl' crazy what wit your back and forth. Hain't never seen ya like this before."

"Don't exactly know, Clem. Jes thinkin' 'bout the mass tonight an' that man lyin' there." Saul waved at the door to the kitchen and stared at it for a moment. "Kinna got me excited, ya know."

"Well, calm yerself. Ya gotta git ready to deal with Sister Semantha when she comes."

"Yeah, thinkin' maybe I should jes go an' do it now, ya know. Kinda get it over wit."

"Somehow that don't seem righ', Saul. Ya thinkin' Semantha's gonna try an' stop ya?"

"Maybe. Some folks gonna go along wit her if she does. Should'a got rid of her when I had the chance."

"Hope she don't fuck things up. But forget that for now. You hain't tol' me how Semantha got inna picture?"

VIII

"Ajax beat up little Semantha pretty bad," Calissa told Pappie when she called. It had now been almost two years since their conversation in the family dining room after the will reading, and they had not talked since.

"He's gone wacko. I guess he's been drinking and taking lots of pills."

"That does not surprise me. We predicted such a thing when we were last together." Pappie recalled what a pig Ajax had been at the will reading, right down to his bad manners and sloppy clothes. *No brother of mine*, he thought.

"This morning, they took her to the hospital. Ajax made some excuses, but, to me, it was a clear case of child abuse. I don't think it's the first time."

Calissa paused, then she continued. "We need to act right away. The next beating could be her last."

"That's sad. Poor little girl," Pappie said in an indifferent tone. He wondered why Calissa was so upset. He did not see this as their problem.

"You talked with him then?"

"I did. He called…was pretty high on something. He was slurring his words, hardly understandable. But I did hear '…payback time…'"

"Did you report him to Child and Family Services?"

"No, that's no solution. Don't you read the stories about all the abuse that goes on in foster homes? Semantha is our flesh and blood. We can't let that happen to her."

Pappie thought, *well, okay then you deal with it, Calissa. Keep me out of it.* He let her continue, but momentarily held the phone away from his ear as she chattered on. Eventually he returned to listening.

"...so this is a family problem, and we will deal with it as a family. Despite everything, we still are a family, Theo. Don't you agree?" Pappie was getting worried. He did not like the direction Calissa was taking.

"What is it you have in mind?

"Here's the scoop. You are going to take her in. You are living in the family home after all."

"Who, Semantha? Goodness, mercy, I am not able to do that. I have my work for the Circle. That takes all my energy." Pappie could not imagine what it would be like to suddenly have to take care of a little child, probably one pretty emotionally damaged.

"Time to give up that mindless crap, Theo. What's more important, playing around with the madness of Devil worship or the future of your own flesh and blood?"

"Good Lord, Calissa, sometimes you sound so like Mother."

Pappie and Calissa debated back and forth about what to do about Semantha. He acknowledged that Calissa had her hands full taking care of her own children and Jake, who was slowly dying from Parkinson's disease. Otherwise, Pappie came up with every argument he could to avoid getting involved with caring for this girl, including that he was not a fit person to take responsibility for the welfare of a little child. But Pappie was no match for Calissa when she set out on one of her missions. More importantly, he was quite afraid that if he did not give in, she would tell him to move, and he had no place to go.

"Hattie will help you, Theo. Make your plans."

On the scheduled day and time when Semantha was to arrive, Pappie and Hattie stood on the inlaid brick front porch of the Wigmore Street house ready to greet their new charge. They positioned themselves between the two Doric pillars holding up an overarching bronze canopy. The house was deep maroon brick with metal frame, double-hung windows, working shutters, and a green tile roof. Ajax pulled up in front fifteen minutes late. The car door opened and Semantha climbed out, barely clearing the car before Alex sped away. Ajax made his wheels squeal as he left, underscoring his certain indifference and contempt.

Semantha walked alone up the brick walkway toward Pappie and Hattie, her head bowed and her shoulders drooped, moving slowly, timidly. She carried a tattered cardboard suitcase, probably filled with everything she owned. Having just turned six, she was skinny as a rail and had various bruises on her face and arms. Her blond hair fell limply from her scalp as if it had not been tended to for a long time. She wore a dirty yellow crepe dress, which looked like it had been purchased at a used clothing shop. But she had a sweet Shirley Temple face and beautiful blue eyes.

Before that day, Pappie had rarely seen her, only from a distance during the few holidays the family had celebrated together before their parents' death. It had been his plan to keep it that way after she moved in. He thought he would turn her over to Hattie and wash his hands of her. But now, standing here before him, this poor forlorn girl touched him. He was deeply saddened by what he saw. This youngster looked every bit as abused and terrorized as Calissa had described. Rather than just saying hello and then beating a quick retreat, he leaned down to talk to her.

"Semantha, this will be your new home. My most sincere hope is that you will feel protected and safe here. It is going to take some time for us all to adjust to each other. In the meantime, please let me or Hattie know if you need anything."

Pappie expected some sort of reply, at least a small smile; but she just stood there like a statue, emotionless, looking down. He was not sure she heard him. Without thinking, Pappie reached out to give her a hug, another gesture he had not planned. She recoiled, but Pappie threw his long arms around her anyway. She did not respond; rather she stiffened and stood there passively waiting for Pappie to release her.

"Let me show you your room," Pappie said, taking her gently by the arm and leading her through the formal entryway, up the thick, carpeted stairs, and to an extra bedroom at the end of the hall on the second floor. She went in and closed the door behind her with a hard thud. Pappie imagined he felt the sound wave from the slamming door hitting his body like a medicine ball right in the gut.

In the first weeks, Semantha kept to herself. She came out only to grab some food and to use the bathroom. Hattie told Pappie that this was unhealthy and that, if Semantha remained so isolated, it would only lead to trouble and more serious problems sooner or later. Based on Hattie's suggestion, Pappie directed Semantha to take her meals with them and to stay at the table for at least thirty minutes at dinner time. She obeyed, but it was obvious that she only sat there until the instant the time was up. Then she scurried back to her room.

During these forced dinner rituals, Pappie tried as best as he could to talk to her about something, anything. It was hard work. Mostly he talked about his memories of when he was a child. He tried to get Semantha to talk as well. He asked her questions about what she liked and didn't like, about her favorite TV shows, movies she had seen, her friends, anything. Usually, she gave one-word answers when she said anything at all. She never smiled. Several times he asked her if she would like to watch a little TV with him. Invariably she said "no."

Pappie fought to understand what was going on with this troubled child, literally abandoned on his front doorstep. Inside himself he cursed Ajax for what he had done to this unfortunate creature. He found himself wanting to help this child if he could, exactly how he was not sure. His idea of pushing Semantha off to Hattie faded more and more with each day.

But then Pappie got frustrated. After several weeks of trying very hard to break through to her, he had just about enough of Semantha's reclusive behavior. His efforts seemed futile. He became uncomfortable around her and was relieved when she retreated after dinner. She was so cold. He considered throwing in the towel. That was certain to evoke Calissa's ire and cause a major family quarrel. Maybe she really would tell him to get out of the house. Again, at Hattie's suggestion, he tried one last ploy.

"Semantha, have you ever been to Chicago?" Pappie asked. "Let us, you and I, go. We can drive in, look around, and go to this big amusement park they have near there. Maybe go to a cinema. What do you say?"

"Sure, when?" Semantha replied without hesitation.

The next day, Pappie and Semantha got in his aging Buick Electra station wagon and drove into Chicago. He showed her around, took her to the zoo, and got her hot dogs and ice cream.

As they were driving down Lake Shore Drive back toward Michigan, Semantha spoke. "Pappie, these buildings sure are tall and there are so many of them."

These were the first words she had volunteered in the three weeks she had been living with him. Pappie looked at her with surprise. "Have you never been here before?"

"Never been out of Benton Harbor 'till today," Semantha replied. Pappie thought he heard a slight laugh. When they got home, Semantha looked at Pappie and smiled, her first smile in three weeks. "I really liked that."

These words touched Pappie like words never had before, especially because he had a good time as well.

This was the first of what became weekly trips to different cities around the area, Detroit, Indianapolis, South Bend, once all the way to Milwaukee. And with each trip, Semantha had more to say and got more involved in seeing the sights. Once in a while she smiled and laughed out loud. Pappie was both relieved and happy. Almost despite himself, he began to like this once sullen creature he had been forced to take in. He started calling her "my little Sama," a nickname she seemed to like.

One night, after a trip to Detroit, Sama and Pappie were having dinner together. It was Hattie's day off, so the two of them were alone in the house. Pappie had prepared her favorite, hamburgers with corn on the cob, and they were eating at the breakfast nook in the kitchen.

Halfway through dinner, with no warning, Semantha began to cry.

"What's wrong, my dear little one," Pappie asked, leaning his head a little to the side. "I had a good time on our trip today, didn't you?"

Sama looked at him for a minute, then tears poured from her eyes and the sides of her lips turned down.

"Pappie, they hit me over and over, no matter what I did, it was wrong. They said I was bad and that I didn't deserve to live. They said I was lucky they did not just throw me in the trash. Sometimes, if I started to cry, they hit me more. Once or twice they wouldn't give me any food. They said it was to teach me to not cry and be such a sissy."

"Poor little soul," Pappie exclaimed.

"A couple of times, Papa lifted my dress and played with me in ways I didn't like. When I said I didn't want him to do that, he smacked me hard across my face with the back of his hand. I had a black eye for days. He said that was what I got for not giving him what was coming to him as my pa."

Semantha continued to pour herself out, and Pappie listened intently until she stopped talking. He then got up and gathered Semantha into his arms. He carried her to her bedroom and sat down with her on her bed. She buried her head in his chest and sobbed. He enveloped her in his arms and held her tight. When she was done and could look at him again, he said, "Sama, please remember what I told you when you first arrived here. You are safe with me and always will be. Forget them."

Eventually the summer ended and September came. It was time for Sama to start school, first grade. Pappie dragged her out of the house and bought her some new clothes as well as school supplies. She asked him why he was buying her these things. He told her that she would need to go to school right after Labor Day.

"Pappie, I like it here with you," Semantha said. "I don't want to leave. I will not go." Pappie told her that she had no choice. She cried and then went to her room, closing the door hard with a bang.

Semantha continued to resist right up until the first day of school. That morning, Pappie knocked on her door to get her up. She did not respond. He knocked again and called her name. When she still did not answer, he pushed open the door and saw her lying in her bed, passed out. An empty bottle of Aphrodite's old sleeping pills was on the nightstand along with a half glass of water. Her face was ashen, her mouth agape, and her eyes open, staring straight ahead. Pappie touched her forehead. It was cold and clammy. She appeared dead.

Pappie immediately called Hattie and they ran her to the car. He rushed her to the emergency room, all the while terrified that his little darling was gone. As he drove, he castigated himself for not being more careful. He knew that his mother took sleeping pills, but he had not thought about the possibility that Sama may use them to try to kill herself. He was beside himself with worry, fear, and self-recrimination.

After Pappie endured several hours of anguished waiting, the doctor came out of the treatment room and told Pappie that Sama was alive. She would be all right. Luckily the pills had lost much of their sedative potency and only caused her to pass out, deeply but not fatally. Pappie thanked the doctor profusely and told him that he would make a donation to the hospital in his honor for saving her.

"Sama, my poor little child, you caused a very big scare," Pappie said to her once they got back home. "I thought I had lost my little darling just when I was really getting to know you. What made you do that?"

Semantha looked at him mournfully. "Pappie, I'm so afraid. All the other kids will make fun of me and tease me. It will be so bad." She threw herself around him and hugged him with all of her might. "Please don't make me go, please no." She started to sob. Her tears wetted Pappie's shirt.

Again Pappie let her cry, not knowing what else to do. Finally, she stopped with a couple of gasps as if she was trying to replenish her depleted lungs. Pappie took hold of her chin with his hand and turned her face toward him.

"Sama, you must not worry," he said in a sweet, calm voice. "Pappie will make sure nothing bad happens. But you must go. I will take you there every day and will pick you up after school. Trust me, it will be fine."

Pappie was good to his word, though the first day was tough. He had to pull her out of the car and walk her into the classroom, where her first-grade teacher took over. That night she came running to the car, bounding from the school like she was fleeing from a vicious beast on the loose. But over time, Semantha got used to the ritual and no longer resisted. She also began to tell Pappie about things that happened at school, first once in a while, then every day. At the dinner table her silence was gradually replaced by a torrent of words. The nightmares she sometimes had became more and more infrequent. Semantha seemed to be on the mend.

"Pappie, you have gotten through to this child," Hattie said one evening after Semantha had gone to bed. "I didn't think you had it in you."

Pappie acknowledged that Hattie was right, although he did not understand how he had managed to penetrate through little Sama's wall of self-protection. What had seemed impregnable shattered like plate glass when hit by a rock.

"What do you think happened, Hattie?"

"You showed her a little caring and attention. That changed her."

Pappie had changed as well. For the first time in his life, he felt compassion, compassion for this unfortunate child, flesh of his own flesh, brutalized by his brother. And each time when Semantha held him, Pappie felt a surge of warmth sweep through his body. This astounded him. He could not believe that he had come to care for this girl so much in such a short time. It felt so good to be needed and loved. These were feelings he had never anticipated or sought out. The little child Semantha had taught him something about himself he never could have learned any other way.

★   ★   ★

IN THE SPRING, PAPPIE went to the school to see Semantha's teacher, one Dorthia Brooks. It was for a routine parent-teacher conference, and he was anxious to see how his little charge stacked up in the outside world. The meeting occurred in Semantha's classroom. Miss Brooks sat behind her desk, looking the part of a stiff, formal school marm.

"You should be very happy with the adjustment Semantha has made after that rocky start," Brooks said. She smiled mechanically as she reached around to adjust the hairpin securing the bun on the back of her head. "Now she leads her class in her lessons. She is obviously a very, very intelligent child. From what I can see right now, I would say she is gifted. She's definitely going to go far."

"Thank you for bringing her along," Pappie responded. He sat up straight in the student chair moved next to Brooks' desk for the conferences.

"She looks a whole lot better than when she first came too. She has gained some weight, her hair shines, and there is a healthy glow about her she did not have before."

"Some of that is thanks to my housekeeper," Pappie said, looking away from Brooks.

"It's more than that. She seems calmer and more content now. She talks about you in glowing terms." Brooks began moving her head up and down in a knowing way. "She idolizes you."

Pappie nodded only slightly in recognition of that last comment. Inside, he burst with pride.

Brooks remained silent for a minute, seemingly searching for words. "But…" She raised her left hand as if encouraging Pappie to listen carefully to what she was about to say. "We are also worried. She is not making friends with the other children. At recess, she stands all alone and watches from a distance as the others play. Sometimes she seems lost inside herself. She appears, how's the best way to say it, glum and dejected."

"That is a worry," Pappie said. He decided not to tell Brooks about Semantha's early years living with Ajax and Penelope. *Strictly family business*, he thought.

"There was also an incident we believe troubling." The pleasant expression on Brook's face disappeared, replaced with a look like she had just eaten a lemon. "Once the playground supervisor found her kissing a boy behind some bushes, and not just a peck on the cheek either. When she was reprimanded, she resisted. She told the supervisor, exact words, 'What's wrong, kissing makes me feel warm inside. Don't make me stop.'"

"I'll talk with Semantha," Pappie said, then stopped speaking for a moment. "Maybe she just needs a little encouragement from Hattie and me to mix more with the other kids. Thank you for your time."

Pappie stood up, shook her hand, and left. He was thrilled that Sama was excelling academically, but he saw no problem with Sama kissing some of her classmates now and again. That seemed pretty innocent. He didn't understand how that could lead to problems. He had enough to deal without adding a couple of kisses to the list. *Maybe this Miss Brooks is just a prude*, he thought.

When he got home, Sama came running. "Pappie, Pappie, what did Miss Brooks tell you? Am I in trouble?" Semantha looked genuinely concerned.

"Sama, Miss Brooks says you are doing very well with your studies and for that you should be proud. But she also tells me that you are not forming friendships with the other children. What's wrong?"

Sama's eyes watered up. "Pappie, nobody likes me. I'm so different. They all have mommies and daddies, most of them brothers and sisters. I don't. They tease me, and make me feel bad. I feel ugly when I'm around them. So I keep to myself. I'm glad when recess is over and can go back to class."

"What do they say to you?"

"They tell me I must have hatched from an egg like a snake because I don't have a mommie. They call me snake baby. They make fun of you too. They call you monk man."

"Dear child," Pappie said as he stroked her hair gently. "Don't pay any attention to those nasty brats. They are jealous because you are so much smarter than them." Pappie had no idea what else to do or say to make Sama feel better. All he could think of was to continue being a good parent in the hope she would come out of her shell. He counseled her about proper social etiquette with boys and that was it.

When Semantha was in her junior year of high school, Hattie heard rumors. The gossip was about Semantha's blossoming passion for boys. She told Pappie that the word was out. Semantha sought out as many sexual encounters as she could find and had become known as an easy mark among the boys in her school. Pappie asked Sama whether this was true. She turned bright red, hung her head down, but said nothing. She was so muted she didn't even ask how Pappie had heard these things. He told her that boys were more than just sexual objects and that she should try to get to know them, not just have sex with them. He told her to control her impulses. Looking very sheepish, she told him she would try, and they left it at that. Pappie heard nothing more and assumed that she had reformed, not imagining that maybe she had just become more careful.

Otherwise, Semantha and Pappie grew closer and closer as Semantha edged toward adulthood. On her seventeenth birthday,

Pappie threw her an elaborate birthday party and invited her few friends. Semantha laughed and talked. After her friends left, she threw her arms around Pappie and gave him a long, warm hug. "Pappie, you are my dad now. You mean everything to me. I love you so much." After that, Pappie contacted his attorney and began the process to formally adopt Semantha.

He adored his little Sama. To him she was practically perfect and could do no wrong.

IX

As SHE APPROACHED HER senior year in high school, Pappie decided that it was time to tell Semantha about his involvement with the Circle and somehow integrate his role as loving father with being a satanist priest. It was a task he did not relish. He feared that once his delightful little sweetheart knew about what he did every night, their relationship would not be the same, that she would not understand. He could not bear the thought of losing his darling, but he did not want to give up his life's work either. What he could not imagine was for Sama to learn about his nocturnal life through rumors at school. He had to tell her and the time was now.

One night after dinner, Pappie asked Semantha to come into the parlor. That's where Sebastianus had conducted meetings with his children when he had something serious to discuss. It was a room designed for formality, with walnut paneling, bookshelves filled with leather-bound volumes, and brass lamp fixtures. Pappie motioned for her to sit down on the same overstuffed leather chair that he had occupied during his father's lectures and began to speak to her from the same desk chair his own father had used when addressing him. The only difference was that he pulled the chair out from behind the ornate desk to be closer to Semantha. Peering over his horn-rimmed glasses, he tried to express himself plainly in a way that a seventeen-year-old would understand. He pressed his fingers together as if about to pray.

"Semantha, you know there are all sorts of forces in our universe. These forces are responsible for how we live, what we do with our lives, and the way we act toward other people. Some people call one of these forces 'God' and they usually associate God with people acting to help other people, love other people, and do good."

"I've wondered why you've never suggested that we go to church like my classmates."

"Because, mostly the people who say they believe in God and doing 'good' don't act that way, they act the opposite." He shook his head. "I don't see God as being the strongest force in the world."

"What is then?"

"Dearest Sama, people are naturally selfish. Greed, materialism, desire, will to power, and ambition, these are the forces that have led humans to dominate the world. Practically everything that mankind has accomplished has been motivated by greed or selfishness, not by love or selflessness. Progress depends on it. The God of love and compassion cannot hold a candle to these basic human instincts."

"So why do you think people are like that?" Semantha asked, tilting her head to the right as if puzzled.

Pappie fixed his eyes on Sama and held his gaze. "I believe that the strongest force in the world is the force that is reflected in human nature. That force is Lucifer. Eventually, Semantha, there will be a grand battle between Lucifer and God. Lucifer will conquer triumphant. He will come to rule the Earth in dignity and might."

Semantha sat, mouth open, motionless as if in a trance, not taking her eyes off Pappie.

"I say we all should bow down and worship the source of these instincts. I have formed a group, which has joined with me to do that. I call it the 'Circle.'" He paused, waiting for Semantha's reaction.

"Pappie, I don't know what to say. This is astounding, the Devil, my gosh."

Pappie and Semantha sat together for another hour talking. Semantha told him she thought Devil worship was odd and that most people would think that too. But Pappie persisted. He fiercely wanted her to understand why he was so committed. He would have sat there forever talking. When she appeared to tire, he opened the upper right-hand drawer of his desk, took out his well-used copy of *The Satanic Bible* and gave it to her. He told her how much of an impact it had on him and asked her to read it. After that, every day or two, they went through another chapter, which Pappie embellished with his own stories about how he had seen Lucifer at work in human experience. She listened but said she still was hesitant about the idea of worshiping the Devil. Pappie struggled to find the means to get through to her as he so strongly wished. He felt he was up against another of Semantha's impenetrable walls.

Two weeks after their talk in the parlor, Pappie came up with a plan. He waited for the right time, said a prayer to Lucifer asking for success, then took Semantha on a walk down the lane between the house on the river and the road. It was a humid summer day; the sky was filled with dark, threatening thunderclouds.

"Sama, my dear child," Pappie said, "now that you have studied about my beliefs, it is time to tell you something I have not told anyone else in the world and do not intend to." He stopped walking, faced her, took both of her hands in his, and peered intently into her eyes.

"Lucifer has appeared to me. Not in a dream, I am saying, but in glorious reality. One night, I stayed here overnight after a particularly powerful midnight mass. I could not sleep so I rose and went for a walk down the road toward Benton Harbor. A blood-orange harvest moon shined overhead, and the smell of burning leaves hung heavy in the air. As I perambulated next to a cornfield, which had just been harvested, I focused my attention down the rows and, in the dim moonlight, peered upon a magnificent half man, half beast with green skin and a perfectly sculpted, intensely black goatee. He towered high above the dry corn stacks around him. His eyes glowed like molten embers and his hair blazed like white-hot flames. He raised his arms overhead, revealing the hands of a giant ape-like beast. In a resonant voice, which seemed to echo in upon itself, he said only, *Ἔλα*, 'come' in Greek. Then he disappeared. Instantly, I felt my heart strangely warm. My spirit caught fire and has burned passionately ever since. That was my true conversion."

At that moment, the wind from an approaching storm blew through the trees and the brush on either side of the lane began to violently sway back and forth. *Lucifer's breath,* Pappie thought.

Semantha shook. "Pappie, I want that feeling," she blurted out. Her eyes filled with tears. "Tell me what to do and I will follow you. Anywhere you say. Thank you, I love you." She threw her arms around Pappie and held him tight. Pappie was both relieved and happy that Sama had come to believe. Lucifer had answered.

Semantha began attending Circle meetings and black masses. She was a curiosity to other members, so young, pretty, and innocent. Out of respect for Pappie, they treated her like a princess in their little kingdom. But she really did not fit in. They were a bunch of malcontents and lonely outsiders, folks with sordid and seamy backgrounds. Some hardly had the means to survive. By comparison, she had been living like a child of privilege under Pappie's protective wing. And to begin with, she was too bookish and shy to mix it up with these folks, especially considering the difference in ages.

Before long, Pappie let her assist with some parts of the mass. Once in a while, he would allow her to speak to the Circle about her adoration of Lucifer and the Circle's work of bringing his rule to the Earth. When guided by Pappie in what to say, she spoke plainly and openly, making his words seem her own. Folks listened respectfully, yet they did not appear to be roused by what she said.

Pappie did not see that. He was delighted with how Semantha presented herself to the Circle when she spoke. He also noticed that, as time went on, Semantha learned how to socialize with the other members. He was quite happy that she was coming out of her shell. *That will help her when she goes to college,* Pappie thought. *If she can be friendly and warm with these folks, she can be anywhere.* Once again, he thanked Lucifer for help in raising his daughter.

Shortly before Semantha graduated, Pappie decided to go to Scotland to assist with the restoration of Boleskine House on the banks of Loch Ness. It was the former home of the now deceased great magician and satanist, Aleister Crowley. He was to be gone for a month and Semantha could not go with him. Since Calissa was overburdened with Jake, who was in the late stage of his disease, and Hattie was recovering from heart surgery, Pappie took Semantha to stay with his cousin Issac. Issac lived well in a very nice house. Pappie thought she would be safe there until he returned.

When Pappie came back, his top priority was to pick up Semantha and bring her home. He was shocked by what he found. She had started to wear makeup for the first time and a rather gaudy gold chain hung around her neck.

"Pappie, why don't we have a nice car like Issac? This old Buick is such an embarrassment," Semantha said. She then went on about all of the electronics, beautiful furniture, and expensive things Issac had all around. "He even has TVs in the bathrooms."

Pappie drummed his fingers on the steering wheel as he drove. "We just said hello after being apart for a month, and all you can talk about is Issac's TVs, Why?"

Sama scowled. "Issac said you don't know how to live, what with our run-down old house and tired furniture," she said arrogantly. "He said that you need to learn how to spend some of that money you inherited. Let yourself go. He's right. It was so much fun being with him."

"Semantha," Pappie said sternly, momentarily taking his eyes off the road and staring directly at her. "I am so very disappointed to hear these words coming from you. Certainly after all of this time, you know what I think is most important. Those superficial temporal things have no value. I thought that was a conclusion you had reached for yourself as well."

"But, but, but..." Semantha tried to speak.

Pappie was not done. "I thought you wanted to focus your life on developing the Circle with me, not go chasing after such unnecessary material possessions." Pappie shook his head. "They are here today and gone tomorrow, so unlike the everlasting and compelling worship of the eternal."

"I do want to be with you Pappie, but..."

It took Pappie weeks to coax Semantha to give up the ideas she had absorbed living with Issac. Eventually she did, but Pappie remained concerned about how easily Issac's passion for material things had corrupted her. He did not understand why she couldn't think for herself. It was like every stiff breeze could blow her over. He hoped she would develop a sterner mettle as she grew older. He had no idea how to help her do that, but he was sure she would somehow.

X

Shadows were beginning to form around the oak tree where Saul and Clem were sitting. Clem opened his eyes after a little alcohol-induced nap. He found Saul throwing pebbles down the lane and gazing intently at the kitchen door.

"Stop," Clem said. "Yer drivin' yerself crazy. We's not got much longer to wait for the mass. Relax yerself."

Saul paid no heed to Clem. He was getting more and more excited. *Only the beginning, holy shit,* he thought. Every so often, his body pulsated. He wanted to go in and do the deed right then, but he knew he had to wait. *Gotta do this righ'…part of the mass…be so purdy…*

"So, Saul you've tol' me about Pappie and Semantha. How's 'bout ya, Saul. How'd ya git into this?" Clem seemed to be looking for a way to distract Saul from thinking about the man in the kitchen.

"Hain't I ever tol' ya, Clem? Thought sure I had. Well, anyway, it's not much of a story."

Sweating profusely, Saul took out a handkerchief and dried his forehead. He then cleared his throat. "Ahem," he said and began.

"Seems like yesterday. I was sittin' in the ol' bar at the VFW hall over in Berrien. I liked that place 'cause nobody was much ever there exceptin' some ol' half-baked WW II vets once in a while. So I was jes havin' a beer when I saw this man walk in. Firs' saw 'im reflectin' in the mirror behind the bar as he was jes comin' in. Kinda got me righ' then, dressed sorta strange, all up in a three-piece suit an' the like."

"Pappie, righ'?"

"Yep, well he looked 'round, then he came an' stood righ' next to me. Put his foot on the brass foot rest and his elbows onna bar, sort of like I was standin'. Kinna creepy. Thought he was a tryin' to sell sumpin,' couldn't think why else he was there. Looked sorta outta place."

As Saul said that, a flock of starlings flew in, perched above them, and began to cackle loudly. They sounded like a choir from hell.

"Before I knew it, he was a talkin' to me, kinna strange the way he talked. All flowery and big words, ya know. Then he asked me if I wanted a drink."

"What ya think then, Saul? You's gotta be careful now days with all them fags everywhere."

"Yeah, well, I tol' him I was jes there to sorta unwind after work an' didn't want nothin'. Then I figgered, whoa, wait a minute, Saul, ya crazy, why not get a free drink. I tol' him I wanted an Old Grand Dad Bonded."

"So he raised his hand and gave a wave to the bartender. Guy was always there, wearin' this white apron roun' his waist. Went down to his knees, sort of like he was from the ol' world, ya know. Big fat guy. Pappie yelled out, never forget, 'Kind sir, please bring what my friend wants and one for me too.' So smooth, like he owned the place."

Saul was interrupted when one of the goats in the pen bleated loudly. The other two joined in. "Time to get 'em fed," Clem said.

"Fergit 'em, Clem. I'm tellin' my story.

"As I was sayin', before ya could say 'shit', we'd had a couple of drinks an' I was feelin' pretty good. So he started talkin 'bout what's on his mind.

"Tol' me he was on sorta a mission, wanted to talk 'bout some stuff he'd been readin' 'bout… bein' selfish an' 'bout evil."

"Shit, like some sorta preacher man, Saul."

"No shit, Clem. Tol' him to be on his way. Didn't want no church stuff, 'specially when I was out at a bar jes drinkin' peaceful-like, ya know."

Clem took out a packet of Skol and bit off a piece. He began to chew. He offered some to Saul. Saul held up his hand as if to say "no."

"Ever git religion, Saul?" Clem asked.

"Naw. My dead ma used to go to church and believed in God and Christ, or so she said. Could never figger out why she went 'cause she was a mean ol' biddie all the rest of the time. Jes got religion on Sunday mornings."

Clem spit out some of the chew.

"Sometimes," Saul said, "She would drag Pa along when he was sober, which was almost never."

"Yea, like my pa."

"Ma made me go every so often but I got kicked out for hittin' the other kiddies an' tryin' to feel up a little girl." Saul laughed and rubbed his crotch.

"So then what, Saul?"

"Well, so here's wha' happened. He tol' me he weren't no preacher."

"Well, okay, then what, I thought. So he starts to go into this thing about the Devil an' evil an' how he wanted to start a coven. Tol' me that evil is already winning. Said people is stealin' lyin', gittin' by wit murder, 'specially if they's rich. Said Lucifer's behind all that, he's gonna win inna war with God. Sound familiar?"

"Yeah, guess we's heard that a few times."

"Try a few thousand times. But, shit, there was sumpin' so powerful 'bout his eyes, sort of magic, hypno-tized me. An' those big words. Didn't understand a bunch of what he was sayin', but he was real strong. I figured someone talking like that must know what he was sayin', ya know."

Saul stood up and went behind the tree to take a piss. He returned.

"But anyway, Pappie kinna got me righ' there in that ol'VFW hall. Seemed he was saying he wanted to git a bunch of people together to do bad shit, sorta mess up people, ya know. I was up for that. Seemed like my kinna thing."

"Well, bad shit didn't happen." Clem stood up and stretched. A garter snake slid along the ground on the other side of the lane.

"I know," Saul said, "but that's sumpim' else. Back then I was jes amazed wit wha' Pappie was a sayin'. An' Pappie, I jes couldn't believe anyone so full of power an' so, well let's say, smooth an' sort of elegant-like, was wantin' to talk to me, me, imagine. Think 'bout that, Clem."

"Yeah. I could see…"

"So, that's how I got in this here thing. At first, we jes had a bunch of meetin's where he went over this and that, some stuff a million times. An' then later, when other folks began to join, he made me, I guess, like a priest, sort'a his assistant or sumpum. Had a ceremony an' everythin'. An' for a while it was like livin' in a different world with Pappie talkin' 'bout Lucifer and this big war inna sky an' all that. Didn't end up so good, but then it sounded real fine."

SAUL STOPPED TALKING. HE'D said enough for one day. But telling Clem about how he got involved with the Circle put his mind to thinking about what his life had been like before. Good because that kept his mind somewhere else besides the kitchen.

He had been a loner, and he pretty much liked it that way. His only human contact was as a night janitor at a small manufacturing company on the outskirts of town. He had no friends and his family had long since disappeared or died off. He felt angry most of the time. To him, people who pretended to be happy and pleasant were disgusting and hypocritical. He liked to think about how enjoyable it would be to cause them pain, unhappiness, discomfort. Having these thoughts excited him.

Growing up, his home was an emotional cesspool filled with anger, jealousy, and spite. Saul's mother dominated his indifferent father. He hated both of them, and, as soon as he could, he spent as much time as possible on the streets. By the time he was a sophomore in high school, he was out of control. He misbehaved in class, skipped school, and failed in every subject. He planned on dropping out as soon as he could. One time after another, he was picked up by the cops for petty theft, unlawful possession of a weapon, drug charges, disturbing the peace, pretty much everything wrong and bad a young person could do in a little town like Benton Harbor.

All that changed when he met Shena, a transfer student who moved to town from a very small village in the coal mining region of West Virginia. She was plain looking and socially backward but physically developed, beyond her fifteen years. Saul and Shena met quite by accident when they both were trapped in an elevator in the Berrien County Courthouse building. It took two hours for the elevator guy to come to extricate them. Saul would have never talked to Shena if he had seen her at school or on the street, but while confined in the elevator there was not much else to do but talk.

They both sat down on the dirty carpeted floor of the car.

"My name's Shena, what's yours?"

Saul stroked his little goatee. Shena looked at his hand rubbing the whiskers. Saul thought it was one of his most sexy facial features.

"Saul," he said.

"Saul. Nice name. What ya come here for?"

Saul put his hands behind his head and stretched, revealing his stomach and a little of his still youthful chest. While his face was distinctly pear shaped, and his eyes like two little black lumps of coal, he had a boyish look and had not yet developed the acne that would later scar his complexion.

"Wanna get my driver's license, and you?"

Saul couldn't stop looking at Shena's breasts. The way she held her body so erect made them stand out even more. One of the straps from her bra peeked out from under her blouse. He wanted to reach over and give the strap a snap.

Saul's eyes shifted from right to left and back. "See it's like this, I got a rep with the cops in town, so they's always pickin' me up and sayin' I done things I didn't. So I gotta come here an' see the judge alla time. He hates me too. Calls me a loser and scum right in the courtroom, but what am I gonna do?"

"Sorry to hear about that." Shena saw Saul staring at her chest and smiled slightly. "You go to school?"

"Yeah, I'm a sophomore at Berrien County High School, but I gotta git out of there as soon as I can. Gonna get me a job and make me lots of money. Wanna get a car and drive to California."

"Got a girlfriend, Saul?" She sounded like she hoped the answer was 'no.'

"Nah. All the girls at school is stuck up an'want to hang with football player types. They don't want me. That's fine wit me 'cause I don't want them neither." Saul knew that was a lie.

"That's too bad, Saul, 'cause I think you're sorta cute."

Saul got out his comb and tried to straighten out his cowlick. He hated the way it dropped down from his hairline onto his forehead.

"Really, Shena? Well, you's cute too." He liked her small nose and heavy black eyebrows.

After they got out of the elevator, Shena and Saul continued to talk for a while. Saul suggested they get together later in the evening, and they did. Saul had his first, and, as it turned out, his only girlfriend.

For a couple of months things went well, surprisingly well. Saul liked being with Shena, and, under her influence, he settled down quite a lot. He loved having sex with her, and, at school, he felt like he was finally somebody. He was getting laid regularly and he knew the other boys were not. He thought about staying on after he turned sixteen if Shena would stay with him.

Saul didn't expect what Shena told him one night. Shena's parents were out; they were in her living room, lying in each other's arms and watching reality TV.

Shena turned to Saul. "I'm pregnant, Saul. It's your baby."

"How ya know?" Saul's right knee began to twitch.

"I've only had sex with you since I came."

Saul sat up and moved away from Shena. "Whoa, Shena, that's a little more than I thought was gonna happen. What's ya gonna do? You gonna keep it?"

Shena stared at the floor. "I'm not ready to take care of no baby, so I want to get me an abortion." She then looked Saul in the eye. "Problem is abortions cost a lot of money and my folks are strict about that. They say gittin' an abortion is a mortal sin. They want me to go live with my auntie in Alabama, have the baby, and put it up for adoption."

"If ya moves away, what's gonna happen to you an' me. I was jes gettin' used to havin' ya 'round. I don't want ya to go. I guess I sort of feel sumpin' for ya." Saul put his hand on Shena's leg and rubbed it a little. Saul was quiet as he thought.

"Shena, why don't you and I have the kid?" he asked after a few minutes. "I think I can handle it an' maybe its gonna make me settle down. I'll get a job over in the washin' machine plant an' we'll be jes fine." He became excited thinking about a happy little home with him, Shena and little Saul. *Could be a real purdy place,* Saul thought.

After a couple of days, Shena gave him her answer on a star-filled night on a Lake Michigan beach near town. Saul had suggested they go there because he liked to watch the big waves crash against the lighthouse, and that night the winds were kicking them up. He wanted Shena to see. She was not interested in looking at waves though. She announced that she was going to move to Alabama. Those words hit Saul like a kick in the groin. He was overwrought with anger and disappointment. Tears streamed down his cheeks.

"Fuck ya then, an' all yours," he screamed. "An' fuck that thing inside ya."

With that, Saul was through with romance. He was also pretty much through with other people. He sank into sullen isolation. But for the rest of his life, he mourned his loss each time he recalled that momentous night on the beach.

★   ★   ★

JOINING THE CIRCLE HAD jarred Saul out of his bitter solitude and changed his life dramatically. He became pretty enthusiastic about the group and tried to help Pappie recruit new members. Not that he got anyone to join. He was too crude and rough around the edges. It was Pappie's golden tongue, natural charm, and grand style which drew them in, not Saul's churlish temperament and mean demeanor.

The one exception was Clem. Like Saul, he hailed from the hills of West Virginia. Saul met him immediately after Clem's mother died. She left him some money and the old beat-up house on the river where she and Clem had been living. Saul sensed that Clem was very much like him, a loner and filled with anger. Like Saul, Clem had no family or friends now that his mother was gone. Saul and Clem thought alike, although Clem was definitely on the dense side. Saul talked Clem into joining the Circle and giving it the house along with the money he had inherited. The house was especially useful. It gave the Circle a place to meet, Saul a place to live, and Pappie a place to dock the sailboat he had always wanted.

★   ★   ★

AS THE YEARS WENT on, though, Saul got frustrated with Pappie and the Circle. It became boring and repetitive. People joined, people disappeared, but it was always the same. A mass at midnight, Pappie's oration, some partying, and maybe a few social events once in a while. Eventually, Saul decided to complain. He and Pappie were sitting together in the kitchen at the house on the river having shots of whiskey one night after mass. Everyone else had already left.

"We's been at this Circle thing now for a long time, sumpin' like seventeen years," Saul said, feeling the effect of the drink. "Long, long time. An' jes, talk, talk, talk. Nothin' more. We needs to get more nasty and mean, doin' bad shit, like we always said. Ya know, messing people up. Right now, we's like an ol' ladies club, sittin' 'round an' gossipin', with you spoutin' these crazy ideas 'bout a big war inna sky. Theys sound good, but they don't mean shit."

Pappie began squirming in his chair, shifting away from looking at Saul.

"Listen to me, Pappie," Saul paused. Pappie turned back to Saul. "An' we needs to make sure people knows that it's us a doin' it. That's gonna get more folks to join than all your flowery talkin'."

Pappie grimaced, drumming his fingers on the table.

"No reason why we can't do some while the mass is goin' on, cut up some critter or something more, what's ya say. I's been doin' some of my own readin' and I've learnt about other groups doin' that."

Pappie sighed and rubbed his forehead. Then he poured another shot and downed it in a single gulp.

"When you and I first encountered each other back in that old VFW Hall," Pappie said, "I had grand ideas like what you are eloquently expressing about the power of evil acts. Back then, I thought that Lucifer wanted us to engage in mayhem to support his struggle with the God most people worship."

"Okay then, you get what I'm talkin' 'bout."

"No Saul, hear me out. As time has passed, I have thought better of that sort of thing. I don't like the idea of including violence in our rituals, even destroying an animal. I do not think Lucifer wants that; it is so senseless. Gradually, I have come to the firm conclusion that we must patiently and faithfully wait for a sign from our dear Lucifer as to how he wants to call upon the awful power of our group. While we are anticipating that, we must continue on, resolutely building the Circle, making it stronger and stronger. Nothing more."

After a hesitation, he added, "...and no sacrifices."

SAUL WAS EXASPERATED THAT Pappie rejected his ideas so categorically. At first, he was afraid to do anything to rock the boat. He knew Pappie was in control and believed he had no choice except to go along. Anyway, he was not completely sure that Pappie's predictions were wrong. He did not want to miss out if things really did begin to happen as Pappie had repeatedly promised they would.

But as Saul grew older, he became increasingly disgusted. He started talking behind Pappie's back, telling other members that he wanted the group to become active, not just sitting around chanting. He talked about desecrations, inspiring hate between people, demonstrations, using humans in their services, and other acts of violence. Some of the members felt the same way as Saul, but they, like Saul, were a little afraid that, if they crossed Pappie, he would disband the group and they would have nowhere to go.

Emboldened by the support he got, Saul decided to confront Pappie again, but this time he resolved he would not be talked down. His opportunity came when he and Pappie were having lunch at a hamburger place near the Circle's house.

"Pappie, enough is enough. No more jes talkin' 'bout sacrifice. We's want to cut up somethin' durin' the mass. Make it more meanin'-ful an' real."

"We have been through this before, Saul," Pappie responded. "No sacrifices."

"Guess you don't understand, Pappie, we's gonna do this whether you like it or not. So screw ya."

Pappie's face turned scarlet and a bead of sweat appeared above his lip. The glass he was holding began to shake.

Not used to anyone talking back, Saul thought. *Maybe now he won't be such an ol' stick.*

Quivering a little as he spoke, Pappie replied, "Saul, you, you, you frighten me. You have n…n…never talked that way to me before." Pappie stopped, then after a pause, continued. "But, uh, uh, well, since you feel so, let's say, strongly about it, perchance we can try out the mass with a rabbit just one time. But only once. Possibly, you are correct that it would enhance the experience."

From that day forward, animal sacrifice became a regular fixture of the celebration. But Saul knew that Pappie had gone along with that only to placate him, which, itself, pissed him off. His fury continued to build.

SAUL'S EXASPERATION REACHED A crescendo early one Sunday morning, right after one of Pappie's particularly long-winded, late-night sermons. He was alone in his bedroom and couldn't sleep. A wave of frustration and hostility swirled through his body. He got so angry that he sputtered out loud.

"Pappie's jes an ol' coot, full of wild-eyed dreams, nothin' more, nothin' ya hear, nothin'. He's jes a big ol'… stupid, uh, fuckin' dreamer. Hain't never done fuckin' shit." Saul took his fist and hit the wall, causing a picture of Clem's mother to tilt to the side. "All he's done is get a bunch of people to-to-together to listen to him go on an' on an' on about meaningless, uh… shit. He's been wastin' everybody's time wit all these crazy ideas of his. Fuck 'im."

His tirade woke up Clem, sleeping in the next room, who, still half asleep, hollered that he should calm down and go back to bed. Saul ignored Clem's words. He got dressed and drove over to Pappie's home, feeling full of spite and ready for a showdown. He had never been to the house before, never been invited.

When he got there, he walked in without knocking, muddy boots and all. He interrupted Pappie and Semantha sitting at the dining room table in their silk bathrobes reading the Sunday *Detroit Free Press*. She was finished with graduate school and ready to begin work as a teacher at the local junior college. They were drinking tea from bone china cups surrounded by Aphrodite's antique oriental furniture and artwork. When he entered, their jaws dropped open. Semantha, about to take a sip, stopped, momentarily holding her cup near her mouth, then putting it back in the saucer. Pappie put his cup down as well and stiffened up. It was Pappie's rule, well known in the Circle, that no Circle member ever came to the house on Wigmore Street and no Circle business was ever conducted there. Never. Pappie clenched his teeth when Saul walked in but said nothing.

Recovering from Saul's surprise entrance, Pappie gestured to Saul to sit down.

"Saul, my dear brother, welcome," Pappie said, sounding like an exasperated father. "Please make yourself comfortable. We are so very delighted to see you. What causes the honor of your visit? Hattie, bring our special guest some of our wonderful green tea."

"Don't bother, never drunk the shit," Saul said, as he plopped down on one of Aphrodite's favorite side chairs, still wearing his wet muddy overcoat. Pappie scowled but again said nothing.

"So Pappie, we's got some business to talk over, and it's between jes us men so Semantha should be on her way till we's done."

"Saul, any business you have with me you have with Sister Semantha," Pappie said with a determined but polite voice. "What is on your mind?"

Saul paused for a minute as if he was thinking about what Pappie had just said. "You's gettin' old," he finally stated. "You need to step away an' let me take over. I feel ready. I heard the voice of Lucifer speakin' to me. He says he wants me in charge. Says you gotten too soft and friendly like, especially wit Semantha."

"So Lucifer converses with you?" Pappie asked, furrowing his brow, apparently concerned that Saul was becoming unhinged.

"Shore do. I hear voices inside myself every night when I'm all by myself at work. It's purdy quiet there, ya know." Saul was not afraid to make up stories to get his way and he was pretty good at it.

"What else does he impart to you?"

"Told me that, if I take charge, more folks will join and we'll be ready to become a real force for evil righ' 'ere in western Michigan, gettin' this place ready for when he comes. He wants us tough, mean, and prepared to fight."

"Anything more, Saul?"

That's purdy much it."

Pappie responded to Saul sweetly, patiently, now like an old man talking to his favorite grandson.

"Saul, my friend, we have been together for such a long, long time. Over the years, we have built up a grand Circle, which we both can look on with significant pride. You have done great works, and I am sure Lucifer will reward you handsomely. I know I am getting a little on in years. I grant you I don't have quite the reserve of energy I had when I was younger..."

"Okay den, it's settled. Tell everybody I'm in charge an' we's done."

"No." Pappie held up his hand. "Let me finish. Despite my age, I still feel Lucifer's vital power streaming inside of me and giving me the strength to continue to carry out his purpose and will on Earth. I am not ready to give up." He then stopped a moment. "But I do want to think about what you just said. Excuse me."

Pappie stood up, turned, and walked out of the dining room, leaving Saul, Semantha, and Hattie sitting there, looking uncertain as to what was going to happen next.

Pappie went into his refuge, the old walnut-paneled parlor. Closing the door, his mind went into motion.

He had given the issue of who would succeed him a good deal of consideration. He wanted Semantha to become the next high priestess. Her beauty and youth would create a very good image, and her sharp mind and persuasive tongue could carry forward Pappie's vision. He was sure that she believed, as he did, that a cosmic Lucifer would prevail in the eventual battle with God for control of the universe and that the compelling power of human instinct would vanquish the useless, gooey concept of brotherly love.

Saul, on the other hand, was only about petty evil and trash thinking. His version of satanism was singularly banal. To him, the worship of Lucifer was only about causing pain. He didn't go deeper. As helpful as he had been to Pappie, Saul was just a nasty, two-bit lowlife, not a true leader or visionary.

What Pappie had not thought about before was how or when to tell Saul. He dreaded doing so. He knew that he would be upset. Now, he had no choice but to lay the matter to rest and tell him. Saul had put the question on the table. Pappie could not let it fester. Anyway, better now than to have him find out at the reading of his will.

Pappie returned to the dining room, smiled patiently, and assumed his chair at the head of the table. "Saul, my friend, my companion, my confessor," Pappie said using his best dulcet voice. "As long as we are talking frankly, it is time to tell you I have been thinking about my successor. I want to tell you now what I have decided. You will find out soon enough anyway."

Saul jumped in. "Pappie, you's never gonna be…"

Again, Pappie raised his hand, signaling to Saul to stop. "Hear me out, Saul. Last week, I made out my last will and testament. In it, I name Semantha to be my successor as high priest of the Circle."

Both Semantha and Saul gasped. Semantha swallowed hard and her mouth dropped open. She turned as pale as the bone china sitting there on the dining room table.

"Fuckin' shit," Saul hissed. Making a fist, he hit the side of the cabinet next to him hard. The delicate crystal candelabra on it clinked.

"I will resolutely ask all of the members of the Circle to recognize her and acknowledge her authority as my successor in this vale of tears," Pappie continued. "I ask you Saul right now to do the same."

Saul would do nothing of the sort. He exploded. "You's a fuckin' shithead ol' coot. How's you gonna do that to me after all I's done standin' beside you all of these years. This hain't right an' I am sure it hain't what Lucifer wants. You's cain't think that I'm gonna jes sit by and watch this happen, do ya?"

"This is my decision. It is for the best interest of the Circle." Pappie stood up as if to say the meeting was over. Saul was not done.

"Fuck yer decision. You's fuckin' blind when it comes to this here broad Semantha. I's a little sorry to say this, with her sittin' righ' here, but you's the one who said she stays. She hain't no leader of no satanic coven. She's only a fuckin' girl an' too purdy an' too young. She like walkin' around wit her head up there in them clouds."

Semantha looked down and her face turned red. She began running her hand through her hair over and over.

"An' you's knows as well as I does, tha' she cain't keep herself away from fuckin' as much as she can. Seems that's the only thing that gets her movin'."

Semantha began crying as she held her face in her hands.

"I'm done, Pappie," Saul said. "Jes fuck yourself."

Saul stood up. His pointy little black eyes grew large, the corners of his lips turned upward in a form of a half smile like a sinister clown, and he gestured madly, uncontrollably waving his hands up and down.

"An' one more thing, ya ol' fool, we's gonna use some human durin' a mass, so git yourself ready," he said as he turned to leave.

When Pappie saw Saul this way, he had a disturbing premonition that he would get to do what he wanted by one means or the other.

Saul departed without bothering to close the front door. A cold draft from outside blew into the house and chilled the dining room where Pappie and Semantha were sitting.

XI

Calissa drove up to the house, anxious to see her brother again after so many years. It was a little after sunset and Pappie had turned on the front porch light. The house looked warm and inviting from the outside. Light reflected through the sheer curtains in the dining room, to the right of the front door. The house was otherwise dark. *It doesn't appear anything has changed,* she thought.

Pappie had called the day before and suggested a reunion, and she had agreed without hesitation. She wanted to put their old disagreement over his vocation behind them. Jake was gone and who knew how much longer Pappie would live. It felt like she was running out of time. She was a little worried since it was just two weeks after knee surgery, and she sort of hobbled around with a cane, but she did not want to miss the opportunity. As she approached the house, her mind was filled with memories of their days together as a family. Many were bad, but some good.

She walked up the steps to the front door and noted that it was ajar. *That's a little strange,* she thought, but maybe Pappie had left it that way to be sure she got in. Then she heard some pounding, like a mallet striking a nail. The cadence was slow and heavy, each strike making a thud as the mallet or whatever it was hit its mark. *What could he be doing?* she thought. *He can't even change a lightbulb. Could be he has finally learned how to work around the house?*

She decided to sneak up on him. Maybe she could scare him like when they were kids. She used to love to do that. He always got so angry, but he fell for it over and over. She tiptoed to the door and pushed it open very slowly. She moved quietly, ever so quietly, through the door and into the great foyer of the house. The heavy Persian rug masked the sound of her footsteps as she went. She was sure Pappie would not hear her, particularly with the racket he was making with the hammer.

When she got inside, she made her way to the arch leading to the dining room and looked in, thinking she was about to see Pappie actually doing something useful around the house. She planned to yell "surprise" and laugh. What she saw was very different. She saw the back of a large man crouched over Pappie's body and pounding his chest with a steel mallet. He was striking methodically, putting the mallet behind his back and swinging it down hard, building momentum for each strike. As the hammer hit Pappie's chest, the man groaned loudly, "umph" and Pappie's body jerked. Parts of one of her mother's vases were scattered around and there were several deep cuts in Pappie's head. A large can painted red stood next to the body.

At first, Calissa froze as she watched in horror. "Umph…thump… umph…thump…umph…thump." Then she came to her senses and screamed. "Oh my dear Lord in all of heaven." A shiver ran up and down her spine and her hair stood on end. She felt a rush of adrenaline, turned around, and ran outside with all the speed her tired old body could command. As she scrambled down the steps, she dropped her cane and her leg gave out. She fell face first onto the brick walkway, hitting her head hard against it. Blood started dripping from her forehead and her head began to throb. She managed to pick herself up and continue her run to her car, to open the door, and to get in. Before she could find her keys, she saw little pinpoints of light like stars in a dark purple luminescent field. Her mind started to darken. Everything then went black.

XII

—┣═══┫—

SEMANTHA WAS NOT EXPECTING Hattie's call. It was just after the big confrontation between Pappie and Saul. She had gone to Ames, Iowa to attend a summer seminar on teaching science to college freshmen. Semantha was in her hotel room, getting ready to go to the day's session when her cell phone buzzed. She panicked when Hattie's name appeared on the screen.

Crying as she spoke, Hattie said. "Oh my God, Sama, I finally reached you. Something terrible has happened, so awful. It's hard to say." She let out a moan. "I found Pappie's dead body this morning lying in the dining room when I went in to set up for his breakfast."

For a minute, Semantha was silent. Then she cried out, "No." Another silence, a louder "No. This cannot be." Tears rushed down her cheeks. She wailed, "No, no, no." She dropped to the bed and began running her hand through her hair over and over, moving her head back and forth as she did so.

"God help me, a stake was driven into his heart."

Semantha gasped. She shook her head. "No, please God, no." A wave-like pain shot through her body. Semantha put her hand over her heart. She could feel it pounding fast.

"Someone must've knocked him out before killing him. There were some deep cuts on his head and one of Grandma's Ming dynasty vases lay in pieces all around him. I would've called you right away, but I couldn't find your number. I had to get it from the school."

Semantha began shaking. "I'll come home right now. Is Pappie still in the house? I want to see him where he fell." She felt the urge to hold him tight, to lie with him even in his death.

"He's already gone. Saul and Clem came to pick him up a few minutes ago to take him to be cremated. Saul told me one of the Circle's members runs a funeral parlor and would do it right away, no questions asked. He said that's what Pappie wanted."

"What, no, no, no. I'm Pappie's daughter. This should be up to me." She cried more loudly. "How did they get involved?"

"When I couldn't get a hold of you, I called Saul. That's what Pappie had told me years ago to do immediately if there was a problem. He had written Saul's number on a piece of paper and taped it to the inside of a kitchen cabinet."

"Saul said he would handle everything, part of his job as priest for the Circle."

"Oh, good Lord, what lies, that miserable creep." A rush of anger flowed through her. *I am going to kill that monster.*

Semantha began crying uncontrollably. Then she became quiet.

"My God in all the universe, Hattie, who would do such a thing, why?

"Well, the house was ransacked. Looked like a botched robbery attempt. I don't know what the killer was looking for, but he went through everything before he left. I can't see that anything is missing, though."

"But a stake, my Lord, a stake." Semantha felt her stomach turn. *Why would a robber use a stake?*

"Did you call the police?"

"Saul said he would, and apparently he did. They came over right after Saul and Clem picked up the body."

"And another thing, before I got home, one of the neighbors found Pappie's sister passed out in her car in front of the house. She's in a coma at the hospital right now."

"What happened to her?' Semantha asked, recalling fond memories of her times with Calissa.

"Don't know. She's got a big gash on her head as well. Pappie had told me she was coming over. They wanted to reconnect before something happened to either of them."

Semantha threw her things in her bag, got into her car, and drove back to Michigan, sobbing the whole way. Once she got there, she went straight to the Circle's house. Clem was sitting in that miserable dive of a living room, smoking a cigar, and guzzling a can of beer.

"Sorry 'bout Pappie, Sama," Clem said. "It's bad shit. You's probably want to talk to Saul. I's don't know where he is. Left a while ago with Pappie's urn. He didn't say when he'd be back or where he was a goin'."

"So he kidnapped Pappie's ashes, is that what you are saying?"

Clem gave Semantha his dim-witted look. "Don't know wha' ya mean. I know's he's gonna take um out on the lake an' throw them on the water. Said probably tomorrow. Told me to let you know if I see you that you can come if you wants; otherwise, we's goin' out by ourselfs. Said tell you he already done gone to the sheriff and they's investigatin'."

"Clem, how could you and Saul be so cruel? I should have been the one to decide on arrangements."

Clem looked at her as if he anticipated her reaction. "Saul said you'd be pissed an' cursin' 'bout this. He also said, 'Hain't nothin' she can do 'bout it. Once Pappie is ashes, no way to git him back. Dust be dust.'"

Semantha left to go to see Hattie. As she drove there, she mulled over what this loss meant to her. Some of her initial shock began to wear off, replaced by a growing sense of tragedy. She had always clung to Pappie like an anchor as she tried to navigate through her chaotic and fearful world, filled with ghosts of her early years with Ajax and Penelope. She thought about how far she had come with him since the day when, bruised and unkempt, she stood on his front step. Now she felt adrift.

She harkened back to that day when Pappie had told her about Lucifer's visitation. She had never felt closer or more in touch with him. She saw that it was then when he became, not just an adoptive father, but also her spiritual leader and guide.

Gone now was the rock of her faith and the foundation for her self-confidence. She saw no other family or close friends who could fill the void. She thought, *Life without Pappie is unimaginable.* She wanted to cry out. *How will I continue? Who will give me the courage to go on? Who will tell me the right thing to do, what to believe in? How can I face tomorrow?*

XIII

As DISTRAUGHT AND DISTRACTED as she was, two days later Semantha found herself on *Blind Faith* heading out on to the lake with the urn carrying Pappie's ashes. It was an excruciating experience. After all that had happened in the previous weeks, Semantha was very wary of Saul, particularly because she strongly suspected that he was the one who engineered Pappie's cruel assassination. But as much as she detested and feared him, she also could not imagine missing the moment when the worldly remains of her beloved Pappie were committed back to the Earth, and she could not get Saul to do this any other way or time. He contended that this is what Pappie would have wanted.

She remained frozen and silent during the voyage, made longer because Saul insisted that they head out into deeper water before they scattered the ashes, away from anyone or anything. He wanted total privacy, he said. She could not look at either Saul or Clem the entire time and kept her eyes fixed on the water. Vivid memories of Pappie overpowered her. She thought she heard him gently calling her name. She envisioned him presiding at mass wearing his long flowing robe. He was such a commanding figure. With his ashes next to her, she felt she was in his presence. His mystical power seemed to radiate from the urn. When she looked at it, it appeared to glow. When she touched it, she felt electricity travel up her spine. But she knew that this was a presence she was about to lose forever. She wept with reckless abandon. Once or twice she moaned quietly.

XIV

———=———

SEMANTHA CALLED MEMMIE THE next day after they had scattered Pappie's ashes. She needed some advice and Memmie could be trusted to give it. Memmie was a long-standing member of the Circle and Pappie's close personal friend. A tarot reader and fortune teller, Memmie was an old, wily matron. She spoke slowly and deliberately, each word seemingly imbued with its own native wisdom. She also believed strongly in Pappie's message about the power of Lucifer.

Memmie's favorite diner in downtown St. Joe was empty when they came in, except for the waitress. She stayed in the kitchen most of the time they were there, leaving them some privacy to talk. They took a corner booth next to the front window. Memmie dressed as she always did, looking the part of a gypsy, complete with a turban-like, multi-patterned headdress. Semantha by now was wearing all black, including a lace scarf covering the top of her head like she was going to mass in the old days.

"Oh, my dear," Memmie said, shaking her head. Her pentagram-shaped earrings swayed back and forth, making a tinkling sound. "I've gotta tell you how heartbroken I am over Pappie's death. Devil have mercy. A real shocker, let me tell you, so awful."

Semantha looked down at the table and cried. She could not think about Pappie without becoming overwhelmed with grief.

"And my goodness, I am so sorry for you, sweetie. Got to have been a terrible loss, my pet."

"Thanks, Memmie." She wiped away her tears with a paper napkin from the Formica-topped table and regained a little composure. She was sure no one could understand the depth of her pain, but she still appreciated Memmie's sympathy. "How do the others feel?"

Memmie looked away for a second. Her glass eye did not follow. "We all hated to see his passing, especially the way he died. Imagine, a stake in his heart."

Semantha closed her eyes and grimaced as she thought about the cold sharp metal penetrating his brave chest. The sonorous noise made by the mallet as it hit the head of the stake. His body jerking each time the stake probed deeper. And then the noble, deep red blood pouring out. She imagined the terrible burning pain, his energy draining away, the cessation of life. She hoped he had thought of her as he breathed his last. *Maybe he said my name.*

"So, Semantha, have you any idea who may have done it?"

Doesn't she already know? Semantha thought. How could there be much doubt?

"There's only one possibility. He'll deny it, of course." She frowned.

"Uh, you're right, couldn't be anyone else. My guess is he just, oh, waited until you were out of town and it was Hattie's day off. Couldn't do it at the house on the river 'cause there are always too many folks hanging around, especially when Pappie was there."

Semantha thought about how everyone loved Pappie.

"But then my aunt must have surprised Saul in the act," Semantha said. "You heard she was at the house when the murder happened? Right now she's in a coma in intensive care."

"Goodness no, how'd that happen?" Memmie asked. The waitress brought two plastic cups and filled them with steaming hot coffee.

"I'm not sure. Maybe Saul too. He's capable of anything. You know, Memmie, right from the time I met him, he scared me. And my experience since, my God. Once I started going to the Circle's meetings, he was on me all of the time. He'd leer at me, try to feel me up, grab my breasts, typical male sleaze stuff. I was afraid to be alone with him."

"Devil have mercy, darling." Memmie took a sip of coffee.

Semantha did not touch hers.

"The worst was a chilly Saturday night after mass, just before I was about to head off for college. After everyone was gone, he grasped me by my arm and pulled me out into the woods. Then he pushed my shoulders against a tree and held me with both of his hands.

"I remember his words. He said, 'Hey Sama, you've turned into quite a hot babe. How about you and I get it on?' He made some uncouth reference to my other sexual encounters, pumped his hips against my crotch, and tried to put his tongue in my mouth.

"I screamed at him to get away and struggled to pull free. I told him 'no' and that I was not interested.

"He then got belligerent. He said, 'What's wrong with me, not a purdy boy or hot jock like some of your fuck buddies?' He asked what I had against him and called me stuck up. He grabbed me by the chin and forcibly rubbed my face against his stubble. I finally managed to get away."

"Scary," Memmie said.

"I was in a tough spot though. He was close to my father."

"And you were how old?"

"Just eighteen.

"That's when he really frightened me. I can still hear him saying these words." Semantha shivered a little as she remembered Saul's threat. 'You just wait, babe, someday you're gonna beg me for it an' we're gonna get it on. Just you wait,' he said. 'Only a matter of time.'

"The thought disgusted me. I ran to my car and left as fast as I could." Semantha wondered if Saul still had designs on her. *Probably.*

"Did you tell Pappie? He would've done something."

"I'm not so sure. As much as I love him, Pappie wasn't so good at dealing with problems. He saw things as he wanted. Pretty much he ignored everything else." Semantha shook her head. "He was blind to the real Saul."

"Maybe a little unfair to our wonderful Pappie, uh, don't you think?" Memmie adjusted her turban.

"No, no. Look at the history. Don't you remember Rod and Jimmie, the gay couple who were in the group for years? They disappeared without a trace. I've heard that their blood was all over their apartment when the police broke in. And all they did was say they thought Saul was a racist. Pappie did nothing about that."

"That was years ago," Memmie responded. "Pappie said Saul was not involved."

"And Sara. She just wanted to move away. They found her cut up, floating face down in the river. Pappie would never talk about that except to say Saul was out of town."

Memmie moved her head back and forth to the left and then to the right as if weighing Semantha's point. "Pappie did have a blind spot or two. Don't we all?" Memmie smiled a little, but Semantha did not see the joke.

"I didn't want to end up like these people." Semantha shook her head. "I thought, better to keep quiet." The waitress came over and offered more coffee. Semantha's cup was still full.

Memmie leaned closer to Semantha. "So, um, tell me, my dear, how went your trip to scatter Pappie's ashes? Did Saul and Clem act, uh, decent or were they their typical sorry selves? Tell me."

"What you would expect, Memmie, but we almost hit another boat a couple of minutes before we were going to throw the ashes in the water." Semantha still couldn't believe that had happened.

"Mercy sakes, another boat? What was it doing out there?"

"Not a clue, Memmie," Semantha said. "It was particularly strange because there was a beautiful man on that boat, and he came so close I could almost touch him."

She hesitated for a second as she relived that exquisite moment. Seeing the man had been like a ray of sunshine piercing the clouds on a bleak January day.

Semantha inclined her head even closer to Memmie. She wanted to be sure Memmie heard every word.

"There was something sweet and loving about him. It was almost as if he could feel my pain across the water, appreciate my heartbreak. Like he too was grieving. I smiled at him in spite of myself. Sad to say, I'll never see him again."

She longed for this man's compassion. But it seemed that a millennium separated her from that treasured interlude.

MEMMIE'S FACE CONTORTED A little. "But, my dear, you said you had, uh, something on your mind when you called. What's troubling you sweetie? Tell me." Memmie extended her hand in front of her as if offering her services.

"Memmie, I'm worried about what's going to happen to the Circle. Pappie's will names me to succeed him." Semantha's stomach felt like it was filled with squirming snakes when she thought about the implications of Pappie's act.

"My Lord in all of hades." Memmie slapped her own leg. "Does Saul know that, sweetie?"

"I was there when Pappie told him. It happened just before Pappie was murdered." She recalled Saul's audacity in showing up at their home uninvited on a Sunday morning.

"By the Devil's tooth, Sama, I'll bet against bet, Saul didn't like that." Memmie shook her head and again her earrings danced.

"To say the least. He was furious and threatening."

"Not surprising. And now Saul's goin' 'round talkin' with everyone, that includes me, I'll have you know. Saying that he is, uh, a natural, so to speak, um, to take over. And the way I see it, in some ways, he's right."

"My God, Memmie, why do you say such a thing?" Semantha clenched her teeth. The thought of Saul in charge of Pappie's proudest creation appalled her. *What a black day that would be,* she thought.

"He's just plain as evil as anyone I've ever got to know. Mercy sakes, got hate flowing out of every pore."

"I can see that but…"

He's tellin' some, um, big fat fibs too. Sure is. Says he's brought in many converts, some dropping a lot of money on the Circle. Course, we know that's a lie, Saul couldn't convince a snake to eat a rat, except for Clem who's lots cruder than Saul."

Semantha ran her hand up and down her arm as she thought a moment. "I'll bet he's saying bad things about me." Semantha could imagine his insults.

"Ugh, you got that right. Brace yourself for this, sweetie. Uh, says you must have been giving Pappie nookie of some type or other."

"Nookie? What do you mean, Memmie?"

"I mean sex, you know, in exchange for saying you should take over when he went to Lucifer, you see. Says Pappie was off his rocker at the end, chasing after you, will you have it. So he says, oh you know, uh, don't pay attention to his will. Says you tricked him into signing it."

Semantha shook her head in disbelief. "That's so wrong. I couldn't have influenced him to do anything even if I wanted to. It was the opposite. I needed him so much he had total control over me. His thoughts were my thoughts, Memmie."

Semantha began to sob. Memmie reached over, took Semantha's hand, and gently stroked it. "Please, sweetie, calm yourself. I know it's so hard." She then took both of Semantha's hands in hers and lightly squeezed them. "It will be okay, my dear."

Semantha felt Memmie's warmth flow into her. *Memmie's a sweet old lady*, Semantha thought. She wondered what she was doing in a coven. Then she remembered how Memmie had told her how much she felt accepted in the Circle, looked forward to the monthly black mass, and enjoyed spending time with others like herself at the house on the river.

Again Semantha regained some composure. "What else does that creep say?" She felt her rising anger. She thought, *I don't deserve this. Why do I need to endure it? I just want a normal life like everybody else.*

Memmie rubbed her forehead. "Let's see, uh, uh, uh… Oh my, how could I forget? He lays it on thick when he brings up your relations with men. Oh my gosh, Sama. Brutal, just brutal he is. Calls you a floozy nymphomaniac. Now, I tell you, sweetie, there's a word I had to look up. Says if you were in charge you'd be, so to speak, chasing tail all the time, forgetting about the Circle."

Just then, Semantha looked out the window and saw one of her old sex partners from high school walk by. *Why'd he choose this precise minute to show up?* Semantha thought, realizing at the same time that it was just a coincidence. It did make her think about whether Saul was right; maybe sex distracted her too much.

What people didn't realize was that, for her, sex was far more than a physical release. When she was having sex, she could ignore her omnipresent internal demons and escape to freedom, at least briefly. Always had been that way, probably always would be. She recalled that she had tried to stop when Pappie called her out. She could not. At college, she had gone to see a psychologist. He told her not to worry about it unless it interfered with her life. Maybe it was a psychological habituation, maybe a chemical imbalance. Hard to really trace or pinpoint a cause, he had said.

Semantha thought of chasing after her old partner, Francisco was his name. It would be good to catch up and maybe… But she still had more to discuss with Memmie. Semantha stared at Memmie.

"Does Saul have a chance of taking over?"

"Sweetie, oh my, now there's a question. Sure does have some folks behind him, especially the ones who think we should be doing bad stuff and riling up the town. By Lucifer's purse. Got a few people thinking that right now the Circle has no reason to go on otherwise. One said to me, exact words, 'Right now the Circle's as useless as tits on a boar hog.'"

The waitress brought the bill and Semantha took out her wallet.

"Do ya wanna be high priest, my dear?" Memmie asked. The seriousness in Memmie's voice scared Semantha.

That question had been haunting her since Pappie had made his announcement at the house a couple of weeks before. She was anything but sure about her next steps. She had hoped that her meeting with Memmie would help her figure that out.

"That's complicated, Memmie." She ran her hand through her hair. "With all my heart I want to see Pappie's legacy continue. I would call that a passion. If Saul takes over, I am quite sure the Circle will crash and burn. He is so radical, ironically too evil."

"By the Devil's concubine, that's my mind about things too. Oh, Saul, um, would scare most everyone to death. They'd sneak away, one at a time, leaving a few crazies like Clem wandering around terrorizing and killing until they got thrown in the slammer for good."

"I also want to see that the murderer pays for Pappie's horrible death. If Saul takes over, I worry Pappie's death will be swept under the rug."

Semantha took a spoon and aimlessly stirred her coffee.

"Does it matter that Pappie named me in his will?"

"Uh, sure does, but still you, uh, gonna need to convince the members you're the one, my dear. That won't come free. Sure won't."

"Nothing ever is. What would I need to do?"

"Sweetie, that's easy. Got to tell 'em, uh, what you believe in. Show them some of Pappie's power and energy, his conviction. Make 'em feel it. Not that easy, sweetie, but I think you have it in you, and so did Pappie. I saw it comin' out of you when you talked to the Circle before you went away to school."

Without knowing it, Memmie had just hit a soft spot. Semantha was anything but sure of her beliefs. With Pappie present, it was easy. She felt the strength of his convictions. When she spoke to the Circle in her younger days, it was really Pappie's words channeling through her. But when she was away from him, her fervor seemed to weaken and her certainty wane. She was easily distracted by new or different ideas.

Her college experience did not help. What Pappie had taught was hostile to everything she heard in school. It now seemed arcane. This whole thing about an epic battle between good and evil felt like a leftover myth from the Middle Ages. If Semantha would need to speak forcefully about her beliefs to become high priest, her doubts made the task much more daunting, maybe impossible. She was not good at faking it.

Her questions about the whole Lucifer thing were not the only problem. Along with the loss of her belief in Pappie's message, she no longer felt confident in herself. His unbounded belief in her had supplied that as well. This seemed to be another roadblock to convincing the Circle she should be high priestess. How could she make others believe in her if she herself was faltering?

Semantha saw the odds were heavily against her becoming high priest, and there were plenty of reasons for her not to do it. At the same time, Semantha felt trapped, absolutely cornered. She was convinced that, if she tried to leave, Saul and Clem would track her down and do her in, maybe torture her beforehand, just like Rod, Jimmie, and Sara. She did not see going to the police as an option. They had investigated the other murders and found nothing. Saul and Clem were very clever at covering their tracks and the police in Benton Harbor pretty ineffective.

She also could not imagine staying in the Circle with Saul in control. She knew he would not leave her alone. She remembered what he had said to her that late night he tried to rape her. Also, he would see her as a grave threat to him regardless of who was in charge. Saul would do anything he could to subdue her and subject her to God knows what.

Although her heart was not in it and she worried that she lacked the conviction to succeed, she saw no choice but to try to assert herself as high priest, to expose Saul, and to save herself. It was a long shot, but it was her only shot.

"Which side are you on, Memmie?"

"By the footstool of Beelzebub, dearie, you don't need to ask, not at all, no not at all. I'm with you, one hundred percent, two hundred percent if I could be." Memmie smiled like a grandmother.

"I'm going to need your help."

"That's no problem."

Semantha managed a half-hearted grin as the staggering weight of her plight seemed to ease some. She could feel a bit of her self-confidence return as she tapped into Memmie's certitude.

"Thanks, Memmie. Just talking to you makes me feel better."

"Mercy sakes, Sama, it's easy to perk you up. Keep on thinkin' positive like that, ya know."

Semantha laughed and took a drink of her now tepid coffee.

"I'm gonna talk with some more reasonable members of the Circle to see what they say," Memmie said. "Oh, in the meantime, we should keep our little talk just to ourselves. Loose lips sink ships and all of that, if you know what I mean."

Semantha nodded in agreement.

"Uh, I'm also going to consult the tarot and look at the stars, maybe plot a horoscope. It's always a good idea to find out what the spirit world can tell us, dearie."

Semantha chuckled silently. She thought that whole thing was silly, but she was not about to say that to Memmie, especially at this critical juncture.

"We need to act quickly," Semantha said. "We both know Saul. He's loud, domineering, and pushy. He's not going to sit on his hands, waiting for folks to think about things."

"Now there, you've hit on the real problem, my sweet. What are you going to do about Saul? You're gonna have to, erh, uh, let's say, dress him down one way or the other, you know. Hard to see how you get from here to there otherwise, my pet."

"You are so very right, Memmie. How do I handle him? Good Lord, everything says he killed my father, and I know he tried to rape me. Plus there are those other murders. How do you dress down a man like that?" Semantha felt a twinge of terror.

"You're gonna need to be strong, look strong even if you don't feel it, you know. Dig deep, find Pappie's power. I know you got it inside you. Just got to find it."

"You think so?" Semantha was not so sure.

"Way I look at it, Saul's not gonna do anything unless he feels the Circle's behind him. Play on that, and, mercy sakes, my guess, Saul will back down, fightin' and cursin', but he'll back down." Memmie nodded her head up and down a little. "That's my advice for right now."

Not convinced she could pull it off, she said in a soft, meek voice, "I'll try. I'm not sure I have a choice, Memmie."

"We do have a little time, though. Nothing's going to happen right now, especially before Pappie's memorial mass tomorrow. If anything was afoot, um, by a black cat's whiskers, I'da heard it. Let's talk again, uh, right afterwards, okay, dearie?"

"Okay, Memmie. You know he agreed to make that into a remembrance for Pappie only because we were going to have a mass anyway."

"Is there gonna be a sacrifice?"

"Yep, Clem told me Saul bought a poor rabbit to cut up. Aren't you going to come?" Semantha desperately wanted her to be there.

"Sorry, dearie, oh, I hate to miss it, my first one in a long time. But I've got to go to Grand Rapids to see a doc. My sciatica is acting up again, this time real bad. Got a big pain right in my leg. Can't sleep a wink, barely can walk. There's a chiropractor over there who knows what he's doin'. One visit and I'm fixed up for quite a while."

"Good luck with that, Memmie."

"Good luck to you too. Remember, think of Pappie and his love for you. Be strong and I think Saul will cave in. You can do this, my sweetheart." She reached over and gave Semantha a peck on the forehead, then departed. Almost instantly, Semantha felt a twinge in her back and her stomach began to burn as her anxiety swelled.

XV

The day after her conversation with Memmie, Semantha drove over to the house for the mass, worried about what was to come but somewhat buoyed by the support and encouragement Memmie had provided. She parked her car on the road and walked down the lane to the barn. She always got the jitters when she walked down that lane alone. It was so dark and spooky with all the thick vegetation and overgrown trees. She felt like there was something lurking in the bushes, ready to pounce, even during the day.

Ten members of the Circle were already there, representing each of the Circle's cells, and a woman who would perform the role of the human altar during the mass. Saul and Clem were inside the barn, setting things up. As soon as she walked up, Clem came out.

"Semantha, Saul and I got sumpin' to talk wit you 'bout. Git in the barn righ' now, ya hear," he said, waving his arm as if herding sheep.

Semantha felt herself stiffen as she went inside. It was dark and cool there, away from the hot July sun. "Okay, Saul, what's up?" she asked.

"We's got a man tied up in the kitchen," Saul responded. "He says he's the man who was drivin' the other boat last week when we went out to toss Pappie's ashes."

Semantha's mouth dropped open. "Unbelievable! Are you sure? How'd he get here?"

"He says some sort'a magic force pulled 'im here. He came from Chicago on the train and walked out here all by hisself. Leas' that's wha' he says."

Semantha could not believe her ears. This man she thought she would never see again was here, actually here, tied up in the kitchen. Her first instinct was to go and throw herself on him.

"Why's he tied up?" Semantha asked.

"Caught him snoopin''roun' the house. Looked like he was tryin' to spy on us, suspicious like," Clem volunteered.

"Did you ask him what he was doing?" By now several other members of the Circle had entered the barn.

"Yep. Jes said he was drawn here to find out more about us an' wha' we did here," Saul said.

Semantha saw her chance. "Wait a minute, Saul, let me see if I understand. This man says he was drawn here by an unseen force, wants to find out more about us, and you tie him up. What sense is there here?"

Members muttered and shook their heads, apparently in agreement with Semantha. One yelled out, "Yeah, Saul, what are you doing? We need new members, not new victims." Someone else said, "Right, what gives?" Semantha felt that they were behind her. Her confidence soared.

Saul stood there mute as if he could not answer her question. Semantha thought she had stumped him, made him look the fool. She felt on her way to really taking charge. *That wasn't so hard. Memmie was right about Saul,* she thought.

"I'm going to let him go," Semantha said. "It's crazy to hold him against his will."

Semantha turned to head toward the door. "Whoa, hol' yer horses, there, Semantha,' Saul said. "You's the one whose gotta think some. Nobody but us know this man's here. This is our chance to do wha' we has been talkin' about for a while. We can offer up this man to Lucifer tonight and nobody gonna ever find out."

Hearing these words, Semantha realized what this was about. This was more than just some man tied up in that ratty, bug-infested kitchen. The battle between them was on.

"Think about what he said," Saul continued, shaking his left finger at Semantha. "He said he was pulled here by some force. Seems like Lucifer sent us this man to use, and if we don't, we'll offend 'im. After all, it's our time to sacrifice something. He's showin' up righ' now gotta be a sign. Who's to say, ya know. Pappie always said Lucifer works in ways we cain't figure."

By now everyone had entered the barn and was standing around listening intently.

Semantha thought about what could have caused this man to show up. It seemed implausible that somehow he had been drawn to the house by an otherworldly force. Much more likely that he had been as attracted to her as she was to him. Then he figured out a way to find the boat. She was intrigued.

"Lucifer's plan? I don't think so," she said, squinting. "I'm pretty sure this man came here looking to meet me. You must have seen us looking at each other when the boats met. I don't think Lucifer had anything to do with it."

Semantha thought maybe that was not quite the right thing to say as she saw several surprised looks. One member whispered something she could not quite hear. May have been the word "nypho," but she was not sure.

"Semantha, that's jes so much bull crap. An' besides, what's you gonna say as to what got us close on the lake inna firs' place. Lake's pretty big. What's the chance of we ever getting that close to this here other boat. 'Bout none. Somethin' needed to get the two boats together. I says it was Lucifer, and you's cain't say it weren't."

"It was just chance, Saul."

"Chance? Shit. This ain't got nothin' to do with chance. Far as that goes, how did this man ever git all the way over here to Michigan inna firs' place. We's not all that easy to find so far up the river from the lake. Think about it. Ain't no big sign in the lake sayin, 'Good fuck this way.' I say Lucifer got inside his mind an' gave him a push. I say this is all part of Lucifer's plan to show us Pappie's murderer."

That comment shocked Semantha. She was sure that the last thing on Saul's mind was revenging anything, let alone uncovering who killed Pappie. This was Saul's ploy to sell the idea of using this man. Claiming it was Lucifer's idea made it sound less brutal, almost spiritual. She was sure the members would see through Saul's transparent ruse. She intentionally fixed her gaze on Saul and held it for a long minute, like she was trying to stare him down.

"Come on, Saul, who are you trying to kid," she said. "You're living in a dream world. What you want to do is insane." She stopped talking and waited for a minute. "No," she yelled.

After her declaration, she continued to gaze at him as if daring him to say anything more. He remained silent, looking a little sheepish.

Semantha finally turned, left the barn, and headed toward the kitchen, confident she had put Saul in his place and assured she really was in charge now. She felt so proud that she had overcome her fears and stood up to this man. She felt empowered. It did not occur to her that Saul was only biding his time.

AFTER SHE LEFT, CLEM looked at Saul and, in front of everybody, asked "Hain't you gonna do nothin', Saul? She's gonna fuck 'im, then let him go."

Saul did not respond because this was exactly what he wanted. He was convinced that every groan from that kitchen would show up Semantha as a wanton slut. She was playing right into his hand.

Saul looked at each of the members, one by one, saying nothing and letting the silence build tension.

"See there goes yer fine new high priest," he finally said, motioning in the direction of the barn door. "Only thinkin' 'bout gettin' herself grati-fied on this man and defying Lucifer after he sent him to us. She's purdy smart wit words, but ya didn't hear nothin' 'bout how it happened the boats got so close or how this man got here in the firs' place? No. An' you all knows why. Lucifer did it. Weren't no man on a boat who got all hot an' bothered to chase her all the way here after jes one little look. Cummon."

One person said, "She's a slut." Another yelled, "Whore." Others seemed to mutter in agreement. Those who were loyal to Pappie and his wishes remained mute.

Saul could feel sentiment swinging his way.

"Yeah, all she's wantin' is to fuck alla time," he said. "Hain't got no thoughts in nothin' else. Not none of you, not the Circle, not the memory of our dear slain leader, Pappie, nothin'." He paused. "As long as we's here, that man hain't goin' nowhere. We all knows what we gotta do." Saul thought, *This broad ain't seen nothing yet. Fool's not gonna git in my way no how.*

XVI

STILL TIED UP IN THE kitchen, Marco felt like he had been in that hot, stuffy hellhole forever. He heard the barn door open and close, signaling the arrival of more people. He could hear them talking, but he could not make out their words, except he did hear a female voice yell, "No" and someone else say "Whore." It sounded like a nasty fight underway. Marco became hungry, thirsty, and he had to take a piss. Eventually, he pissed in his pants.

★   ★   ★

BEFORE SHE OPENED THE door, Semantha paused. She knew herself too well, what she was about to do. Here was a man of extraordinary sensitivity and understanding, worthy of getting to know. She had felt it profoundly in their brief encounter on the lake and seen it in how he had managed to find her. She thought about Pappie's counsel when she was in high school. Get to know someone first. But then she winced as she imagined the sting when Ajax's hand slapped her cheek. She needed soothing the only way she knew how to get it.

★   ★   ★

WHEN SHE WALKED IN, Marco recognized her instantly as the woman from the boat encounter. He was incredibly relieved to see her. He thought she had been very attracted to him on the boat, and now he could see lust in her eyes. *Translate that into a little help, and I'm out of here.*

Feeling relieved and hopeful for the first time all afternoon, he let himself give her a good look. She was every bit as sexy and desirable close up as she was from a distance. The word *Melissa* again came to his mind. *So, so much alike.*

She was dressed in a beige tank top and white, form-fitting jeans, with a gap between revealing her trim stomach and belly button. Her lips were supple and naturally colored, her completion clear and blemish free, her eyes soft and inviting. She had a kind and intelligent look, a sweetness that spread over her countenance. *Perfect,* he thought. She did not look the slightest bit evil or like a witch.

She came to where Marco was tied up and stood next to him, close enough to smell his odors, those like a farmhand just in from a day in the barn. She smiled, highlighting her dimples. Marco jumped when he saw them, pushing against the restraints.

"It's okay," she said, seeing him struggling with the ropes. "My name is Semantha. Some call me Sama. I heard you were here and I just had to meet you." She reached down and removed the dish towel stuck between his teeth. Marco shook out his mouth and his beautiful curly hair waggled a little.

"What's your name?" Semantha asked.

Her voice was soft and disarming, a little deep and mysterious, so different from the other brutes, so different from everything there. To Marco she was like a rose in a field of thistles, a filly in a pen with donkeys. Even the way she dressed did not fit in, so fresh and clean. After hearing the sweetness in her voice, he was sure she would help him escape. *Play along with this. It's going to work out,* he thought. A rush of calm swept over him.

"Marco's my name."

"How did you get here?"

"As I told your friends, I was the captain of the boat you passed last week and ever since I felt compelled to come here. Not exactly sure how I got here, believe it or not."

Sama's face turned serious. "You lie," she said. Those words frightened Marco. Maybe she knew about the powerboat and how he really got there. But then a coy smile replaced her frown.

"You know very well what got you here. I felt the energy passing between us—a sort of dynamic tension. I can't explain it in words, but I felt it and apparently you did too."

"I…" Marco began to speak.

Semantha interrupted by putting two of her fingers on his mouth. "Your compassion and sorrowful look overpowered me."

"I saw a sadness in your eyes as well," Marco said as the two stared at each other for a second.

"The only difference between us is that you came looking for me. I thought I would never see you again."

"Please help me get out of here."

"Don't worry, Marco. You are not in danger. Believe me." Semantha put her hand on his shoulder.

"How can you be so certain?" Marco asked. "This is a witches' coven, right, and those guys who pointed a gun at me and tied me up are Devil worshipers. Not exactly model citizens. Are you involved with all of this?"

"My father, we all called him Pappie, founded this group over eighteen years ago to worship Lucifer. Until he died, he was its leader and high priest. His will appointed me as his successor, and I have assumed leadership. I am now in charge."

"Those thugs still around?"

"Saul and Clem? They can be rough and violent, no doubt about it. Sometimes, they do things they shouldn't, and this was one. But they can't do anything without my say-so, and the other members of the Circle are behind me. Saul and Clem are under control. Believe me, you are safe."

"I heard that man Saul say that I may be of 'use' during the ceremony tonight. When you walked in, I thought I was on the way to being a human sacrifice--quite a terrifying thought. Is that the plan?"

"It's not my plan. Don't worry Marco, I am not going to let anything bad happen." She bent over and brought her face close to his. "Do you need to hear that more plainly?"

With these words, Marco felt the weight of his confinement lift. His cravings stirred despite the surroundings. He wanted to reach out and touch Semantha but couldn't.

"Regardless of what you told the boys about the mysterious force that got you here," Sama said, "I suspect you went to a lot of effort. I bet it wasn't easy. So, in return, let me offer you a little token of my gratitude."

Her face grew even softer. Focusing her eyes on his and speaking in a calm, low, innocent voice, she whispered, "I want you and I want you to have me."

After a minute, she ripped off her tank top and revealed her fresh supple breasts. They were smallish and round, just like Marco loved. She straddled the chair where Marco was strapped and pushed them into his face, softly rubbing her nipples back and forth, lightly touching Marco's nose and open lips. Passion overtook him, sending an electric pulse directly to his balls and shaft, which filled up and pushed against his pants.

"I stink," he said.

"I know. Doesn't bother me."

"I cannot move to touch you."

"Let me change that," she said, removing the belt and the ropes.

"Aren't you afraid I will run?"

"You can leave if you want. But I hope you stay for a little while. I think we can make a little black magic together." She winked at him seductively and smiled.

After she freed him, she guided one of his hands under her pants and then down to her throbbing moistness. As he pulled his hand out to touch her breasts, he smelled the sweet fragrance of her desire. She was right about one thing. Right now Marco's mind was on anything but escape. He had left this dump on the river and had entered into a glorious world populated by only the two of them where nothing else mattered but pleasuring and being pleasured. No time existed except the moment, no past or future, and no other except each other.

They lay on the floor and explored with their lips and tongues without inhibition or limitation. He rubbed his cheeks against hers and kissed her dimples with his tongue. *Oh sweet Melissa,* he thought. His shaft pulsated hard. He rubbed his whiskers against her neck. She groaned. He delighted when she nibbled softly on his ear. He relished the aromas of her body, potentiated by the moistness of her skin on that hot summer night. Sama's hips began to rythmetically gyrate as Marco pushed against her erogenous zones, teasing her with his virility. She emitted soft, measured groans, which gradually increased as her desire overtook her. She pleasured his shaft with her lips, and he her privates with his. She rubbed her nose under his arms and in his pubic hair.

Marco lifted Sama off the floor and gently laid her on the table. He entered her, thrusting more and more deeply and powerfully until he built to a final crescendo. His passion burst out of him and flowed into her with a free and potent release. She emitted a loud gasp and he a long groan. At that moment he was nothing except his maleness, and she was nothing except his vessel.

He lay there for a bit, remaining inside of her, his form hot and trembling. He felt her blood pumping through her; they fit together that well. Then he withdrew and sat upon the chair which, until a few moments previous, had been the scene of his confinement. She sat up on the side of the table and looked at him. His eyes met hers as they drank each other in while their bodies calmed. Neither said anything with words, but they explored each other's thoughts through their eyes.

Finally Marco spoke. "Beautiful."

Semantha smiled.

"I hope you don't get pregnant."

"Would that be so bad?" She reached out and began gently stroking his hair.

Marco, surprised by that statement, took her hand and began caressing her fingers. They smelled mossy and sweet. A sugar-coated image of a happy little family flashed across his mind. *She may be the life partner I have been looking for,* he thought. *She is smart, beautiful beyond belief, and classy. And those dimples.*

You think we have a future together?" he asked as he put his hand on her thigh and began rubbing it.

"Wouldn't that be nice?" She took his hand and guided it toward her privates.

"But you worship the Devil."

Semantha looked away. "Not exactly," she said, as if to soft-petal what the Circle stood for. "Pappie used to talk about dark energy. There is much more dark energy and dark matter in the universe than matter and energy that we see and feel. Black holes are the most powerful concentration of energy there could ever possibly be. Pappie chose the prince of dark matter because that is where the greatest force resides."

"You sound like a scientist."

"I teach science at Berrien County Community College, my first job after getting my masters in physics. I guess that makes me a scientist."

"Most scientists say that science led them away from spiritual beliefs. You are still worshiping some mystical force. That's unusual."

Sama, not delving into her own doubts, said only, "Faith is blind."

Marco was quite intrigued by that response but decided that the kitchen of a rundown farmhouse was no place for discussing philosophy.

"What do you mean when you refer to this so-called 'Circle?'" Marco asked.

"The more conventional name would be, as you suggest, 'coven.' Pappie did not like that word, so he called it a 'Circle,' a symbol of unity and infinity. Circles have no end. Circles also have special meaning in our rituals."

"I heard your friends saying that your ceremony tonight is in memory of Pappie."

Tears came to Sama. "A couple of weeks ago, someone knocked Pappie unconscious and drove a stake in his heart." She trembled.

Marco reached over and hugged her.

"When we came close to you on the boat the other week, we were about to scatter Pappie's ashes. It was a sad and solemn occasion for us. We expected we would have some privacy, but you came out of nowhere."

"Now I've done it again, I guess, showing up just before your memorial."

"We hope Lucifer will come to us tonight and reveal Pappie's murderer."

"And I presume there is a reason why you were on a sailboat, maybe it's a cover?" Marco asked.

"Right, Saul and Clem used the boat to dispose of our sacrifices, sort of part of the ritual," Semantha responded.

"…and sailboats don't attract a lot of attention." Marco snickered. "Everyone knows that sail boaters are naive nature lovers, not into much of anything." Sama let out a "ha."

"Besides that, Pappie had this idea that eventually he would spend his summers sailing up and down the coast of the lake. It was his boat."

"You know, the electronics went out on our boat when we passed. Some of my crew members think that you had something to do with that."

Sama smiled shyly. "Pappie claimed he could do that sort of thing. I never saw it."

"And what about the way you were dressed, that veil and in a bikini on such a miserable day? You must have been freezing."

"The bikini was my thought. I put that on just before we were going to scatter Pappie's ashes. To me, it symbolized that we come into this world with nothing and that's the way we leave. It was cold, but that only added to the solemnity."

"And that sort of veil affair...why that thing?"

"Saul insisted I wear it. He said his grandmother wore it at her wedding. He claims that it has spiritual powers. Said it brings good luck and money. I put it on because I didn't see any reason to fight with him."

Semantha's forehead wrinkled. "Why don't you stay and attend the mass tonight? It will be interesting for you. I'm sure you have never seen anything like it."

"I only want to get out of here, Sama. Don't get me wrong. Meeting you has been wonderfully unbelievable, and I would like to see you again. How can we arrange that? Maybe another time?"

"Another time? How about now?" Semantha touched Marco gently on his lips and let him caress her finger. Then she continued in her sweet low voice, "My darling, stay just the way you are. I'll bring you some food and a little wine. It's still early. I would love to do a little more, uh, well, mutual exploring."

She winked again and smiled seductively. "Don't get dressed. I've got a little Circle business to take care of. I'll be back in just a couple of minutes. It will be so hot; bet on it."

Sama dressed and walked out.

Now's the time to get out of here, Marco thought. But then he thought some more. *Wait a just a second, one more roll with Sama would be great.* Since Sama was in charge, Marco had no reason to fear Saul, Clem, or their nastiness any longer.

If Sama wanted more, he was quite ready to deliver. *It would be silly not to grab the chance. Got to make up for lost time after my long dry spell in New Mexico.*

XVII

WHEN SEMANTHA GOT BACK to the barn, Saul was there, and the other members of the Circle were standing around, for sure waiting to see what would happen next. By now they had all dressed in their black robes. Along with the velvet curtains hanging from the rafters, their garb gave the feel of midnight inside the barn even though outside the sun was setting. Saul yelled at her as soon as she walked into the barn door.

"So Sama, you have a good time fuckin' the man Lucifer sent me?" His voice was heavy with sarcasm. "We's all could hear ya goin' at it all the way out here. Sounded like you's got fucked real good."

"Mind your own business," Semantha said tersely, not expecting Saul's aggressive tone but feeling herself turning a little red.

"Whoa, wha' happens to this man is my business. As I told you, Lucifer sent 'im to me to use, an' I'm a gonna do it."

Some of the members began to murmur. Everyone's eyes were on Saul and Semantha. No one moved.

Semantha's body tightened. She braced for a struggle as she realized her battle of wills with Saul was not over. She began to sweat and her mouth dried. Her voice quivered a little, but she still tried to sound brave.

"No, Saul. I w–w–will not, uh...uh permit this brutality. Pappie was against using humans. He thought, uh...animals were more than enough."

Several members chuckled and she heard someone say, "Brutal, that's what we're all about." Semantha had a sinking feeling in her gut.

Sensing her weakness, Saul moved close to Semantha. "What's ya mean ya won't allow it? Who the fuck do ya thinks you is and where do ya thinks you get off running things around here? And sure it's brutal. Sure, it's evil… but that's why Lucifer is gonna do great by us, 'cause we's evil and brutal. Ya gotta get your head screwed on right and deal with who we is. Ya also needs to face up to what Lucifer wants. We better do it or Lucifer gonna git pissed."

"But Saul…" Semantha hesitated as her resolve pulverized into dust.

"Anyway, Semantha, you's against this cause you's a little nymph and you's wants to keep 'im as yer little fuck toy. All ya wants is to use this man yerself, maybe in a different way than we wants to use 'im, but at least for us it's to worship the almighty power of the universe. For you, it's jes yer own animal lust a drivin' ya."

"You tell her, Saul," someone shouted. A couple of other members began to stomp their feet. By now the members loyal to Pappie had moved away from the fight and were standing along the walls looking frightened.

Semantha swallowed hard. With this last comment, Saul had hit her right between the eyes. She felt exposed and defenseless in the face of Saul's powerful, commanding force, further intimidated by the comments from the crowd. Desperately trying to follow Memmie's advice, she took a deep breath and summoned up courage one more time. Tears filled her eyes.

"H-h-how d-d-dare, you Saul. Pappie willed me to be the high priestess. It's, it's, it's, t-t-time for me to take charge. If we start doing this sort of thing we will, uh, attract too much attention. The-the-the Circle will be destroyed and, uh, we will all pay a terrible price."

"Cummon. That's stupid," someone said.

Saul sidled up behind Semantha, grabbed her arm, and twisted it behind her until she gasped. She tried to struggle free, but she was no match for Saul. He only twisted that much harder. She felt his erection pushing against her leg. He got so close to her that she could smell the rancid garlic on his breath. She could feel the scratch of his prickly whiskers on her neck. He put his face right up to her ear and spoke in a powerful, mean whisper.

"Ya listen here, ya floozy cunt. I don't give a damn 'bout what yer fuckin' stepfather wrote 'fore he died. Wes all know he was half senile and that he did what ya wanted. He probably wanted to fuck ya too like half the men in Michigan. Could be you let 'im so he'd leave ya things. He deserved to die."

Saul squeezed a little harder. "We's gonna do this tonight and that's all there is to it, so git yerself used to it. Your littl' lover boy's a goin' to Lucifer."

Upon saying this, Saul threw Semantha against the table. After she recovered a bit, she turned and stared at him. Semantha's thoughts raced in disordered torrents. She was both terrified and red with anger. *What can I do now? How can I take on this monster? He is winning. He is the Devil. He will destroy everything.*

"You killed Pappie, didn't you, you miserable scumbag," she screamed. "You wanted him out of the way so that you could take over the Circle and make it the way you wanted."

"No cunt, you killed Pappie one day at a time, lovin' the hate out of 'im and makin' 'im useless to the Circle and to Lucifer. You turned 'im into an ol' fool, worthless to anyone but you. By the time you was done with 'im, Lucifer's high priest was already dead."

Saul paused, quieted down a little, then spoke, sounding somewhat defensive. "Besides, I hain't the only one in the Circle who wanted Pappie done gone. Lots of folks could a gone an' did it."

After she heard this, Semantha grabbed the large dagger lying on the table. She came running toward Saul, holding it high in the air as if to strike. But as she approached him, he just grabbed her arms, squeezed them hard, and the dagger dropped to the ground. He held her close and again whispered in her ear quietly so only she could hear him.

"Whore, you better be careful, ya hear. You's askin' fer trouble comin' after me. Nasty things can happen 'round here especially late at night in the middle of the berry patches. Ya know Clem. He does wha' I says. He don't care what it is and he don't care if it's nasty. He kindda likes it when it's nasty. He sort of sneaks up from behind and people don't know what hit 'em. We's sure would hate to see anything bad happen to your purdy body and them sweet tits."

"Oh Saul, please don't do this." She then dropped to her knees and threw her arms around Saul's legs. "I think I love him. Maybe he will give me a baby to carry on the work of Lucifer here on Earth," she pleaded. "I'll give the baby to you."

Saul looked down at the miserable animal clinging to his legs, degraded as she was in front of everyone. He yanked her to her feet, held her shoulders, and leered at her. "Fuck ya an' any of yur offspring" Then he spit on her face. One of the members of the Circle let out a gasp. The others stood motionless in seeming amazement.

Saul then turned Semantha around, twisted an arm behind her back, and marched her outside away from the crowd. Again he whispered. "Semantha, ya gotta know by now, this thing gonna happen, but it will make this a whole bunch easier for all of us, 'specially you and this man, if ya don't fight wit me any more. I'll give ya some drugs to put him out, easier for 'im, easier for me. An' fur you."

Saul grabbed her chin and yanked her face close to his. "But we's got some time. If ya wants, you's can go and bed him down again. I don't care. Let 'im get you pregnant if you can. But like I tol' ya before ya went away to that there school, after you's done with this man, ya gonna be my bitch an' my bitch alone. You's gonna do what I says, everything I says. An' don't forget it."

Semantha groaned.

"Groan all ya want, don't matter. Here's the deal. You gets some more action now, you stays with the Circle, and ya don't get hurt. You's happy, I is happy, the Circle is happy, best Lucifer is happy. What's ya say? Otherwise, jes git yourself outta here an' we's gonna deal wit you later. I can tell you righ' now, if I gotta come after ya, it hain't gonna be no fun for you.

"And one more thing," Saul continued, "you's gonna be up there with me at the mass tonight so everybody can see we's in this together and we's one big happy family jes like Pappie wanted. And tomorrow you's gonna put on my grandma's veil jes like you did before so everybody knows you's my wif. We all gonna take what's left of yur lover boy out on the lake, weigh him down, and toss him in. You's gonna give the final push, an' you's gonna have a big smile on yur face when you do."

Bringing home his point, Saul took the back of his hand and slapped her hard on the side of her face, so hard it knocked her to the ground. There she lay sobbing. He pulled her to her feet by her hair, pointed her toward the road, and said: "Now bitch, you go git your mind screwed on correct and when you come back, git ready to do wha' I say." He gave her a push.

SEMANTHA BEGAN TO WALK down the lane. By now it was close to dark and the lane was filled with shadows. She almost walked into a large spider web. At first, she was in a daze, her mind blank. Then, as her head cleared a little, scattered thoughts returned. *Where am I headed? Am I done? Can anyone save me? Where's Pappie when I need him? Even Memmie has abandoned me.* She felt desperately alone, defenseless. She thought she heard a chorus of shrill voices calling her name over and over.

And Lucifer? Where is he in this? She recalled how sure Pappie had been about Lucifer's power. She knew that if Pappie were still here, he would say that this is all part of Lucifer's will and plan. *Could it be that Lucifer will use this mass to expose Pappie's murderer? Maybe he will appear in the incense smoke and resolve everything.* Semantha prayed he would manifest himself just like he had appeared to Pappie late that night in the cornfield.

The thought that Lucifer might appear comforted Semantha's troubled mind. She agreed with Saul about one thing. This man's appearance at precisely this time seemed to be too unlikely to have happened only by chance.

Did Lucifer send him? Is Lucifer my only hope? Will he help me out of this? She didn't know what to believe.

Her mind veered in a different direction. *Maybe I should just run. As far and as fast as I can. But there's no use to do that. Where would I go? Saul will find me. He would make me pay big for trying to escape.*

She heard something hiss and a shadow like a bat flew in front of her.

Saul's image appeared in her mind. *Wait a minute, he is in control now. He's the law. He is so powerful and sure of himself in his hate.* She thought more and more about his power and willfulness as she walked. *Should I just submit to him? He is so strong.*

She stopped walking. *Do I have a choice?* She did not see one.

These thoughts replayed themselves in Semantha's mind, circling faster and faster like dry leaves caught in a whirlwind. She became dizzy, sat down on the ground, put her head between her legs, and wrapped her arms around them. The ground felt cold, clammy under her. By now it was dark.

Closing her eyes, suddenly she was transported back to her days living with Ajax. She could see him vividly as she stood before him, taking his blows and abuse. Once again, she felt the sting of the extension cord as it struck her body. The terror of her early days overtook her as her spirit seemed to drain from her body. Her mind went blank again. Feeling nothing, a vapid peace settled over her. The force of Saul's evil consumed her. Pappie's little Sama was no more.

A crow cawed once just over her head. She thought it was Saul saying "mine."

Her animal passions flamed. All she could think about was having sex over and over. Like a zombie, she turned around and headed back toward the kitchen.

SAUL HEARD THE WOODEN screen door to the kitchen squeak open and then slam shut. He smiled. He knew he had her. *She's a pretty horny bitch,* he thought. *She took all that from me an' she still wants a fuck this man some more. Best watch her. She's still purdy strong. Will need more breakin' in. Got ta start tha' righ' away.* He smirked. *That's gonna be fun too, get one over on that ol' coot Pappie for the last time.*

Things were definitely going Saul's way.

XVIII

WHEN SEMANTHA WALKED BACK into the kitchen, Marco said, "Hey, what took you so long. I thought of coming to look for you, but, you know, no way I wanted to run into that creep Saul."

"Wise choice," Semantha said coldly as she pulled off her clothes, dropped to her knees in front of Marco, and took his penis in her mouth. She again brought him to orgasm as she pleasured herself with her finger. This time, there was no magic or extraordinary sensation, only mechanical copulation. The sweetness and passion were gone. After it was over, she looked at him with an expressionless face and said, "I guess I promised you a glass of wine. I'll see what I can find."

She dressed and walked out, leaving Marco feeling empty and confused, not imagining what had happened to his seductive beauty. Then he heard a chilling sound, the sound of Semantha locking the kitchen door from the outside. Running to find another escape route, he found all the other doors and windows either barred or locked. Again, he was trapped. His one and only chance to escape had evaporated. He kicked himself again for letting his lust overtake his reason.

★　　　★　　　★

SEMANTHA RETURNED TO THE barn. "Okay, where's the drug." Saul told her to get dressed in her robe for the ceremony. After she did so, Saul had another woman member of the Circle braid her hair, making it look like an anaconda slithering down her back ready to strike. Saul pinched her cheek. "Real nice," he said. "Get yourself ready. After the mass, we's gonna get it on. You's gonna know what it's like to get screwed by a real man, none of this city boy faggot shit." He gave her a hard slap on her rump and she squeaked impishly, like a can-can dancer in a burlesque. It was a put-on reaction. Inside, she felt numb.

Saul gave her a red plastic cup filled with wine and infused with the drug. "You see's he drinks all of this, an' no funny business, ya hear. That would not go so good for you or him."

SEMANTHA, DRESSED IN HER robe, went back to the kitchen with the glass of wine. "Maybe I should've told you that I was going to lock the door," she said. "Saul is upset that I am going to let you go. I didn't want him going into one of his rages and beating you up. So I locked him out. Here's the wine."

Marco didn't know whether to believe Semantha. By now he was suspicious of her intentions. She seemed so different from when they first met. Now she seemed unfriendly, casual, brusque. *Is she saying these things just to keep me calm?* he thought. But he did take the glass. He was incredibly thirsty and needed a drink. Marco was about to drink when someone from outside called for Semantha. She left again, again carefully locking the door.

That interruption gave Marco time to look at what was in the glass. It was wine all right, but it was sort of cloudy and it did not smell that good. *I don't think I should drink this. It might make me sick, and I still need to have my wits about me to get out of here.* He took the glass to the sink and poured it down the drain. He tried to run a little water to wash it away. He discovered that the water was turned off, probably had been for many years from the looks of things.

Semantha came back and saw the empty cup. "Good. You drank it," she said. "Do you feel better? I hope you don't mind, but I put a little relaxer in the glass. You seemed to need something to calm you down. It will help ready you for the mass."

"Semantha, I told you, I'm not going to your whatever it is. Just want to leave, you know. Now. I'm going to dress and be on my way."

"You're not leaving," Semantha said in a robot-like monotone. "Saul is high priest now, and he has selected you to serve in a very special role tonight. We are sure that your presence will be of use and pleasing to Lucifer. We want him to appear and point us to Pappie's murderer."

Marco's body quivered with fear. His worst fears were confirmed.

"H-h-h-how would I e-e-eever please, uh, Lucifer?"

Semantha frowned. "You'll find out soon enough." She then walked out, not bothering to lock the door. Terrified and shaking all over, Marco felt like he was naked in the freezing cold. A few minutes later, Marco heard her saying, "He drank it all. He should be out completely. I'll go and check. Let's get this thing over with."

Marco, panicked as he was, managed to gather himself together enough to think about whether there was still a way out. His only hope now was to outfox Saul and his gang. Maybe if he played along, when their guard was down, he could make his run for it. It was going to call for all of the talent as an actor he could muster, not one of his natural skills, but now his life depended on convincing Semantha and her assembled troupe that he was out and powerless. So when he heard Semantha coming back, he let his arms fall limp to his sides; his head dropped so that his chin was touching his chest. He closed his eyes.

Semantha came over to him and lifted his arm. He let it fall. She gave him a slap. He did not react. She forced open his eyelids. He continued to look blankly straight ahead. She grabbed his crotch and squeezed hard, sending a wave of intense pain through his body. He managed to react only with a slight groan.

Then she kissed him on the forehead. "Good-bye Marco. It's been wonderful. Happy landings," she said softly.

She opened the door and yelled to Saul. "He is ready. Bring him into the Circle. It's almost midnight."

Two of the congregants dressed in black robes, hefty furniture-movers in the outside world, came into the kitchen. One of them grabbed Marco under his arms, and the other his feet, carrying him into the barn. When they got him there, they heaved him like a sack of wheat into a large wooden armchair. He landed with a thud, sending a ripple of pain through his legs, behind, and back. Marco needed to remind himself to play unconscious regardless. The brutes did nothing more, and he lay there, stretched out, limp, naked, and appearing to be unresponsive.

Marco tried to imagine how a person drugged with heaven knows what would act. These people would certainly be on the lookout for any signs that he was faking it. Too much moving and squirming around would be a tip off, but probably even a person pretty doped up moved at least a little, likely groaned once or twice, and occasionally briefly opened and closed his eyes. Doing that much would be essential to keep his body from aching and becoming so stiff he would not be able to mobilize quickly when he had the chance. And his curiosity demanded that he open his eyes once or twice to look around.

What a scene he saw when he stole a look. The walls of the still empty barn were covered with the long, pleated black drapes he had seen before he was captured. There were few adornments except an inverted pentagon painted high in the gables above the rafters. Lighting was provided by four very large flaming torches, smelling of kerosene and giving the room a feel something like a meeting of the grand Spanish Inquisition. The table upon which the altar would lay sat at one end of the barn on a platform about a foot above the floor, which was mostly straw and dirt. A black drape covered the table. A large open saucer sat on the table with burning charcoal in it. A skull of a goat sat adjacent to a statue shaped like a phallus, and, next to it, a chalice, which appeared to be of gold in the dim light emitted by the torches. A dagger was also lying there. It was long and sharp with a metal pentagram at the end of the handle. The chair upon which Marco had been thrown faced the table about fifteen feet away. Ten chairs, five on each side of Marco's, formed a semicircle with the table.

Marco could only imagine what was about to happen.

XIX

———

SAUL WATCHED AS THEY brought the limp, drugged man from the kitchen and heard him hit the chair. He was hyper-anxious to get the mass underway. Why he had no idea, but the image of that old girlfriend of his, that girl Shana, came to his mind. A current of rage and hostility surged through his body. *That cunt*, he thought. *Things coulda been so different…*

Saul summoned the Circle. "Ring the gong and lets get started," he said, looking at the person who had been selected to serve as altar. "Semantha git behin' me.

"May Lucifer triumph," he bellowed out, sounding in charge.

The altar tapped the gong twelve times and Saul led the procession into the barn. As priest and priestess, Saul and Semantha entered first. Saul wore Pappie's black robe with an inverted cross in red embroidered over his heart. Semantha had donned the crown with the veil she was wearing on the boat. The altar, a middle-aged, rather rotund female dressed in a black robe open in the front, followed. Her salt and pepper hair was frizzly and long. Ten other congregants then entered, men and women, all dressed in plain black robes extending to the ground. The last one closed the barn door and secured it with a latch.

Semantha and Saul walked behind the table and each made a deep bow. The altar came up behind them and did the same. She then slipped out of her robe, letting it fall to the ground and reveal her naked, flabby torso. Each of the others assumed positions standing in front of the ten chairs. Saul and Semantha stepped up on the platform and bowed again.

Saul gazed down at Marco's still nude body lying there, appearing to be out cold. *Real purdy* he thought. It excited Saul to think about plunging the dagger into this man and sending him to eternity. *...too bad he's out like' this...* he thought. *...doin' it when he's awake, real slow, one stab at a time, hearin' him scream an' moan...that's the way...So much sweeter...next time wit no Semantha fuckin' things up, that's what I'll do. Maybe I'll do it to Semantha after she's all used up.*

He invited the altar to come up and assume her position. She climbed on the table, laid down, and located her body at right angles to the table's length, her knees at the edge widely parted and her arms extended across the table. Saul placed a tall burning black candle in each of her hands. Then he moved up between the woman's knees, giving him access to her breasts and vagina so he could easily reach them when it was time to desecrate the host. A ritual book was propped on a pillow right under the woman's left extended arm. Saul knew some of the words to the mass by heart, but he read from the book because, if he read slowly and carefully, his West Virginia hills accent more or less disappeared, and he sounded almost elegant, a little like Pappie.

Semantha read the invocation she had written out:

"Oh Lucifer, prince of darkness and dark energy, we have assembled here tonight to celebrate a Black Mass offered up to you and as a memorial for Pappie, our father, leader, and guide, who was cruelly taken from us at the hands of one of your enemies still unknown. We pray to you tonight for your guidance and assistance to right this terrible, unspeakable wrong, offense to your majesty, and shock to our circle of believers in your ultimate triumph. And we thank you for bringing us this man before you now. You know he willingly came, brought to us by your power, and is now before

you without restraint. We will use him to show you our devotion to your authority and sovereignty. We pray that you will appear to us in this sacred smoke and reveal the murderer of your servant, our beloved Pappie."

She then took a ladle, filled it from a pail behind the table, and poured its contents on the coals. Individual streams of thick black smoke arose from each charcoal ember and ascended to the rafters, intertwining and forming multiple hazy shapes and puffy nebulous forms, driven around by a draft from a vent in the gable at the top of the roof. Occasionally, they collected together, forming miniature thunder clouds or taking on ephemeral shapes, at times a vague ghostly human form, sometimes something like a face, then a finger, then a phallus. Mostly they created amorphous abstractions from which many different things could be imagined.

Saul scanned the smoke intently looking for any sign of Lucifer. After what he had felt in the lane that afternoon, Saul almost expected him to appear and proclaim Saul high priest. *That'd be so purdy*, he thought. Saul's body shook with anticipation.

Semantha chanted:

"Oh prince of darkness come to us;
Oh prince of darkness come to us;
Oh prince of darkness come to us.
May our sacrifices to you this night be pleasing to you and a sign
of our extreme devotion."

Sacrifice, YA BET, whoa, what a sacrifice, Devotion, SURE, devotion righ' to the toes, Saul thought. Then he took over from Semantha, evoking the Devil. He chanted:

"In nomine magni dei nostri satanas. Introibo ad altare domini inferi.
"Santus, santus, santus, dominus diabolus sabaoth."

The assembly replied in unison:

"Santus—venirel; santus—venirela; ave satanas, ave satanas; tui sunt caeli'; tue est terra; ave satanas.

They repeated this responsive chant over and over, creating a deep resonant chorus like the monks of old. The cadence and the chime increased each time they echoed the verse, pounding like an orchestra of massive kettle drums steadily pulsating in rhythm. The incantation became as a grand wave building its force to break. Then they began stomping their feet in step to the rhythm, driving the mantra to the corners of the old barn. It seemed to quiver as if possessed by a mysterious force.

Suddenly, Saul raised his arms and they all stopped, leaving the room in eerie, penetrating silence. *Powerful*, Saul thought. *Lucifer's done come.*

Saul then proceeded through the lengthy ritual, each a perverted version of the Christian ceremony. Semantha regularly stoked the charcoal, causing more streams of smoke to rise to the rafters, creating additional swirling shapes, and eventually filling the barn with thick puffy clouds as it circled back down. The resulting haze, combined with the diffused light from the torches, caused the room to take on an otherworldly, supernatural glow.

Saul loved this part of the mass. It was like he and the Circle were together in a different world, a world where he was Lord.

Semantha watched, hope against hope, for a sign in the swirling smoke. She had a feeling that something extraordinary was about to happen. In the past, she had seen incredible images form from the smoke, demi-Devils, grotesque distorted faces, gargoyles consuming wild animals, snakes coiling around vague moving forms, once or twice something almost like the face of the Devil himself. *If he would only come now and reveal Pappie's murderer,* she thought each time she added more incense to the coals.

MARCO SOON DISCOVERED THAT no one was paying the slightest attention to him, certainly not either Semantha or Saul. They were preoccupied by the ritual and the forms the smoke was taking. So the time he spent opening his eyes and looking around became longer, as he became bolder, searching his surroundings for the best way out.

But Marco sensed he was running out of time. This thing could not go on forever. Any escape would require that he plow directly through the tight circle of congregants sitting on either side of him. He would have no choice but to jump up and push through, hoping that the element of surprise would get him to the door with enough lead time to run for it. It would be a heroic and risky venture, but he had no alternatives. He began to gather his resolve just when Saul pulled out a large, struggling white rabbit, held it in the air, and carefully read from the ritual book:

> *"O mighty and terrible Lord of Darkness, we entreat You receive and accept this sacrifice, which we offer to you on behalf of this assembled company, upon whom you have set your mark, that you may make us prosper in fullness and length of life, under Thy protection and may cause to go forth at our bidding Thy dreadful minions, for the fulfillment of our desires and the destruction of our enemies. In the unity of unholy fellowship, we praise and honor first Thee, Lucifer, Morning Star and Beelzebub, then Belial Prince of the Earth and Angel of Destruction; Leviathan, Beast of Revelation, Abaddon Angel of the Bottomless pit and Asmodeus , Demon of Lust. We call upon the mighty names of Astaroth, Negral, and Behemoth of Belphegor, Adramelech and*

Baalberith and all of the nameless and formless ones, the mighty and innumerable hosts of Hell, by whose assistance may we be strengthened in mind, body, and will."

After he spoke these words, with his free arm, Saul raised the dagger high above the squirming animal. Semantha poured more incense on the burner and a great puff of smoke, thicker than before, filled the area around the altar. Saul invited the congregants to step up and encircle the table and altar so that they could each share in the blood from the rabbit. They left their chairs and crowded around to watch the evisceration close up.

Marco could not believe his good luck. They now all had their backs to him and were hiding him from Semantha and Saul. That meant that he would have just enough time to get to his feet and sprint to the door before they realized what was happening. It was now or never.

At the moment Saul thrust the dagger in the rabbit, Marco jumped up and began his run; but he accidentally kicked one of the chairs into the next one as he passed by. Saul immediately heard the noise, turned his eyes, and saw Marco running out.

"Fuck," he said. "Holy shit. Git him NOW." The others turned and watched as Marco cleared the barn door and ran outside.

By now Marco was out in the dark cool air, running for his life. A brilliant moon lighted his way around the house and toward the river. He could hear the crowd in hot pursuit, likely about fifty feet behind him. Now he had the advantage. Not only was he strong and athletic, but he was not burdened with long flowing robes. He ran like a gazelle pursued by junkyard dogs.

Someone yelled, "Get the gun." Someone else, "Let Zano out."

As he approached the water, Marco considered whether it was better to go for his little runabout with its quirky motor or take his chances swimming away. He elected the latter. If he could get 100 feet offshore, it was dark enough they would have a hard time finding him. He could cover that distance in a matter of a few seconds. So when he got to the river, he dived in and swam underwater for as far as he could.

The cool fresh river water invigorated him. Exhilarated by his escape, he felt a pulse of energy flow through his body. His only thought was to get as far away as he could as quickly as possible. Spurred along by the current, his long graceful body slid through the water as his powerful arms, fueled by adrenaline, propelled him one long stroke at a time further and further from danger.

A rifle fired a few shots, but by now he was close to out of range and most likely pretty well out of sight in the dark. He heard a couple of people jump in after him, but he could tell by the splashing and yelling they lacked the capacity to make it a race. The dog, in hot pursuit, barked, then apparently lost Marco's scent at the edge of the river and went no further.

Saul yelled, "Get me the boat keys."

Shit, Marco thought. Certainly the boat had a searchlight to help them navigate upstream at night. And with the light and the boat, the advantage in this deadly-serious fox hunt would be theirs. Marco had no choice but to continue to swim. As he did, he listened for noise from the engine. Nothing. He stopped for a second to be sure. Nothing. He was quite sure that he was close enough to hear if the engine had started. Those clunky older diesel motors were exceedingly noisy and the night very still.

After a few minutes, Marco concluded that Saul could not get the motor started. For a second time that night, fate smiled on Marco. *Another motor that will not start--is this Pappie's revenge for the stake in his heart?* Marco wondered. *Or, could it be there's a God?* Either way, for all intents and purposes, Marco had escaped.

Marco slowed his pace. He wanted to put some additional distance between himself and the coven, but he was not in such a terrible predicament any more. Of course, he was swimming nude in the middle of a muddy river at 2:00 a.m., but he was clear. He swam until he reached the last opening bridge up river. If they ever got the motor on that old tub started, he could hear them coming from a distance and could escape simply by swimming to the other side of the bridge.

Suddenly Marco was overwhelmed by exhaustion. But this was no time to sleep. He needed to stay alert. Maybe though, he could afford a few minutes of rest on the shore. It was still way too early to get any help, and he would have some explaining to do. No clothes, no IDs and a story straight out of a horror movie. So he swam up to the shore, pulled himself up on a grassy ledge, and allowed his aching body time to rejuvenate.

Finally safely away, Marco's first thought was gratitude and his second penance. *Lord, have mercy. Thank you, God, thank you. Once I get back, I will perform a solemn novena to the Blessed Virgin for getting me out of there alive. No, not just that. I'm going to reorder my priorities with women.*

★   ★   ★

BACK AT THE HOUSE, Saul, still wearing his robe, was frantic with rage.

"What the fuck's happening. Now we's in real trouble. That fucker could git away an'go righ' to the sheriff. Then all hell'll break loose. How could this be happenin'?"

At that instant, Saul saw Semantha alone at the shore line, looking passively in the direction Marco had swum and running her hand through her hair. She had let her robe drop to the ground and was standing there unabashedly in her underwear. *That cunt*, he thought. *She defied me an' helped him get outta here.* He decided that she must have told the man not to drink the wine and had dumped more incense on the coals to give him cover for his escape.

This be all her fault. She's gonna pay and pay big.

Saul pulled out the dagger from his ankle holster and ran over to her. He grabbed her from behind and held the dagger hard against her neck. It was still covered with the rabbit's drying blood.

"You's a miserable cunt, you put yer own sex passions ahead of the rest of us, the Circle, and Lucifer. And now we's in real trouble. I oughta slit yer throat right here and now. The only reason I don't is ya deserve to die real slow and painful like. Maybe ya should live on all uglied up."

He pushed the dagger harder against her throat. "Ya helped yur lover boy escape, didn't ya?" The blade cut lightly into her skin.

Semantha let out a groan. "No. I wanted him to drink the wine. I swear, I swear. Could be he decided drinking it was not such a good idea. Could be you did not put enough drug in it. I don't know what happened, I don't. Please believe me, Saul, please. I know I'm yours."

"Then why did ya keep puttin' more and more incense on till it got all smoky?"

"I was hoping that Lucifer would appear in the smoke and make everything like it was before."

Saul quieted down a little and said, "So you's our last chance. You's gonna go an' git that man. Finish him off."

"Saul, please no. The only way to catch him is to swim after him. I can't swim that well. You know that."

"Well, ya better learn real quick, now. You gotta find him and do what ya needs to do, say what ya needs to say. Let him fuck you again. Jes git him. He'll stop and rest somewhere down the river. You'll find him."

He then took the dagger holster off, put it on her leg, and slid the dagger in it. He grabbed her by the chin. "One more thing, ya bitch," he said. "If ya don't git him and the sheriff comes, we's gonna blame you for everything. You'll be spending the rest of yur lif' in jail, maybe git the 'lectric chair. An' if ya runs away wit 'im, you knows we gonna find ya and it's not gonna be purdy. Only way out fer you now is you gotta bring me this man's privates in this here bag." He shoved a small plastic bag in her hand. "Now git."

Then Saul gathered the Circle together. "We's been betrayed by that miserable cunt and now we's in real danger," he said. "We's don't know what she's goin' to do. She may jes fuck 'im again and try to run away wit 'im. We gotta clean up all our shit an' git outta here. Clem, go an' see if you can figger out wha's wrong wit the boat. An' take down the mast, throw it in the river. We's not gonna want to wait for the bridges to open." Saul thought, *Fuckin' Pappie and his sail boat.*

The Circle gathered up the few things that they had there for the mass, took them to the boat, and cleaned up the blood from the rabbit, which had splattered all over everything in the barn. They shooed the goats out of the corral and sent them running down the road. After about an hour, Clem found a loose connection going from the battery to the starter and got the motor to start.

Saul and Clem took one last walk through the house to be sure they got everything. That's when they found Marco's clothes with his wallet and keys. Saul took the wallet and looked through it.

"Christ, this fucker works as some sort of doc at this here place called Fermilab," he said. "Ya know what that is, Clem?"

"No clue, Saul. Sounds like he's some sort'a big wig, though."

"Well, whatever it is, we's let 'im jes slip through our fingers. Real bad. This would a been somethin' to talk about.

"At least there's $500 here. Nice of him to leave us a little cash." Saul held up the greenbacks and gave a little smile.

"Bring the wallet and the clothes, Clem. I have a feeling they's gonna come in handy. Thinkin' we's goin' be seein' him again."

XX

SEMANTHA WAS NOT AT all sure that she would be able to kill Marco and dismember him as Saul had ordered. The idea was so foreign, so completely hostile to who she was and everything Pappie had taught her. It was one thing to submit herself to Saul's brutality or even be forced to watch as he committed unspeakable acts. What choice did she have? It was another to savagely destroy another human being, especially one with whom she had just made passionate love. Despite everything, she cared for him. She could not forget the day they first saw each other, his smile, so understanding, so filled with pathos.

Nonetheless, cowed by Saul, Semantha waded into the water and began her swim. She was not in particularly good physical shape for such an arduous task. She would paddle and crawl for a bit and then float on her back to rest for a while longer. It was lucky that there had been a cloud burst earlier that day. The river was swollen with water and its current stiff. It carried her quickly downstream, and, she hoped, closer to finding Marco. Despite her grizzly mission, the gentle flow of the river, the cool summer air, and the tranquility of a moonlight night in the country brought Semantha to a state of transitory peace. She sensed these were the last moments of calm she would ever enjoy. From that day forward, Saul owned her.

Every so often as she swam, she would cry out in a weary, mournful voice, wailing like a siren, "Marco… Marco… Marco… Where are you? I love you. Please, Marco."

★   ★   ★

BEFORE TOO LONG, MARCO, still resting on the shore, heard her voice pierce the stillness of the early morning, then the sound of her swimming his direction. His years of experience in the water told him she was alone. She was not leading a posse out to catch him. What he could not figure out was why she had followed after him. What could she want? *Probably not anything good*, he thought.

As she drew closer, he heard her speak, this time in a much softer, sweeter voice. "Please don't leave me. I love you. I want to marry you. I want to spend the rest of my life with you."

When she spoke these words, Marco could hear how weakened she was. The effort of speaking was almost more than she could muster. He could tell that he could easily overpower her if necessary, or just swim away for that matter. But in spite of all she had put him through, he felt a twinge of the same protectiveness toward her he had felt the day their eyes first met. And her voice, it was so sweet, so innocent, so sad. He suspected a trick, but still, he was intrigued. A part of him even now wanted the seductive beauty to whom he had made glorious love only hours before. He decided to reveal his location, keep his distance, but find out what this was about.

He slipped into the shallow water adjacent to the shore. "I am over here, Sama."

She began to swim in the direction of his voice. As she got closer, Marco could make out the outline of her face, strikingly angelic bathed in the soft sheen of light from the setting moon. She gasped for air between her words.

"Marco, you must believe me," she pleaded. "I am the one who killed Pappie. He controlled me. I could not escape his power. I was desperate. Killing him was my only hope. Then you came along and I found a reason to want to start again.

"Please. I love you," she said.

Having seen her again, Marco's first thought was, *Melissa*. This time, though, he didn't fall for the illusion. He imagined Frank saying, "*She is NOT Melissa.*"

Semantha was now standing in the water about twenty feet from him.

"Hold it right there, Semantha." Marco said, raising his hand. "Let me get this straight, you killed your own father and blamed Saul. That makes no sense."

"Oh please, Marco, you must believe me," she said. One of her hands went to her side and then underwater. Marco noticed but did not think anything of the gesture. "Please come here so I can explain, let me hold you. Please, babe. I want you so much."

Marco thought about going to her. *What could that harm?* Suddenly Frank's face appeared in his mind and said, "*No Marco, NO.*"

"Don't move. Stay right there, Semantha."

"Why, Marco? I could never harm you. Saul wanted me to, but I couldn't, couldn't. Can't. Really, believe me, please, oh, please. If you let me, I will prove it to you."

"More lies."

Upon Marco saying that, Semantha's voice changed from seductive to hard. Her tone said she was angry. "Lies? That is so unfair. You have no idea what I have gone through, what my life has been like, my vain search for peace and comfort. Then you came along out of nowhere. I did hope, still do."

"Hope for what? A life together? Well, I guess you sort of blew that one, didn't you?" There was arrogance in his voice.

Semantha moved closer; Marco backed away.

"Who are you to be saying that to me, so high and mighty," Semantha said. "I'll bet your romantic life is not so hot either. Why did a man your age set out on a crazy mission to look for a woman he saw only for a few seconds out in a boat? Must be something missing, Dr. whoever you are. Don't play mister superior to me. You've got your own problems."

"'A man your age,' what kind of a crack is that? I didn't hear you object to my age as you wantonly seduced me back in that old kitchen. Seemed pretty content with what I could do for you." Marco could feel his anger swelling inside.

"We all make mistakes, don't we?"

"Now I've heard them all, a two-bit pretend witch in the middle of nowhere dressing down a theoretical physicist. Watch yourself, Semantha. So what if you are young and beautiful. You just tried to have me killed."

"Yeah, and I'm sorry it didn't happen. You deserve it. You're a typical haughty male, thinking you can use women for whatever and then just move on. Who cares if you are drop-dead handsome. Really. That doesn't give you the license to do anything you please to anybody you want. Time that ends, Mr. Marco.

"You deserved to die," she screamed.

Rage and hatred comingled in Marco's body. It was the sort of hatred that could spring only from intense passion. In his heart, his hatred of her lay ever so close to that love. He remembered the beauty of their first encounter but then how sinister she looked in her robe standing next to Saul, undoubtedly about to enjoy the spectacle of his grisly death. *Perverted slut,* he thought. *Who deserves to die?*

Emotionally at wits end from his scrape with death and his harrowing escape, now red hot, Marco lost control of his impulses. Without thought, he dove underwater and swam straight to her. He grabbed her legs and pulled her down under the surface. Her arms flying, she struggled and tried to go for the dagger. Before she could unsheathe it, he placed her in a body lock from behind. Both of his arms held her tight immediately below the same breasts which only hours before had been the focus of his desire. She flailed around a little more with her forearms and kicked her legs wildly, but she was no match for him. He stood up and held her under water until she stopped struggling. Then she ceased breathing. After a few more seconds, he checked her pulse. Her heart had stopped. She was dead.

As she floated to the surface, Marco saw the dagger in its ankle holster, the same one which had dispatched the rabbit. *My God, surely meant for me. She was so clever. Almost got me.* This was his second brush with death in one day, he thought, both times caused by this woman. With her gone, justice had been served. He felt relieved, like he had put a little more distance between himself and the whole sorry episode. Someday, he would need to tell Frank the story and thank him for the warning. Maybe he would write a book.

Marco then turned Semantha's limp body over, once again showing her face, her sublime chest, and her privates clad only in her underwear. Her face bore the look of terror, but her sorrowful, enchanting, eyes were still open, still enticing. The river water dripping from her face seemed like a torrent of tears. Marco felt a twinge of regret about what he had just done, but without thinking more, he blurted out loud, "God, I just barely escaped."

With the first light of morning appearing on the eastern horizon, Marco decided it was time to go get help. He kissed Semantha's remains on her forehead. "Goodbye, Sama," he said without emotion. "It's been wonderful. Happy landings." He gave her body a push out into the open water.

THE NEXT DAY, MARCO and three deputy county sheriffs armed with search warrants went to the farmhouse and barn. The gate to the complex was gaping open and no one was to be seen. The place had been cleaned out, not even the goats remained. The table where the rabbit had been sacrificed was still in the barn. While it had been hastily washed, there were still drops of animal blood on the platform around the table, apparently missed in the clean-up effort. The chairs were also there as was the large chair where only twelve hours before Marco had awaited his fate. The only other unusual sign was the pentagram painted in the rafters. In the kitchen, the table and chair remained, but the wine glass, ropes, and belt were removed. Out on the river, the runabout was just as he had left it and a gold-looking plastic chalice, obviously dropped in a hasty evacuation, was lying on the ground near the dock.

Blind Faith was gone.

It was late morning when a mastless *Blind Faith* reached the first opening bridge. Clem was at the helm and Saul was sitting in the cockpit, head down, with his arms folded, immersed in thought. This time they were dressed like respectable sailors, their beards trimmed and neat.

Clem saw something floating in the water, being held to one of the bridge casements by the current. When they steered the boat over, they saw that it was Semantha's body, floating face down. Her legs were a little under the water, but the dagger was clearly visible.

"Wha' happened to her, ya think?" Clem asked.

"Don't know," Saul said. "She couldn't swim so well. She cudda' got tired an' jes drowned."

They looked at her floating there. "Well, don't matter how," Saul said. "Tha's the end of her. She made shit of everything. Good she's gone to Lucifer." He then reached down and took the dagger and holster off her leg and thought, *Be needin' this again.* They loosened Semantha's body from the casement and pushed her out into the middle of the river. "Next stop for you's the big lake," Saul said. "Happy landings."

"Good riddance, floozy," Clem added.

They then proceeded down the river and out into the lake, wanting to get as far away from St. Joe and Benton Harbor as they could. En route, they passed time gossiping about the events of the last few weeks.

"Define-tly time to blow outta there anyway," Saul said. "Them police were askin' too many questions."

"Yeah, like wha' happened at Pappie's house? Ya never tol' me neither."

"Was gonna be purdy, Clem, sendin' Pappie to his rest the good ol' way, then pullin' out the stake an' settin' the place on fire. But some broad, don't know who, came from outta nowhere an' barged in. Thought better get outta there. I picked up the gas can an' runned out the back door."

"But you's the one who called the police."

"Good way to mak' 'um think I didn't do it."

"Yeah an' we already got the body."

"Now you's beginnin' to think, Clem. After how many years?"

Pulling a dinghy they stole as they went down the river, Saul and Clem traveled as far north as the gas on the boat would take them, a few miles south of Muskegon. There they opened all of the sea cocks and, for good measure, punched a few holes in the hull under the water line. They threw a bag with their things into the dinghy, climbed aboard, and watched as *Blind Faith* slowly sank to the bottom in fifty feet of water. Later that night, the two reached a stretch of deserted beach, scuttled the dinghy, and started the walk into town. They were on their way to settle a score.

XXI

FRANK GOT A CALL from Marco as soon as he returned from Michigan. Although it was Saturday, Frank was in his office, busily preparing for a trial, the defense of a big-time physician who had been accused of Medicare fraud. The trial began with jury selection the following Monday, and Frank was way behind. Usually when he was in trial prep mode, doing anything else was a distraction and a very low priority, even when he was completely ready. But he always could make time for Marco. Besides, he was anxious to hear about his trip. He told Marco to come over.

When Marco arrived, he sat down at Frank's large conference table. Like the rest of the furniture in Frank's opulent office, it was of cherry-stained walnut but now was scattered with papers for the trial. Jeannie and Chris were also at the table, helping Frank with jury instructions. After a hasty "hello," Marco got down to business.

"What do I need to do to make this conversation attorney–client privileged and totally confidential?" Marco asked. "I want to be sure."

Frank, Jeannie, and Chris each gave the other a sideways glance. Frank rubbed his eye, and the look on his face said amazement. He wondered what could possibly be driving Marco to make such a peculiar request. Frank told Marco to give him $10 as a retainer and that he would bill Marco for his time. Marco got out his wallet and gave Frank the money.

"What about Chris and Jeannie, is it okay if they're here?" Marco asked.

"They work for me and so the privilege applies. But I sense that you are about to go into something, well...sensitive. Is it okay with you if they stay?"

"Sure, Frank. Their input may be good."

Jeannie began to take notes, but Frank told her that would not be necessary. Then Marco proceeded to tell them the whole story from the first encounter with Saul and Clem all the way to sending Semantha to her death. He got fairly graphic about his sexual experience with Semantha and the black mass. He said that he was sure that if he had not escaped, he would have been sacrificed as part of the ritual.

Frank, Chris, and Jeannie sat not moving, looking astounded, as they heard the story unfold. It was dramatically different from anything they had heard before, unique in Frank's experience as a former prosecutor and now criminal defense attorney. He was used to stories about assorted stabbings, killings, robberies, rapes, and extortions, not about anything as bizzare as human sacrifice. If it had been anyone but Marco telling him these things, Frank would have been incredulous, but Marco was level-headed and not prone to wild storytelling, especially about something as darkly outlandish as this. Plus, there was something inherently believable about how he told the story. It was graphic, detailed, and real.

"Did you go to the sheriff after you escaped?" Frank asked. Knowing Marco as he did, he was afraid of what he might hear.

Marco shrugged as if irritated by the question. "First thing I did. Wouldn't anybody?"

"Did you tell the sheriff about killing the woman?"

"No, I didn't know what to say about that so I said nothing. Seemed safer, you know."

Jeannie scowled and began pulling on her earlobe. Frank thought, *Already a problem.* He fidgeted with his pen. "How did you explain being at a black mass in the middle of the night in the middle of Nowhereville, Michigan?" Frank asked.

"Told them about coming up the river looking for the woman, but then I stumbled into this house where I was shot at and tied up. Also I told them about my encounter, our encounter actually, with *Blind Faith*. Didn't mention you or *Provocateur*. I tried to keep it simple and straightforward. You know what I mean? Just like in physics, simple is almost always the most likely, right?"

"Didn't they think it odd that you had gone to such great lengths to find this woman?" Jeannie asked.

Good question Jeannie, Frank thought. *She is learning.*

Marco shook his head 'no.' "I just told them that I was a frustrated bachelor coming up on forty looking for love anywhere I could. I emphasized the frustrated part. Right."

"That's a little different from what you told me when we had drinks together," Jeannie said, turning her head a little to the left and raising her right eyebrow.

"Well, after my year in New Mexico, it was true." Jeannie gave a knowing smile.

"Also told them about my work at Fermilab. And that I was trying to find new ways of doing super fast computing using quantum theory. They became quite interested, especially the sergeant who had read a little about how that works. He asked me lots of pretty good questions. They seemed a little starstruck by me and my work."

"What else did they ask you? " Jeannie said.

"Not much. After we talked for a while, they took me to the house. When we found nothing, they said they would be in touch and let me go. They left me with the impression I would not hear from them again. I'm pretty sure I won't."

If Marco's story was peculiar, the county sheriff's reaction, as Marco described it, was bizarre. In all of Frank's years working with law enforcement, he had never encountered such a cavalier attitude. Something did not seem right to Frank.

"Didn't they ask you for details? Didn't they try to push you or test you in any way? They had a naked man with no IDs standing there saying that he was a big-time physicist and that he had almost been used as a human sacrifice." Frank shook his head. "That's plain weird."

Marco nodded in agreement. "Yep, sure is."

"Things like this do not happen anywhere let alone in a small town in Michigan," Frank said. "I would expect such a story to perk up the ears of almost any law enforcement person anywhere, even in little old, run-down Benton Harbor, Michigan. It is incredibly hard to imagine that they bought your story hook, line, and sinker."

"Well, they did," Marco replied. "But it's not quite as strange as you just laid it out. By the time that I got to the sheriff's office, I had gotten some clothes. Right. An old man fishing from a dock behind his house gave me a shirt, a pair of pants, and some old gym shoes. Surprisingly, they fit pretty well. And he gave me a cup of coffee."

Great, Frank thought, *another person in the equation. Not good.* "What did you tell him about why you were swimming naked in the river at dawn?" Frank chewed on his pen.

"So, I didn't want to get him involved or tell him what had happened, you know. So, I only told him that I had got a little high and went for a midnight swim up river. I said I was overpowered by the current and couldn't find my clothes in the dark. He didn't seem too interested in how I got there, you know. A little strange."

"What was he all about?" Chris asked. "Do you have any idea?"

"My hunch is he wanted sex. He sort of came on to me." Chris frowned. "He asked me into his house and offered me a shower. I nixed that. It wasn't just that I didn't want to have sex with this old dude, more that I didn't want to get into another compromised position. Too many crazies in Michigan. Way too many."

"Understandable," Chris said. "You never know about old coots on the make." He smiled as if he had personal experience. "How'd you get away from him?"

"I told him that I needed to get to work. I left and walked into town."

Oh terrific, Frank thought. *Two inconsistent stories. This is definitely not good.* Worried, he began to doodle on his legal pad.

"What about the body?" Jeannie asked.

Marco told them he had no idea what happened to it. Marco looked around the room, then continued, almost whining.

"You've got to understand, guys. I was not in the best of condition. You know, I was dazed, like in shock. My gosh, my life had been threatened. I had nothing to eat or drink for twenty-four hours and just completed a marathon swim for my life. My adrenaline level was way in the stratosphere, for God's sake. I wasn't thinking clearly or objectively. You know, by then I was only reacting."

Marco shook his head slowly. "How do you think you'd be if you had gone through what I did?"

Marco waited for an answer. When none was forthcoming, he continued. "So you've been acting as if there's a problem. So many questions, like an interrogation. When I came here, I thought this was really nothing. Now I'm scared."

Frank stopped doodling. He dropped into his lawyer mode.

"My dear friend, here's the situation." Frank's voice deepened. "You have killed a woman and not in self-defense. At the time you attacked her, you had no reason to believe that she was any immediate threat to you. You had every reason to believe the opposite. According to what you told us, she was pleading with you to give her a chance to escape with you. Whether you believed what she was saying or trusted her intentions is beside the point. You intentionally let her get close to you. You could have swum the opposite direction and disappeared."

"But Frank, she wanted to sacrifice me to the Devil."

"Regardless as to whether you believed she was part of what would have been a gruesome crime against you, it was not up to you to take the law into your own hands. Saying that is trite, but here it one hundred percent applies, one hundred percent."

"What about the dagger? I am sure that was intended for me."

"Just having a weapon like that is not a crime. Nor is it evidence, in and of itself, that she intended to harm you," Frank said.

"Unless she gave you a reason to believe she was going to use it," Jeannie added. "Did she? She looked askance at Frank.

"I didn't see any," Marco responded. No one said anything for a couple of minutes.

"Chris, Jeannie, anything to add?" Frank asked. They both shook their heads 'no.'

"So, Marco, this is a lot. What's your reaction?"

Marco fidgeted in his chair a little and cleared his throat. "Frank, please believe me. I had no intention to end her life when I first heard her calling me. As a matter of fact, a part of me wanted to believe her. I mean, for Christ's sake, she was intelligent, beautiful, and the sex we had was my best ever. My first impulse was to come to her, comfort her, and make her my own. She was so much like Melissa, my gosh."

"You should have left it at that."

"I can't really explain what happened in my head. When we were standing there in the shallow water, we had a little argument, nothing serious. Then something took me over. Not sure what. I don't remember every detail ya see. The whole thing is a blur."

He looked away and stopped speaking as if he was mulling over what had happened that night in the river.

"I do know that I was consumed by the vivid image of her standing next to Saul in that black robe wildly stoking the incense pot, probably fondly anticipating my demise. At that instant, I equated my own survival with doing her in. I could only imagine a horrible fate if I gave in to her charms. At the time, going for her did not seem wrong."

Frank took his reading classes off, placed them on the table, and peered at Marco. "There are hundreds of cases that discuss whether this type of spontaneous change of heart mitigates your act from first-degree to second-degree murder," he said with an indifferent tone. "Either way, you don't get by with it. Sorry."

Marco sat stiff and quiet in the chair. As Frank's words sank in, he closed his eyes and the corners of his lips turned down. He looked like a remorseful schoolboy standing before the stern, unforgiving principal. He focused on Frank.

"You're saying I'm a murderer. Is that correct?"

"I don't like the label. But I guess that's where I come out."

Marco put his head down in his arms on the table and cried for a while. Frank, Jeannie, and Chris sat quietly. Then he sat up. Tears streamed down his face.

"Lord in all of heaven, what am I going to do?"

"Well, you have two choices," Frank responded. "You can go to the sheriff over in Michigan, confess, and beg for mercy. You will probably get some prison time, and afterwards you will be a convicted felon with the loss of citizenship rights that goes with it. I can check on the lay of the land over there, but probably you will get at least several years plus a few more on probation. I can also check to see what kinds of prisons they have, but they are probably not very nice places to spend time."

Marco shook his head and looked down.

"You can also wait and see what happens. If they never find the body, your chances of getting a pass go up quite a bit. They will forget about the wacky Chicago professor with his curious tale."

"What if they find the body?" Marco's knee twitched.

"If they find it fairly soon and have a forensic examination, they probably can come to some pretty good conclusions about the cause of death. I would be quite concerned that some of those stupid rent-a-cops you talked to would then put two and two together and come up with five. If the body shows up quickly, they could pinpoint the time of death with your appearance on their doorstep."

"And then?" Marco asked. Frank could hear the terror in Marco's voice, but he knew that this was no time to paint a false rosy picture.

"Then you are in deep trouble, especially because you did not mention the girl to them. They would take that as evidence you intended to kill her. And if they ever connect with that old fisherman, you are all the deeper in the fryer. If you do not voluntarily surrender to them and they come after you, you would probably face more jail time. How much I do not know but probably a lot."

"Jesus Christ. You are saying my choices suck?"

"A fair way to put it."

Marco ran his hand through his hair, slowly pulling it back and revealing his high gothic forehead. "Gotta think this over," he said. Abruptly, he stood, scurried to the door, and left. The bounce in his step had disappeared along with his swagger and self-confidence. It appeared as though he had been drained by some terrible and malevolent disease.

Frank wrinkled his brow. "That was sudden. Poor guy. I'm worried."

XXII

MARCO GOT IN HIS car and began to drive. He didn't care where he was going. Getting away, escape was all he could think about. He began driving faster and faster. He left the city and drove out into the country, eventually down a deserted rural highway . Panic overtook him as he pushed the accelerator pedal on his classic BMW 2002 to the floor. The speedometer read 110 miles an hour. As he approached a side road, suddenly a farmer driving a large tractor pulled out in front of him. He was on a direct collision course. He slammed on his brakes as hard as he could and skidded toward the tractor.

"God help me," he screamed. He heard a bang, the sound of glass shattering, and the noise of twisting metal. He came to a stop with the hood of his car jammed against the large rear tire of the tractor.

Wet with sweat, he shook like a frightened puppy. But he quickly realized he had not been hurt and calmed down. He jumped out of the car as the farmer descended from the cab of the tractor. Running toward Marco, the farmer yelled out.

"You okay, bud?"

"Guess so."

"Well, you's one lucky fella, let me tell ya. Good Lord must be watchin' down on ya. When I seen ya comin', I thought this guy in this little car gonna get frickin' creamed. But ya just hit my tire, that's

175

all. Another six inches an' you'd been a goner. Probably taken me with you."

"What about you, you okay?" Marco asked.

"Yeah, you pushed me to the side a bit but nothin' more. Also lucky I wasn't pullin' nothin'."

Marco and the farmer exchanged insurance information, and he drove away.

BACK IN HIS OFFICE, now alone, Frank sat consumed in his work. He had not moved from his seat at the conference table for hours when Marco walked in.

"Frank, I must talk. I'm frantic, beyond words. Please," Marco said.

Frank dropped his pen and motioned to Marco to sit down on the chair next to him. "I wondered why you left so quickly, with not even a 'see you later.'" Relieved to see Marco back in one piece, Frank smiled.

"I had to run, you know, had to get away, get away from what you had told me, more get away from you. I sort of went into a tailspin after I left, crazy driving, you know, reckless, speeding, out of control. Insane. Wild. I hit this guy driving a tractor."

"Oh good Lord, was anyone injured?"

"Luckily it wasn't serious. Thank goodness. The accident sobered me up some. I knew I had to talk this out. You are the only one who would understand."

"You wanted to get away from me, why?"

"I'm so embarrassed, beyond belief embarrassed. You know what I mean? I was afraid you wouldn't respect me anymore. Can't bear the thought. Your friendship means so much to me, now more than ever." He leaned close, put his hand on Frank's shoulder, and looked directly into his eyes. "Dear brother, help me."

"Okay, my friend, calm down. You've got to get yourself under control."

Frank got up, grabbed Marco by the arm, and guided him over to his couch. Sitting down next to him, he brought his face close to Marco's and touched his knee.

"Marco, let me make this crystal clear." Frank said softly, then he paused. "You have made a mistake, that's all. It was a big mistake, but everyone makes at least one big mistake. In my mind, you are the same energetic, insightful person I have always known. Nothing will ever change that. We are brothers, right?"

Marco put his head down and began to cry. In between sobs, he gasped in anguish, "no, no, no."

Frank picked up a box of tissues from the coffee table in front of the couch and handed it to Marco. He touched Marco gently on the shoulder. "Come on Marco, please do calm down. I care for you, maybe now more than ever, maybe more than you know. The truth be known, I am honored that you came back, that you trust me that much, not just as a lawyer."

Marco stopped sobbing, sighed, and slid down a little on the couch.

"Believe me, I appreciate what you are going through, I do," Frank said.

"I don't think so, not actually." Marco took a tissue and wiped away some of his tears. "When I came to see you earlier, I had no idea that you would tell me that I had committed a crime. None. Thought maybe I needed some legal input, but murder? No way. When you said that, it felt like a 350-pound lineman had just flattened me."

"Most of my clients have similar reactions after I tell them about the consequences of what they did. How you reacted is not all that unusual."

"No, Frank." Marco looked miffed. "I'm not like your other clients. From what you have told me, they always have some sort of, uh, checkered backgrounds."

"I've represented some seamy human beings, no question."

"That's not me. It's not. I have always played the game totally above board. Right. I worked hard in school, got good grades, did the sports thing. I was raised to be a good kid, a model citizen, you know." Marco shook his head again and took another tissue.

"I know," Frank said. "I was with you as you grew up, remember."

"It's not that my parents shoved this down my throat either. This is the life I wanted for myself all along."

Marco rubbed his forehead and coughed a little. He looked exhausted.

"Okay, granted once in a while I shaved the rules a bit, but nothing serious, smoking some dope or cheating on the results of a few lab experiments when I was behind."

"I know, I know," Frank said with a note of irritation. "You don't know how many times your pop told me what a straight shooter you were."

Marco again shook his head. "There you have it. With that upbringing, I cannot imagine how I could ever have done something this terrible. Even if it was in the heat of the moment. Committing a crime. Killing someone. Heaven help me."

"I understand, Marco. I'm sure nothing like that was on your mind when you went to Michigan."

"All I was looking for was a little passion, more some magic. But now I am facing time in prison. Holy shit. Prison. That word keeps bouncing around in my mind like an echo in a canyon. I can't believe this is happening, I cannot, cannot." He put his hands over his eyes and began to sob again.

"I know it's hard, my dear friend." Frank hesitated, thinking about how to best comfort Marco. He reached out and put his arm around Marco's shoulder, pulling him close. Marco fell into Frank's arms, whimpering like a frightened child. "Take a few deep breaths," Frank whispered. "My dear, dear boy, panic never helps."

Frank held him while he cried. Then Marco stopped and sat up, pulling away from Frank. His face was ashen, his eyes puffy and red, his hair disheveled. Marco looked like he had aged five years in the last thirty minutes. Frank pulled some more tissues and handed them to Marco, who then patted his eyes and blew his nose.

"Killing Semantha at the time seemed so natural and justified, but now it feels vulgar and cruel. Maybe I'm not such an upstanding person after all. Could be I am a faker and a fraud, just another creep like those lowlifes who tried to do me in. Do you think?"

Frank struggled to come up with the magic words that could assuage Marco's feelings of terror, guilt, and remorse. *In all likelihood,* he thought, *there are none that can.*

"Come on. You are letting your mind spin out of control. Get a grip," Frank said, frowning. "Most assuredly, you are not like the people in Michigan."

"And then there is the religious thing, Frank." From their many conversations about theology, Frank knew that Marco gave some credence to the idea of a God and held as important his connection to the church. But he wavered between a vague belief and studied agnosticism. He was Catholic more out of a sense of tradition rather than strength of belief. Yet Marco always had abided by the church's ethical precepts, at least the serious ones.

"What I did violates the church's strong moral teachings. In the eyes of the church, I have committed a mortal sin." He shook his head back and forth as he spoke. "If I don't confess and atone for it, I can expect everlasting damnation. And atonement will certainly mean telling the police what I have done and probably going to prison. No room to maneuver around this one."

Frank went to his office bar where he poured two Scotches and added a little ice. He handed one to Marco and sat back down.

"Look at things a little differently, Marco. There is another perspective, one which may help you live a little easier with what you have done." Frank put his hand on Marco's chest.

"From the way you described it, Semantha was inherently evil and part of a cabal intent on using you, first to whet her sexual appetite and then to offer you up for what would have certainly been a painful, slow, gruesome death. How could any sane person think otherwise?"

Marco nodded his head as if to agree and took a large swig of the drink.

"In my view, it was perverted to have sex with you when she surely knew that you were about to be cut up and brutalized. No normal person could do that. It is almost like necrophilia."

Frank paused and took Marco's hand in his. "Think of your act in the context in which it occurred. It was not good, but it was understandable."

"And another thing," Marco said, "I had every reason to believe that she was out for me. How could I, you know, trust her professions of love and passion in the river that morning. Think of the dagger. That was not there simply for appearances, you know."

"Yep. And then there's the whole grotesque scene into which you were thrown," Frank continued. "That man, Saul, the way you described him. What a brutish rogue, mean, disgusting, and crude."

Marco winced and his lips puckered. "It makes me sick to my stomach to think of him and Semantha together. I wonder if she got it on with him. Could be she was a wanton nymphomaniac, giving herself to anyone as often as she could. To think I may have put my lips and tongue where he may have been. Oh holy Christ." Marco's body shook visibly as he looked away, apparently reliving the entire repulsive experience.

Marco took another sip from his glass, waited a few seconds, then emptied the drink down his throat. He placed the glass on the table and smiled at Frank as if to say, "That helps." He looked relieved.

"Another?" Frank asked, pointing to the glass. Marco shook his head 'no' but fought back more tears.

"That leaves only the question you asked me, Frank." He rubbed his chin as if considering his next words. "Why didn't I just swim away. Wouldn't be sitting with you now burning through your trial prep time."

Frank nodded.

"What scares me is that maybe I did it because I could and wanted the thrill. That possibility weighs me down like a ton of bricks. You've heard of the . . . the Leopold and Loeb murder down in Hyde Park? The wealthy kids in the 1920s who wanted to commit the perfect crime just to say they did it?"

Frank could not let Marco continue to reprove himself like this. It was too destructive. Frank cut off Marco's thought like a guillotine doing its thing at an execution.

"Listen to me." His stentorian voice filled the room. "Stop beating yourself up. Right now. I know you so very well, could be in some ways better than you know yourself. It's not your nature to murder in cold blood for the thrill. You have enough on your mind without thinking paranoid thoughts like that."

Marco stopped talking and looked away for a minute. "Frank, I'm so exhausted thinking about this. What's left is to decide my next step, correct? Please give me some advice. What should I do?"

Frank stood up, walked to the window, pulled the drape aside, and looked out. After a few minutes in thought, he turned to Marco.

"Marco, as I said before, you are not in an easy position. There are grave risks no matter which way you go, whether you turn yourself in, or hope they never find the body. No one can make this decision for you. It is so intertwined with your own value system and what you hold dear."

Frank walked back and sat down next to Marco. "Here's the question you must answer. What is important to you? Is it the good life... your own moral values... your everlasting soul? Answer that question and I think you will know what to do."

FOR THE NEXT WEEK, Marco spent virtually all of his waking hours mulling over that question and his answer to it. His preoccupation got him no closer to a satisfying answer. He was torn between expediency and his ethical values, fearing that who he was did not measure up to the person he wanted to be.

Gradually, Marco's primordial urge for self-preservation gained ascendancy. He concluded that he had to end the debilitating, imponderable philosophical debate raging inside of him and return to normal. As much as he could appreciate the nobility and morality of confessing, he could not imagine time in prison, especially some rundown and dangerous dump in Michigan. He would come out a permanently diminished person in ways he could only imagine, if he came out at all.

Inside, this effort at rationalization failed to fully satisfy him. He could not elude a nagging disquietude. *You are a coward. Do you not have the strength to face the consequences of your actions? What is your life about anyway?* Thoughts like these hammered Marco to the point of distraction.

With these questions still unanswered after days of self-reflection, Marco finally determined to bury them as best he could and try to put the Michigan incident behind him. It was time to get back to the lab and focus on his work. He fervently hoped that doing so would be the ultimate resolution. Work had always been his refuge. He hoped that a few weeks of hard work would free him from these thorny perplexities.

Trying hard to put the cork back in the bottle as he returned to the lab, Marco took a cue from Frank. He focused his thoughts on Saul and Semantha. *These were very bad people*, he thought. *I owe them nothing. What use would a confession be? Semantha got what she deserved.*

End of story. Or so Marco thought.

XXIII

ONCE MARCO GOT BACK to work, his life quickly returned to what it had been before, surprisingly quickly. After his week of self-flagellation and doubt, being back in his office and working felt comforting and peaceful. His office was his sanctuary, a small, simply furnished space without any windows, away from the bigger, fancier rooms of his co-workers. His bookshelves were stuffed with all kinds of different works about science, philosophy, literature, the arts. He had read each one, and he felt reassured having them around him as he worked. In one corner, there was a gray, oversized government-issue metal desk so heavy it took two people to move it. On it, Marco had placed a small desk lamp with a shade to warm up the otherwise sterile atmosphere created by the fluorescent lights overhead. Only his PhD diploma from MIT hung in a simple black frame on the beige-colored cement block walls. These were modest digs, but Marco liked his office especially because it was only a bit down the hall from the accelerator he used to perform his experiments.

A couple of days after Marco returned to the lab, Gordon Fellsteon dropped in unannounced. Gordon was head of Marco's department at Fermilab and an internationally known theoretical physicist. Marco and Gordon got along well enough, but Marco always suspected that Gordon did not think much of him or his research. He worried that Fellsteon thought him all show and no substance.

Gordon entered without knocking and walked quickly to stand right next to Marco, who was sitting at his desk. His 250-pound, six-foot-six frame towered over Marco.

"Marco," he said, "I need to be direct with you."

These words tipped Marco off as to what to expect. "Shoot, Gordon."

"We were very disappointed about the outcome of your year at the University of New Mexico. Frankly, it was no surprise considering your overall performance here. We had hoped that a change of atmosphere would help you find a new approach to your research. But it didn't."

Gordon cleared his throat as if beginning a lecture.

"Your ideas are interesting, but they do not pan out experimentally. While you have tried, I will grant you that, we are not sure that this position is right for you."

These words sent a shiver down Marco's spine. It was not as if they came as a surprise, but hearing them still packed a wallop. Before Marco was worried he was in trouble; now he was sure. Marco's head dropped.

"Gordon, it's true, my work has not produced the results I had hoped for," he said, avoiding looking up. "But I do believe that I am on the verge of collecting some important data."

Marco felt like a helpless, frightened orphan. He knew his words must sound trite to Gordon, but he could summon no others. Undoubtedly this was not the first time Gordon had made this same speech and probably not the first time that some under-the-gun junior researcher had said pretty much the same thing.

"Well, Marco, here's the bottom line." Again, Gordon cleared his throat. "Your contract runs out at the end of December. I will check back with you before then to see if things have changed, but, if they have not, there will not be a renewal."

Marco looked up at Gordon. "I will come up with the data. Just give me the chance."

"As I said, you have until December. And don't get me wrong, it's not that you haven't made contributions," Fellsteon said, shaking his head. "You've got wonderful energy and enthusiasm for the field. And I trust your integrity and honesty. That's something sadly missing in the new crop of researchers produced by our not-so-wonderful mega-university factories. It's just that energy and integrity don't pay the bills." Gordon turned and walked out.

Gordon's words brought Marco again face-to-face with the moral dilemma he had wanted to bury with work. What would Gordon think about his integrity and honesty if he knew he was looking at a murderer, a murderer who lacked the courage to face up to his crime? What would he think if he knew the entire sordid story from first encounter to grizzly death? Marco thought about these questions for a bit, but he was not about to return to the quandary which had preoccupied him in the week following his talks with Frank. He could not afford spending still more time and energy in that emotional whirligig. He had to focus totally and completely on his research if he was to save his career. And he must save his career.

But Gordon's words did not deter Marco from the challenge of producing the data he needed. Instead, they toughened him up, as a sense of purpose and resolve replaced the initial shock. He knew what he had to do. Try different approaches to his experiments, run the numbers in new ways, rethink his formulas. While he was desperate, he was not hopeless.

He thought about the scientists who had inspired him as a child. Einstein had struggled to get his ideas accepted when he was a humble patent examiner in Switzerland. Then with the publication of his paper on special relativity, he achieved almost instant fame and recognition, pushing himself immediately to the top of his profession. And Faraday could never produce data to back up his theory that light, electricity, and magnetism are all different manifestations of the same force, today a commonly accepted principle. Marco thought about the many other great scientists who were told to do something else until a breakthrough launched their careers. *I'm far from being done.*

★   ★   ★

MARCO BEGAN PUTTING IN long hours, six or seven days a week, sometimes fourteen hours per day, approaching his work with the same passion as a zealot in search of converts. Many nights, and often all weekend, he was alone at Fermilab at midnight in his far off-the-beaten path office.

Marco did not give a thought to being so alone or that his life had been condensed to a single focus. He paid no attention to the "voicemail full" message on his phone and hardly noticed that he went for days not talking to anyone else except the tech who helped him set up the accelerator. His only thought was how to check his data, improve his techniques, modify his formulas. He went without sleep and sometimes forgot to eat. The world outside his project ceased to exist, as he became a unidimensional thought machine. It was a grind, but he was up to it, driven partly by the tight December deadline and his love for physics, but mainly by his iron-clad will to succeed. *Maybe this is what all truly great thinkers have done over the centuries*, Marco thought, pleased with the comparison.

All of this work pushed the Michigan incident and Semantha's death further and further into the background. Consciously, he thought about it very little. Some days, he wondered if it actually happened or he merely imagined it. It was so crazy it ceased feeling real. Most of the time, all he thought about was his research and his theories as he snaked ever so slowly toward his research goal. Once in a while he would have a nightmare and wake with a start, but otherwise he was in his own unique form of denial.

It was late at night, about a month after meeting with Fellsteon, when he saw the shadowy figure next to a tall shrub to the right of his front door. As soon as the lights from his car moved in that direction, it disappeared. He was so deeply immersed in thinking about his research that he was not actually sure he saw anything--it was that ephemeral and brief. Marco thought nothing of it as he drove into the garage and went straight to bed.

Several days later, exactly the same thing happened, again a single fleeting, dark image, disappearing as soon as the headlights illuminated the front of the house. This time Marco paid attention, but it was too dark and too briefly in view to make out who or what this was or whether it was actually anything at all. Marco shuddered involuntarily, but when he got out of his car and went to look around, there was nothing. *Must have imagined it*, Marco thought.

When this happened a third time, Marco reacted rapidly, jumping out of the car to chase after the specter. But whoever or whatever it was got away in the darkness. He thought he saw a shadow running to a neighbor's house, but he was not sure of that. *Could be I'm seeing things*, Marco thought, *and this working fourteen hours a day non-stop does take its toll.* Possibly it was time to take a little breather.

Sometimes he wondered if Saul had found him but then dismissed that thought as too remote. How would he ever find Marco all the way over here? Or could it be something paranormal, Semantha or some other demon haunting him? He refused to consider that as a possibility. It did not fit with his science.

Then things got impossible to dismiss. One night he heard a faint but unmistakable knock on the kitchen door. His watch said it was 2:00 a.m. when he turned on the lights. He looked out the window. No one was there.

A day later, he heard a long, slow scratch on the screen of his bedroom window, distinct and unquestionable. Marco jumped out of bed and impulsively threw open the curtain. Again, no one. He remembered *The Raven*, the scary Edgar Allen Poe poem about mysterious, unexplained noises outside the poet's window. Recalling a line, he thought, *'tis the wind and nothing more.'* But also like the poet,

Marco stood there, 'wondering, fearing, doubting.' The quick beating of his heart told him that he was shaken.

Marco spent the rest of the night tossing and turning, waiting for the next noise. He did not want to involve the police. He worried about where their questions might lead. Finally, in the morning, his fear overcame him, and he called. They came, looked around, and found nothing. They told Marco to keep more lights on at night and install a security camera. They advised him to settle down, work less, and things will be fine. In effect, the cops told Marco he was hallucinating.

Possibly they are right, he thought. Maybe, unconsciously, his guilt was eating away inside and causing him to see and hear things. His lack of sleep was also most likely affecting his ability to think clearly. *Once I get my research done, things will return to normal and everything will be fine.*

Then things began to happen at work. Late one night after everyone else but the cleaning crew had left, he went down the hall and, upon his return, found his office light off and the door locked. He had not left the office that way. *Maybe it was just one of the janitors*, he thought. But the next night, when he came back to his office after spending some time in the lab, his wastebasket was turned upside down on the top of his desk, scattering garbage and left-over food scraps all over his calculations and lab notes. He was sure he hadn't done that. A hint of garlic hung in the air. *Some leftover bit of food*, Marco thought.

Marco called the Fermilab security force. As with the municipal police, they were dismissive. They pointed out that the Fermilab grounds were quite secure and that no one could enter and do the sort of things he described. Like the police, they said he must be working too hard. They told him that it was not the first time that someone at the lab became a little unhinged. Over the years there had been a number of incidents where faculty members had played mind games with each other, and things had gotten a little out of hand.

Sometimes they were innocent pranks, but other times the incidents deteriorated and became deadly serious. They told Marco about a time when a junior faculty member had caused an explosion by intentionally changing the labeling on an accelerator coil to sabotage the work of a colleague he did not like. That's just an example they had said. There were many others.

Marco did not buy what the security police had said. He knew he was not imagining things. There was no question that someone or something was stalking him, intentionally trying to rattle him. He just could not say who or why. He again thought that maybe it had something to do with the whole Michigan thing. He dismissed that possibility as implausible.

Then he thought about his wallet. It had gone missing that horrendous night. In all the turmoil, he did not know where or when he had lost it. Maybe Saul found it. Still, that could not explain how he could get into Fermilab. Marco had reported his ID as missing, and it had been deactivated. Nor would it explain how Saul could have found him at his home. He had just moved and his new address was not of record.

★   ★   ★

THE NEXT NIGHT, AT about 11:00 p.m., Marco was working in his office. His door was open as it usually was. He was sitting on his desk chair, a government-issued matched set with his desk. It was one of those older models with leather padded armrests and wheels that allowed it to pivot around like a carousel. He heard someone shuffle in the hallway. Before he could get up to look around, a hard object slammed against his head with a thud, knocking him out cold.

When he came to, he was still sitting in his office chair but now tightly bound with rope around his chest and arms. His phone was no longer in his pocket, and his mouth was covered with duct tape. A figure stood there, hovering above him like a predatory creature over his kill. It was Saul, not the unkempt Saul of Michigan, but a Saul cleaned up, shaven, and wearing a Fermilab janitorial staff uniform with an ID in a plastic holder. Marco did not recognize the name on the ID, but, with or without the name tag, there was no mistake. His small black eyes and pockmarked, pear-shaped face were unmistakable.

Saul had shut the office door and turned out all of the lights except the desk top lamp, from which he had removed the shade. The light emitted from the naked lightbulb was stark and harsh. Marco's desk phone lay on the floor, the line cut. Saul spoke slowly with a deep voice, like a man with plenty of time.

"Hello there, doc. I's been waiting for ya to wake up from yur little beauty rest, purdy boy. I was jes about to get some cold water to see if that would do the job, but now you's up all by yerself."

Marco tried to speak through the tape, but his words came out as mumbles.

Saul continued.

"You and I have a littl' score to settle, don't we now? Ya thought you could jes break into my lif', get sum pussy from my bran' new wif', ruin my night, and then jes swim away. You's seen that she was dressed up like a bride, my bride, you fuckin' piece of shit. You ain't got no respect fur another man's property."

Saul spit on Marco's face.

"Well, it ain't quite that easy." He stopped speaking as if to let his words sink in.

Then he slapped Marco hard across the face with the back of his hand, causing Marco's head to jerk violently to the side.

"So now it's yer turn to pay for the fuck ya got and what's you's done to me. You's got to be sure that my revenge is gonna be sweet and real slow."

Saul lifted his pant leg and revealed a sheathed dagger. It was decorated with a pentagon on its handle, the same one he had used on the rabbit during the mass and the one Semantha was wearing when Marco drowned her. He unsheathed it, pushed it lightly into Marco's side.

"You thought you got away from my purdy little baby here, didn't ya," he said. "You didn' figure that when my purdy little baby gets her mind to do sumpin', she finds a way to do it. An' every day since we first seen ya last summer, I's been sharpenin' her up an' gittin' her ready, jes thinkin' 'bout ya. And here we is. We's gonna finish off what we started back then. Only difference is Semantha's gone so she's not here to save yur ass or make it easy for ya. And ain't gonna be no drugs to put you out, so you can enjoy every minute."

Saul moved closer to Marco, grabbed Marco by the hair, and yanked his head to the side as if he was about to give Marco a shave. He then slid the blade lightly over Marco's cheek. Marco felt a sting as the blade penetrated his skin and could feel the blood flowing down his face. Saul was now close enough for Marco to smell Saul's fetid garlic breath and see his rotted, stained teeth. He gagged under the duct tape.

Saul grinned when he saw the blood flowing. "There ya go, Mr. Lover Boy, tha's jes for starters...we's gonna have lots more fun tonight."

"But first my little faggot, let me hear ya beg for mercy like ya done before." He violently pulled the tape off Marco's mouth. "What's ya gonna say now to try to save yourself and make me stop. Cummon now, speak, Mr. Pretty Boy. But no groaning, ya hear."

Saul grabbed Marco hard by the balls and squeezed, causing Marco to let out a groan.

"I said no groaning. Your groans hain't enough, shithead. You better do a lot better an' do it now." Saul pointed the dagger directly at Marco's crotch, holding it high with both hands. Marco squeezed the arms of the chair, clenched his teeth, and braced himself. He resolved not to scream out, didn't want the freak to have the satisfaction.

Just as Saul was about to plunge the dagger into Marco's privates, an alarm went off outside Marco's office. It was the accelerator warning bell, indicating the particles were reaching the proper speed for collision. While, to Marco, this was routine, Saul was jolted by the unexpected interruption.

"What the fuck is that," he screamed, turning away from Marco and opening the door.

That split second gave Marco time to act. Using his still strong, still powerful legs, he pivoted the chair on its wheels and charged at Saul, thrusting the back of the chair toward Saul's legs and waist. Upon impact, Saul doubled over and fell back into one of Marco's overstuffed bookshelves with enough force to cause it to topple over on him. He was instantly bombarded by Marco's collection of books and journals, among them a few weighty textbooks. The impact of the chair also caused Saul to let go of the dagger, which then went flying across the room like an arrow shot from an unseen bow. Saul was momentarily dazed but quickly recovered.

"Fuckin' shit," Saul screamed. "You's gonna pay for this, ya faggot."

As Saul dug himself out from under the pile of books, Marco swung the chair around again and propelled himself and the chair toward the edge of the sturdy metal desk. This time, the collision caused the chair backrest and arms to break cleanly off from the seat, leaving Marco's legs free but his arms and chest still restrained.

Both he and Saul went for the dagger, Saul crawling out from under the books, and Marco carrying the chair back. Just as Marco was about to reach it, Saul lunged at Marco's leg, caught Marco off balance, and grabbed him. As Marco began to fall, he was able to kick the dagger well under the desk and out of reach from either of them.

Marco and Saul then struggled on the floor, wrestling, kicking, and hitting, both fighting hard. Although Marco's arms were still tied to the back of the chair, he placed serious blows, sometimes using the chair itself. Finally, Marco was able to land one of his feet squarely and hard on Saul's balls causing him to double over and scream with pain. With this momentary advantage, Marco pulled himself up with the handles on the drawers of the desk, fled the office, and ran down the hallway toward the accelerator lab. There was a button in the lab that he could push to call security.

Saul was not far behind. As they reached the door to the lab, Saul jumped up and threw his arms around Marco's shoulders, trying to tackle him from behind and pull him to the floor. Saul held on with both arms locked around Marco but could not bring him down. Rather than trying to shake him off, Marco used his height and strength to swing Saul around in the air. He spun faster and faster, building momentum as he went. Saul hung on for dear life as Marco moved them closer to the accelerator with each turn. When he was ready, Marco took aim, bit hard on Saul's hand, causing him to give up his grip, and then gave him a heave. Saul catapulted through the air toward the accelerator. He landed directly on one of the machine's high voltage coils.

Saul let out a piercing shriek and then gave an eerie deep moan, as 200,000 volts of electricity gushed through his body. Saul became a massive voltaic arc, like a lightning bolt, causing his body to convulse wildly. For a moment he appeared to be suspended in mid-air. Sparks flew and a fetid, vapor-like green smoke flowed from his ears and nostrils. The air smelled of sulfur and bile. Saul's clothes caught fire and began to burn. His skin took on a sinister, smoldering glow, then melted off, cascading to the floor in glowing droplets and exposing the bones below. His eyes became like two burning, white hot coals. As the flesh on his face incinerated, the skull of a demonic incarnate man-beast with horns and scales briefly seemed to replace Saul's face before disappearing.

Then it was over. Saul's very unremarkable remains lay smoldering and motionless at the foot of the coil. Marco breathed a sigh of relief for having again escaped disaster and shuddered anew as he contemplated the terror he had just eluded. *The events of that day in Michigan hound me still,* he thought. That thought, in turn, brought him face-to-face with his own despicable act, the consequences of which, until this moment, he had buried in his work. All the guilt and remorse with which he had once struggled again surfaced. He stood there, looking at Saul's remains, and silently contemplated the emptiness of his strivings and the bankruptcy of his moral values. His mind returned to Michigan, that old house, and his daring but ill-omened escape.

Marco snapped back to the present when the accelerator again sounded a warning bell, this time signaling the end of the experiment. He found a sharp corner on a piece of equipment and sawed off the ropes holding him to the chair back and arms. He pushed the button to call security and went back to his office. There, an incredible surprise awaited him. He found his computer printing out the results of the experiment he had just completed. As he looked them over, he could not believe his eyes. There it was--the data he had been looking for.

Marco stood there reviewing the printout, almost reverently, mesmerized by what he saw. For a moment, everything else besides that single piece of paper seemed to fade away and become extraneous. He looked for errors, something missing, any mistake. But no, everything was correct and in good form. He drank in this remarkable occurrence. His career was secure. To Marco, all of his past was merely the herald of this delicious moment.

Yet, Marco also knew he had some unfinished business, which, he now understood, would plague him for the rest of his life if not resolved. Tomorrow he would go to Michigan, meet with the sheriff, and atone for what he had done. Two people dead by his hand was enough.

XXIV

———————

THE NEXT MORNING, MARCO again visited Frank at his office. Frank was sitting behind his big walnut desk correcting a brief when, unannounced, Marco walked in.

"Good to see you, Marco," Frank said as he laid down his pen. "All good at Fermilab?" Marco looked silently at Frank for a minute.

"I've decided to go to Michigan and meet with the sheriff about the problem I had a few months ago. Remember the incident?"

Frank's eyes grew large and his jaw dropped.

"How could I forget? But I thought that two-headed hydra was history. What in the name of the Lord happened?"

"Very long story. I'll tell you later," Marco said. "In the meantime, Frank, please come with me and represent me. I need you there so much. I really do."

"Of course I'll help," Frank responded. "Let me make some calls. Come back tomorrow. We can figure out how to best approach this thing."

Frank looked troubled when Marco came back the next day. "I'm afraid I don't have very good news," Frank said. "My friends in the Berrien County trial bar tell me that the county recently hired a young crack prosecutor who spent five years as an Assistant U.S. Attorney in Detroit but wanted a change of environment. She handles this sort of case. She is mean, tough as nails, and known to be a hard ass. She's not likely to be very forgiving or pleasant."

"Just my luck." Marco jerked his head and snapped his fingers as if to say 'Oh shit.'

"Does this change things?"

"No. Why would it?"

"Maybe this will. It has been quite a while and no body has washed up. My friends tell me that they have heard nothing about anyone finding a female victim floating in the river. Apparently, the body drifted out into Lake Michigan and is gone. I would put the chance that anything will ever come of this at near zero, unless of course you go there yourself."

Frank hesitated as if to emphasize what he was about to say.

"Marco, this is not legal advice, this is your older brother talking. Listen to me." Frank stood up and grabbed Marco by the shoulders. "You'd be a fool to turn yourself in now." Shaking his head, Frank grimaced. "Do not go."

"I understand what you are saying, really do. But, fool or no fool, remember your question to me when I was in your office last time? Well, I have answered it. That's the reason why I'm going."

Frank's phone rang. He pushed the 'do not disturb' button.

"The other night," Marco continued, "I had an uncanny encounter with what seemed like the Devil. I'm sure it was just my imagination, but it was still a powerful image. Will tell you about it on the way over to Michigan."

Marco leaned closer to Frank. His voice became firm. "Now I see that my integrity is more important to me than anything else. Right? I've got to take responsibility for my actions and pay the price, regardless of the cost."

Upon hearing this, Frank swallowed hard and a tear came to his eye.

"Marco, This means that you are willing to give up everything you have worked for, your career, your scientific accomplishments, your wealth and, most of all, your freedom, for what could be a long time. Because once you lay out your story, you cannot take it back. This hard-ass prosecutor will be in a position to decide your fate, and we will not be able to do much about it."

Frank rubbed his fingers back and forth on the side of his head.

"And I don't understand what you gain. This woman was quite evil and sleazy. Again, I say, for Christ's sake, don't go."

"My mind is made up."

"Well, if you insist on going and doing this thing, why don't you at least tell them that you acted because Semantha tried to attack you with a knife after luring you to come close. That would make this about self-defense and not murder. They will never know the difference."

Marco squinted. "That makes no sense. I am going to come clean and take responsibility for my acts. Nope, I must tell them everything or not go at all. I'm going."

"You will regret this." Frank shook his head.

"I don't think I will, at least not in the long run. Actually, I'm quite surprised that you would suggest that your client lie to the prosecutors. Aren't lawyers supposed to advise their clients to either tell the truth or not say anything at all?"

Frank's face blushed scarlet and his head bowed a little.

"Yes, you are correct, Marco. I was wrong to suggest that. I guess my protective urge overtook me. It grieves me to think of anything bad happening to you. If you do this, you are in for a long, rough ride."

"Saying that does not make this any easier, Frank." Marco did not need any reminders of the consequences of what he was doing; his weeks of mental anguish had been plenty.

"Maybe this will help. I do admire you for staking out this position and sticking to it. It shows that you are a person of true integrity. But I have one suggestion."

"Okay, what? You aren't going to get me to change my mind."

"When we get there, let me do the talking. Potentially, I can blunt the rough edges around the story and make it sound less…less…well criminal."

"Okay, Frank, but still only the truth."

★   ★   ★

A WEEK LATER, FRANK picked up Marco for the trip to Michigan. Marco did not look good. His eyes were red and bruised with big bags under them; his face was haggard; his already trim body was almost gaunt, and he was ghostly white.

"What happened to you, Marco?" Frank asked.

"Pretty tough week, Frank. Couldn't sleep or eat. I changed my mind about going a thousand times, back and forth, back and forth. Prison time is beyond scary. In the end, I decided to go through with it only because I knew I would eventually hate myself if I didn't." Marco also worried about looking like a vacillating, spineless coward in front of Frank, who he admired. He decided it best not to tell Frank that.

Frank then picked up Jeannie. He had suggested that she come along to put a female on the team. He usually employed that litigation strategy, especially valuable in a case like this involving a female prosecutor and the death of a woman at the hands of a male. Marco was happy to have her along, and he was relieved that they had not had sex after the boat ride. If they had, her presence would have been uncomfortable for them both. And Frank would have discovered that Marco had played around with one of his associates, not a good thing.

On the way to Michigan, Marco told Frank and Jeannie about what he thought he saw as Saul died. He described how that had led him to an ethical catharsis, resulting in his decision to come clean with the law. Even though driving, Frank listened intently, watching Marco in the rear-view mirror.

"Now I understand why you are doing this," he said. "But how do you feel about Saul's death? You killed him as well."

"That was very different. The Fermilab security police were on the scene in about five minutes after I electrocuted him. You know, and the Batavia police as well. They spent two hours interviewing me, checking the scene, dusting for fingerprints, and taking photographs. They put the dagger, the chair, and everything else Saul used in bags to take with them as evidence."

Jeannie turned around and looked at Marco in the back seat.

"Did they ask you if you knew the person you had just killed?"

"They did."

"And what did you say?"

"I told them the same thing I told the police in Michigan the day after I escaped. I told them I went looking for the girl and stumbled into this coven. You know the rest."

"So any reason to believe that they tied Saul's coming after you to the girl you drowned?" Jeannie asked.

"No mention of that. How would they even know? One of the cops did say that I must have really pissed off this creep, escaping like that and ruining his night."

"Did you give them a statement?" Frank asked.

"Sure, why not?"

"You should've called me first. I would have told you to say nothing."

"But I didn't feel under investigation."

"Good Lord, Marco," Jeannie said. "I thought you would have learned your lesson from your experience with Semantha. The law is not that simple. You had just killed another person. In such a case, you always could face some criminal exposure."

"Yeah, well, maybe. But they told me that it was a clear case of self-defense and that I had nothing to worry about. I totally believed them, right."

"For a theoretical physicist, Marco, sometimes you can be so naive," Frank said. "But go on."

"I was going to say, I don't feel the same guilt about Saul as I do about Semantha. It was absolutely him or me, you know."

"I hope that sticks," Jeannie said. "Otherwise, you are a two-time offender, and that's a big issue."

For an instant, Marco felt a twinge of anxiety, but Frank's continued questioning quickly focused Marco's attention on more immediate concerns.

"So tell me," Frank asked. "How did that lowlife get into Fermilab in the first place? Did you ever find out?"

"Yep. They told me that a couple of days before Saul came after me, one of their night janitors failed to show up for work. Saul had his uniform and ID card. He must have attacked the guy and took his stuff, ya know."

"Real slime," Jeannie said.

"Yeah, for sure. I hate to think of what happened to the poor guy. I assume Saul killed him. That would be his way. If he did, count person three dead as a result of my trip to Michigan. That does bother me."

"I'm surprised that none of this made it into the papers," Jeannie said. "It should have been big news."

"It did, but the official explanation was an accidental death of a Fermilab janitor," Marco responded. "Fermilab is good at spinning things. Typical corporate America."

The three continued to speed down the interstate toward Michigan.

EVENTUALLY, FRANK, MARCO, AND Jeannie walked up the steps to the courthouse. After they waited for some time in the rundown marble and terrazzo front hallway of the 1930s style building, the prosecutor's assistant appeared.

"Miss Sandibar will see you now," she said.

The clerk escorted them into Cynthia Sandibar's windowless office. It was small and cluttered with stacks of paper and miscellaneous law books thrown around. Sandibar, looking stiff and stern, remained seated behind her desk as they walked in. When Marco's eyes met hers, she hesitated and looked at him... a second too long. Marco felt a spark. Sandibar quickly caught herself and turned her attention to Frank.

"Well, tell me, how are things in Chicago, Mr. Douglas? And what brings such an esteemed Chicago lawyer and his talented associate to our humble little town?" She spoke brusquely and as the person in charge. "And by the way, this is my assistant Claire Mitchell who will be taking notes of our meeting. I presume you will not mind."

"Counsel, this is my client, Marco Adamos, and my associate Jeannie Auerback," Frank began. "We are here to report a death in which Mr. Adamos was involved. I would like to tell you what happened."

"Proceed," Sandibar said as if she were a feisty old judge at a trial.

Frank began to recount the story, starting with Marco's ride up the St. Joe River. A few minutes in, Marco raised his hand and interrupted him.

"No, Frank, I've got to tell Miss Sandibar about what happened. I do not want this sugarcoated." Marco then picked up the story and recounted every detail, while the clerk furiously took notes. Sandibar listened intently, hanging on every word. He finished by saying "And then I held her under the water until she stopped breathing."

When Marco was done, the room was silent for almost a minute. No one moved. Frank was speechless. Sandibar continued to look at Marco as if she was in a trance, captivated either by the story or the person telling it, maybe both. Finally she cleared her throat and spoke, this time in a voice not at all powerful or commanding.

"Mr. Adamos, that is an incredible story. I would say you are lucky to be alive, sir." Sandibar gave her head a quick jerk to the side, gently throwing her long blond hair to the front of her shoulder. "But please answer me one question. Why didn't you simply swim away when you saw her coming?"

Ever since Frank had asked Marco that exact question back in his office, Marco had been trying to figure out why he did what he did. He still did not have a good answer.

"Miss Sandibar, wish I knew. By that time, I was beside myself with exhaustion, stress, and confusion. Felt like I was sort of out of my mind. I furiously wanted to believe that she was telling the truth about her intentions and that we could make a life together. But I also knew that ultimately she posed a grave threat to me. The image of her standing there in her black robe calmly waiting for Saul to knife me was unbelievably vivid in my mind. No matter what I did, I knew that it was either her or me. I did not think that swimming away would end the problem with these lunatics. No. Regardless of what she said, she was still one of them, you understand. So I acted."

"Well, Mr. Adamos," Sandibar said, again clearing her throat, "we have some forms for you to fill out and ultimately we will want you to sign a confession. Since you voluntarily came here to report this crime, we assume you will continue to cooperate and you are not a flight risk. So I will not have you arrested right now or require bail. But we will be in touch, probably in a few days." She stood up as if to say, 'meeting over.' "Now excuse me, I have a three o'clock court call."

"Miss Sandibar," Frank asked as he too stood up, "How do you see this and do you expect to bring charges?"

"Your client has committed a crime," Sandibar said as she headed to the door. "We will be bringing charges. I will need to consult with my chief and be back in touch." Sandibar's authoritarian voice had returned.

On the road back to Chicago, Frank and Jeannie volunteered nothing about the meeting. Frank kept his eyes on the road, and Jeannie looked out at the sights as they passed by. Finally, with the Chicago skyline in sight, Marco broke the silence. "Guys, you have been too quiet. What do you think?"

"I don't know, Marco," Jeannie responded. "Your story did not sound made up. I mean, for gosh sakes, a young Chicago physicist on the rise does not end up swimming in the St. Joe River in Michigan at 2:00 a.m. unless as a result of some pretty strange circumstances. So, I believe that Sandibar credited what you had to say."

"Well, that's good… I guess."

"And as to the answer to the question as to why you did not swim away, I think you did about as well as you could have," Frank said. "I am glad we had gone over this when you first came to my office. The time you spent thinking over this question definitely helped today. With that answer you went about half the way to a temporary insanity defense."

"That's hopeful…I guess."

"Something was going on in Sandibar's mind, though," Jeannie then said. "I mean, the dynamic between the two of you was charged, charged with what I don't know but charged with something. I could see it."

"I could feel it," Marco said. "I hate to say this, but the last time I felt a connection like that was when I first saw Semantha on the boat that day."

"For Christ's sake, Marco, no," Frank said. He pulled the car over to the shoulder, stopped, and turned around so he could look directly at Marco. "You need to stay away from thinking like that, like miles away. Sandibar is off limits, strictly off limits. Stifle your fantasies before they get you into another big mess. She is a lawyer who has tremendous power over you, nothing else. Get it?"

Marco felt chastened and did not respond to Frank's lecture.

"Sorry I brought it up," Jeannie said as they headed for the loop and Frank's office.

BACK HOME, MARCO CONTINUED to fret as he waited to hear from Sandibar. Time passed excruciatingly slowly. He tried to distract himself by reading a novel, when that didn't work, watching TV, or when that didn't work, playing computer chess. He was too distraught to concentrate. All Marco could think about was how much time he would be forced to spend in prison and how his life was about to forever change for the worse. So often he regretted his decision to go, but, as Frank had warned him, it was too late to change things. He saw no one and did nothing. He became a little unraveled as one sleepless night followed another.

Finally, a week after returning from Michigan, Frank called. It was two in the afternoon, Marco had not shaved for several days, and he was still wearing only his pajama bottoms.

"Marco, I just got off the phone with Martin Dunland. He is the county prosecutor in Berrien County and Sandibar's boss. It was a very peculiar conversation. He told me that Sandibar was off the case and that you and I need to come back and start the process all over."

"What do you mean, 'start over?' I can't go through this much longer. Not eating, not sleeping. Alone with my preoccupation and worry. I need to know what is going to happen. Really do." Marco was frantic.

"Marco, I feel for you, but there is nothing I or anyone else can do. I did ask Dunland what had happened. All he would do is repeat, 'Sandibar is off the case and I need to hear from your client myself. That's all I will say.' We have no choice but to go back."

The next day, Marco and Frank drove back to Berrien County again and met with Martin Dunland. The conversation went about the same as it had with Sandibar except there were no furtive glances or unspoken undercurrents. Dunland had a deputy sheriff there, who arrested Marco. He was fingerprinted and booked on a charge of second-degree murder. He had to appear before a judge who rather reluctantly set him free without requiring him to post bail.

For Marco, the experience was surreal, a living nightmare. While Frank had alerted him as to the process, he was nonetheless not prepared for how it unfolded. Never in his life had ever expected he would be treated like a common criminal. Being fingerprinted and booked, unbelievable. Being treated with indifference by the sheriff and disdain by the judge. Beyond any thought. It was a sobering and degrading experience, bringing him down from the rarified academic stratosphere to the habitat of a societal deviant, all in one horrific minute.

Marco quickly sank into all-consuming despair. Booked on a charge of murder and with every prospect of a long prison sentence, he was overcome with depression and a feeling of unrelenting helplessness. He could see nothing in his future but suffering and pain. He thought about whether it would be better to just end his life, since he felt that was about to happen anyway.

This time, however, his wait was short. The day after they returned to Chicago, Marco's cell phone rang. It was Frank.

"Dunland called," Frank told him. The serious tone in Frank's voice worried Marco.

"Give me the bad news. I am prepared, I guess," Marco said, although he was anything but ready for what he was convinced he was about to hear. He paced back and forth holding the phone in front of him.

"He told me a lot. For one thing, he said that the sheriff's office had been scoping out this little coven and its leaders for a while. They had investigated the grizzly murder of the old so-called high priest but had not positively identified any suspects. They also knew about the gory animal sacrifices and that some members of the coven had met bad ends."

Marco grimaced.

"They also ran background checks on this sleazebag who came to Fermilab. He had a criminal record as long as your arm, mostly for crimes of petty violence involving knives and a history of involuntary confinement in mental institutions."

"Unbelievable," Marco said, but his anxiety was rising. *Why isn't Frank getting to what they are going to do to me,* he wondered. *Must be really bad.* He paced faster and faster.

"As to your lovely miss Semantha, she was going to be arrested and, most likely, put away for a long time. They were planning to charge her for having sex with underage boys she met while coaching the high school science fair. Not one but two of them. Only reason that didn't happen is they couldn't find her. You know how to pick um, Marco."

"Pretty sick." Marco shook his head slowly back and forth. But hearing Frank mention Semantha's likely fate made him think about his own. Walking through the heavy metal gate to the prison, the gate closing with a bang; fingerprinted and given his number; issued his prison jumpsuit; led to his cell by a brutish guard; pushed inside with a shove; the barred door slamming shut with a leaden thud; the windowless gray walls now his world; alone, cold, abandoned, for years. He shuddered.

"Marco, you there?" Frank asked.

"Yeah, I'm sorry. Just thinking, What did he say about me? What they going to do to me?"

"I'm getting to that. Dunland told me that they had evaluated the statements you made about your state of mind when you killed her and believed that we could make out a credible case for temporary insanity before a jury. In any event, he said, they did not want this case to go that far. Dunland had concluded that a trial would become a public spectacle and would only hurt the community. He's right. I would want the jury to hear every bizarre detail if we tried the case."

"Frank, can you get on with it? Give me the bottom line." Frank was making Marco extremely nervous.

"Okay, okay. The bottom line is this. You have not waived your right to a jury trial because you have confessed. A jury could still decide whether your conduct resulted from temporary insanity. So Dunland is offering a plea deal to avoid a trial. Plead guilty to a lesser charge of something called 'second-degree reckless endangerment,' accept a six-month probation, and pay a $1,000 fine. Then we are done. That's just a misdemeanor. You would need to report this action whenever you apply for a job or any professional license, but, other than that, this incident would be history. No jail time, no felony record, no loss of the right to vote."

Marco couldn't believe what he was hearing. He stopped pacing and sat down. "Don't play with me, Frank. That is way too good to be true." Marco was pissed that Frank was making light at a time like this.

"It's true. Believe it."

Marco's tongue failed him as he digested the news.

"You there?" Frank again asked. "You want the deal? The alternative is to go for the possibility of a 'not guilty' verdict after a trial."

"Frank, that's just spectacular. I love you. My God. I love you." A sense of calm flowed through Marco, a peace he had not felt since the day he met with Frank in his office just after he did Semantha in. "Of course, I'll take the deal." He smiled for the first time in months.

"But the last question. Did he tell you what happened to all those people in that strange little coven?"

"Scattered to the winds. Not a trace anywhere, including Clem."

Marco did not know why, but he did not like the sound of that.

"Dunland told me one other thing. As soon as he heard about the case, he discussed it with the commissioners. They told him he needed to handle it personally. Dunland said that this case was too sensitive to relegate to a relatively new assistant. That's why we had to go back."

"Sandibar did ask him to inform us that she did not play any part except to interview you and that she had no role in the decision about how to handle the case. It's somewhat odd, but that's what he said."

As soon as he and Frank finished talking, Marco danced a little jig and then fell to his knees, thanking God for his unbelievable good fortune. His life and his future as a scientist had been saved, like he was born again but with no religious hocus pocus. He got a good night's sleep and woke refreshed, ready to tackle some new research problems. Possibly he would make a clean break by looking into something besides the neutrino, perhaps take up the study of quantum entanglement. His unpleasant discussion with Jeannie and Chris on the boat was still in the back of his mind.

And, no question about it, he needed to rekindle his social life. He had not been too interested for quite a while as first he buried himself in his work and then went to Michigan to confess. This whole encounter had left him exhausted and wary of romantic entanglements, but he also knew he did not want to live alone forever. Maybe he should find a beautiful woman who could help him jump-start his passion.

The next day, his initial exuberance over his newfound freedom quickly evaporated. He discovered the effects of the disabling emotional damage he had suffered when he returned to his office. He had not been there since the night Saul met his end. He had expected to leap back into his research, but, instead, repeated vivid reminders of the terror he had experienced there dominated him, distracting him when he tried to work. Over and over, he imagined Saul about to plunge the dagger into his privates. The image was so real that he shook when he thought about it. He replayed the desperate struggle on the floor. His stomach knotted just recalling it. And he relived watching Saul's fiery demise, chilling his body every time. He could not shake those horrific images.

A return to normalcy was going to be more difficult than he had imagined, if he ever could go back at all.

XXV

MARCO'S PATHWAY BACK TO a semblance of his previous life began slowly. Fermilab was incredibly supportive, not only because Saul's attack was as a result of an egregious breach of security but much more because of Marco's data. Gordon wanted Marco to get busy and publish his findings, expecting great interest from the scientific community with significant residual benefit to his department. He arranged for Marco to get a computer at his home, away from the scene of the assault, and helped him obtain top quality exposure therapy to assist him in coming face-to-face with his trauma. Gradually, Marco was able to return to his office and the lab, first a couple times a week but soon pretty much every day. Adept at burying his problems in his work, Marco's research and writing output came back very quickly. His social life, not so. He still could not bring himself to return to the dating scene, finding the thought of doing so disquieting.

Then he received this email:

> Mr. Adamos, I am planning to be in Chicago this weekend. I hope you don't think this presumptuous, but I am wondering if you would like to have a cup of coffee with me. Please understand, I would be doing this completely personally and not as an employee of Berrien County, Michigan.
> Cynthia Sandibar.

Marco was shocked by the e-mail but intrigued at the same time. He was also wary, recalling Frank's strong warning to stay away from her. He called Frank to see whether he could respond even if he wanted to.

"I guess Jeannie's radar was correct," Frank said. "You certainly got to her from the get-go. Sounds like another woman wants admission to your little harem, Marco."

"Just what I don't need."

"And I'm very surprised. Her contact is somewhat unprofessional. But that's her problem, not yours. Go for it, if you want, that is."

With Frank's blessing secured, Marco wrote back telling Cynthia he would meet her the following Saturday at ten, suggesting a coffee shop called Rocky Mountain Caffeine High near his new townhouse in River Forest. The place was a quaint little store decorated in a Colorado mountain get-away motif and with a big collection of old coffee grinders. It reeked of freshly ground beans. The atmosphere set just the right tone for meeting a new date.

Shortly after he made the arrangement, he began to regret it. *This is not going to be fun,* he thought. *She's just another pushy female attorney, and I have already had my fill of both attorneys and pushy women.*

At first he was going to cancel, but then he decided that meeting a woman like her could be a boost to his tattered ego and maybe help him get his social life back together. *It's not everyday that a woman is so turned on that she goes to such ends just to meet,* he thought. She could be another trophy, a new female conquest, and definitely a confidence booster. Likely it would never result in anything more than a coffee, which was fine with him.

Probably because of his ambivalence, he was almost a half an hour late getting to the coffee shop, and then he did not bother to clean up or shave. Cynthia was still there, looking miffed. She did not stand up to greet him. Even so, he could see that she had gone to some effort. *A little too cleaned up for Saturday morning coffee,* he thought.

Cynthia had shed the look of a bull-dog prosecutor and tough street fighter. Sitting there in the coffee shop, she looked sweet, almost coquettish. And she was beautiful. She appeared to be in her early thirties with riveting hazel eyes, a flawless complexion, and, from what Marco could see, a very shapely body. *This could turn out to be fun after all,* he thought.

"Sorry to be so late. The morning conspired against me. Let me buy you a coffee." Marco felt a little guilty.

"Thanks but no. I've already had my fill. Too much coffee makes me edgy, but so does sitting around cooling my heels." Cynthia looked away and frowned. "I was getting ready to leave when you finally decided to stroll in and grace me with your presence."

"Please do forgive me. I'll make it up to you, I promise. Let me get a coffee and we can talk." As he left to go order, he accidentally kicked the table where Cynthia was sitting, causing her water glass to shake. She instinctively grabbed it and winced. A few minutes later. Marco came back with an espresso and sat down.

"I guess an explanation is in order," Cynthia said. "You must think it rather curious that I would contact you and suggest we meet."

"The thought did cross my mind, yes." Marco sat up in his chair, expectantly waiting to hear what she had to say. But he also noticed how tastefully she was dressed, wearing a light green, low-cut blouse and form-fitting blue jeans. A silver necklace with a single large pearl fell elegantly from her neck.

"You intrigued me so much when you and your lawyers came to my office. Now that the case is over, I just had to talk with you."

That statement was no surprise to Marco. As Frank had suggested, it sounded like this young prosecutor had fallen for his good looks and swagger. So far, this meeting was going exactly as he expected, and he was already poised to bolt. He found himself uninterested in acquiring another member for the Marco fan club. The old sweatshirt and dirty jeans he wore were sending the right message.

"Isn't it a problem for you to contact me? My lawyer was quite surprised." Marco's attention was distracted when a lovely brunette walked by their table. Cynthia saw him look and frowned.

"Oh no, my boss was not concerned. The case is over, and anyway, all I did was the intake. Truthfully, he's afraid I'll leave so he bends over backwards to accommodate me."

"Let me get this straight. You told your boss that you wanted to meet me socially and he said that was okay?" Something did not seem quite right to Marco.

"I wouldn't say this meeting is exactly social."

"If not social, what?"

"What intrigued me about you is your almost unimaginable integrity. I wanted to find out more about what drove you to self-report your crime." She folded her hands together on the table as if she was counseling a client in the interview room.

"Integrity? How so?" Marco was getting a little hot under the collar. It was beginning to feel like he was on display.

"In my job, I am used to dealing with the typical run of the mill criminal who always tries to avoid culpability, usually goes to great lengths. You came when it was pretty clear that otherwise you would get by with it. Why did you?"

"And that's so important to you because?"

"Because I love the criminal justice system and I have been thinking about exploring the criminal mind some more, maybe write a law review article. Talking to you may give me some ideas, if you are willing, that is."

"Because I have a criminal mind, is that your drift?"

"You did commit a fairly serious crime."

Marco bristled at the thought, but he was also a little disappointed that, as it turned out, Cynthia was not another Marco groupie.

"So this meeting today is just a research project about my unique criminal mind? Is that your gist?" Marco crossed his arms tightly in front of his chest. "When I got your email, I thought you were interested in me, and maybe we could connect, you know, socially."

"Sorry, Marco, I hope I can call you that, I don't make a practice of dating my ex-criminal defendants. But can we talk?"

Marco became angry. "About my decision to self-report? Here's my answer. I don't want to be a part of your blankety-blank research project. I've gone through enough already." Marco stood up, ready to leave.

"Cummon, sit down will you?" Cynthia said so loudly, almost angrily, that people a few tables away looked over. She did have a way of making herself felt.

Marco, shocked by her tone, stared down at her in disbelief. What is this woman about, he thought. *Coming all this way to insult me. Why?*

"Please, Marco, don't leave," she said, changing to a diminutive, agreeable tone of voice. She looked sad; she waited a second, she leaned to get closer to Marco.

"Maybe," she whispered, "I'm just a little interested." She smoothed her hair with her hand.

Marco sat back down. He wanted to see how this would play out.

"I'm confused. Did you suggest coffee to get to know me or to study me, which?"

"Can we just talk, Marco? Do we need an agenda? It was a risk for me to contact you. As long as we are both here, let's get to know each other a little. See how it goes." She smiled. "To be clear, you are not a research subject."

"Okay, I'll bite. Why did you take the risk? There must be many men in your world who would jump at the chance to get to know you."

"Men of integrity are sort of my turn on." She reached out her hand as if she wanted to touch Marco's arm. He did not move to let her. "Rare to find in this day and age. And I don't mind taking a few risks now and then, especially when I find something I want."

"Something you want, you mean me?" Anticipation replaced Marco's anger.

"I guess I do want to get to know you at least. Is that so bad? I'm not too shy to say so."

Marco's anticipation changed to intrigue. He had yet to meet a woman, especially a powerful, professional woman like Cynthia, who was interested in him for some other reason besides his looks or his social status. *Refreshing*, he thought. *This woman is different.* He liked that she did not throw herself at him. *And she is very attractive even if she doesn't have dimples.* Her diminutive nose and high cheekbones substituted pretty well.

"I think of myself as being shy," Marco said. His face took on a boyish look.

"Come on, guy, you don't seem like the shy type," Cynthia said in a mocking tone. "I mean, how can you be shy? You're a theoretical physicist at a prestigious institution."

"Well, I guess I'm, uh, shy in some situations and not in others. Definitely shy when it comes to getting to know women, especially if they are strong willed. It takes me a little while to get entirely comfortable, you know." Cynthia focused all her attention on Marco.

"Interesting, Marco. I wouldn't have pegged you that way. You're saying you have a problem with strong-willed women?"

"Maybe, but not because of what you think. Strong-willed women are too unpredictable. I never know where I stand. Take yourself. With your reputation as a tough, unrelenting prosecutor, I was not sure how it would be to talk with you."

"So, is that why you were so late?"

"No, no, absolutely no." Marco responded, but she was dead on target. Marco felt even more guilty for not coming at the time they'd agreed. He lifted the espresso cup to his lip to take a drink, but it was already empty. He looked sheepishly at Cynthia, hoping she had not noticed. She smiled.

"Marco, I do not consider myself to be tough or aggressive. I am only passionate about what I do. That's very different. I know it sounds a little corny because people nowadays are not supposed to be motivated by high-sounding principles, but I just want to see that justice is done."

"So, that's what gets you up in the morning?"

"I guess you could say that, but it's more than that. Behind most crimes are victims who have been gravely harmed. I see my work as vindicating them, and I get very wrapped up in doing that. It could be that comes off as tough and aggressive, but I'm not actually that way."

Marco smiled. He was disarmed by her earnestness and fascinated by her sincerity.

"That's admirable, Cynthia, I hope I can call you that? Anyway, we all need a little passion to get us moving every day."

Both Cynthia and Marco held their gaze on each other as they continued to talk.

"What's your passion, Marco, the behavior of quarks and neutrinos?"

"Wow, where did you come up with that? That's impressive, Cynthia, and I mean that. No question. Most people have never even heard these words or know what they refer to."

"Well, I had to learn a little about particle physics for a case I had a few years ago. It was interesting stuff, but I have not had the chance to follow up and learn more."

"I can teach you a few things, if you want that is." He winked.

"I'm sure you can…" Cynthia's eyebrow went up. "…and maybe you could teach me about quarks and neutrinos as well." Cynthia smiled slyly. "You didn't answer. What's your passion?"

"Beautiful blondes with dazzling hazel eyes," he replied, returning the smile and the innuendo all at once.

Cynthia looked a little embarrassed by that comment. She waited a second. "Sounds more like lust than passion," she said. The meeting, which started out strained, began to flow.

Marco grinned. "Aren't they the same?"

"I don't think so. Passion is important to make life worth living. Lust is a biological instinct built into us necessary for the propagation of the species. People mistake the two all of the time."

"I make that mistake myself, actually a lot. Sometimes my lust leads me to break the rules, and I get into trouble." Marco looked away as Michigan came back to him.

"I am not a rule breaker, Marco."

"Bending the rules a little is not so bad, especially for a good cause."

"True, but it's knowing which rules to bend and when it's actually a good cause…that's the hard part."

"That's why we have great lawyers like you." Marco chuckled.

"Sounds more like the realm of philosophy than law," Cynthia said without hesitation.

"Maybe you are right about that and that's good because philosophy is also one of my interests."

"Mine too, but up until now I've had no one to talk to about that."

"And now you do," Marco said earnestly. "Where do we start? I'm a Nietzsche fan myself."

COFFEE TURNED INTO LUNCH, then a long walk along the lake followed by dinner and a late-night drink at the cocktail lounge on the top of the Hancock Building.

Marco and Cynthia discovered that they had much in common; and, despite what Marco had feared, Cynthia was easy to talk with. The conversation flowed. The periods of silence, natural. She almost convinced Marco that she was interested in his work on the behavior of neutrinos, although in the back of his mind he doubted that she was. It sort of turned him on that she appeared willing to feign interest in his work just to get to know him. He, on the other hand, was genuinely enthralled when Cynthia told him some stories about cases she had tried when working in Detroit. Some of it was pretty steamy.

They both shared stories about their early years. Marco told Cynthia that he grew up being stereotyped as a good-looking jock, with all the negative connotations of that image, but really wanted to be known for his brains. His parents were both entrepreneurs on the rise and not particularly involved in his life. He never felt they took him seriously or cared very much.

Cynthia told him that she was a child of average intelligence reared in a small, midwestern town. Her parents were overprotective, very conservative Protestants absorbed in their church. She broke free from that constrained, narrow environment through the unrelenting pursuit of a career in what she described as a 'power profession.' Her life had been a persistent search for self-identity.

As the hour grew late, Cynthia moved close, took Marco by the arm, and held him tight. "What a great day and night," she said. "Let me be forward once again and ask you if you would like to come over to my room at the Drake. I am sure we can find a bottle of wine along the way to have a nightcap."

Marco pulled away. "Cynthia, I find you incredibly sexy. There's no question. But, you know, for once in my life I want to put first things first and get to know you more before we get physical. I hope that this doesn't put you off because that is the last thing I want to do. Seriously."

What Marco did not tell her was that he had not been with any woman since that night with Semantha and he was still shell-shocked. He needed some time before he could imagine having sex again, even with a beauty like Cynthia. Having a sexual encounter with anyone right now scared him. Anyway, he had not cleaned up all day long. Likely, he did not smell all that great at close range.

Cynthia replied, "Of course, that's fine. We can wait." She then grabbed him and gave him a deep kiss right in the cocktail lounge.

★   ★   ★

CYNTHIA CAME TO CHICAGO almost every weekend after that. She and Marco developed a congenial relationship. Even though platonic, it was a connection that helped Marco distance further from Saul and the nightmares he caused. Coupled with his success at work, his relationship with Cynthia gave a big boost to Marco's healing.

Marco was careful to keep his physical distance, though, ending the evenings with little besides a quick hug and peck on the cheek. He worried that Cynthia would question why he was not more physically aggressive, but all he could do was hope that she didn't force the issue. He still was not ready, and he knew it. He had no idea when he would be or what it would take to be ready to have sex again. He knew that, sooner or later, the issue must be confronted, just not yet.

Two months into their relationship, Cynthia more or less invited herself to stay with Marco for the weekend. Marco did not know what to do about that. She would certainly want to take their relationship to the next level in Marco's bedroom, and he was very apprehensive of how that might play out. He presumed that Cynthia thought of him as an experienced lover, always ready for some action. And now they had gotten to know each other as he had wished, so she would see no more reason to wait.

He could not think of an excuse for not having her stay with him. Nor did he see that he could further avoid a sexual encounter. Anything else would seem weak, hesitant, not manly, certainly not consistent with his own carefully cultivated self-image. He had to hope for the best, but he had a knot in his stomach all week, an anxiousness which increased day by day.

The inevitable nightcap on the leather couch in Marco's upscale Italian-designed living room came all too quickly. Cynthia sat very near him after she poured two glasses of wine from the bottle of expensive Brunello she had purchased for this occasion. She seemed very happy to be there, even more ready to make love. Marco was not. He gulped a wine meant to be sipped to try to calm his nerves. He felt anxious and scared, like a fifteen-year-old, pimply faced boy about to kiss his first girlfriend behind the football stadium, aroused and petrified at the same time.

Cynthia wasted no time. She took a sip from her glass, slid close, and put her arm around Marco's shoulder, bringing her face near his. Marco could smell Cynthia's intoxicating perfume, mixed with her sweet body smells, a combination which both attracted and repulsed him. He placed his hand on Cynthia's leg and began sliding it up her inner thigh, his typical first move in times past. They kissed deeply.

Cynthia sighed softly and put her free hand on Marco's crotch. She began to breathe more deeply and rapidly, moving her hips slightly to the rhythm. Marco felt nothing. The space between his legs seemed empty, a vacuum devoid of sensation. He was tense all over. His palms became sweaty and cold. He pulled away abruptly and looked at her mournfully, his self-confidence in disarray. He was embarrassed and sure his face was blood red. Words would not come.

"Marco, what's wrong?" Cynthia asked softly. "Did I do something to spoil things? Am I being too pushy?" She reached over and tenderly rubbed the back of her hand on his cheek. "I thought that all you needed was a little encouragement."

This was a crossroads moment for Marco. His sexual prowess and competency had always been a secret source of great pride for him. Never before had he been unable to feel aroused or get an erection, beginning with his first sexual encounter at age sixteen. For him, this was uncharted territory. He full well knew that his inability to perform was the consequence of his tumultuous day in Michigan. But he had not thought about how to handle a situation like this where his impotence was out in the open and revealed to his potential sex partner. He feared that healing this injury would be his greatest challenge.

What do I say to Cynthia? Just admitting to her he could not perform would be a devastating acknowledgement of weakness and a confirmation of his inadequacy. He fought to keep from swallowing his words.

"Cynthia… um, you are great," he was finally able to spit out. "Could be I am not in the mood tonight. I guess that sort of thing happens sometimes, right?" He emptied his glass of wine.

"Marco, that's okay." She paused and smiled patiently. "Sex is not the most important thing to me. As I told you when we met, your integrity is my biggest turn on. That has nothing to do with copulation. I mean, I would like to have sex with you, but just being with you is more than good enough."

Marco doubted Cynthia was being totally honest when she said that. It felt like he had just been awarded the consolation prize in a sexual performance contest. But Cynthia's statement disarmed him a little. His anxiety diminished somewhat.

"So, Cynthia, you need to know this." He moved closer and put his hand on her thigh. "I have not had sex with anyone since Michigan. Frankly, I haven't thought about it. See, I've felt comfortable and safe buried in my research." Marco surprised himself when he said that, but it felt good being honest with Cynthia. In the past, he had shied away from telling his girlfriends about his self-doubts and shortcomings. He had thought that he needed to keep up images. Maybe that was the wrong approach.

"I am sure your encounter with that witch caused you a lot of pain. What you went through would be an incredible turn off, Marco."

A twinge of Marco's protectiveness for Semantha returned. He frowned.

"Don't call her a witch. Ultimately, she was a victim too, like me. Right?"

"Witch or not, it would be understandable if you were not ready to perform in bed at the drop of a hat after going through all that. You were a sexual victim, almost like you were raped. Sexual activity got all intertwined with the threat of horrible violence against you, and you barely escaped."

Marco looked away as if in thought.

"That whole thing would have traumatized anyone," Cynthia continued. "Such a thing is not easy to forget and its consequences difficult to shake."

Cynthia's words, comforting as they were, took Marco back to Michigan and its aftermath. So many bad memories he had tried to choke off powerfully re-emerged. He covered his eyes with his hands as the tears flowed out.

"Cynthia, my dear, please understand," he said between sobs, "It's been so hard, so overwhelming. The entire experience crushed me."

Cynthia put her arms around Marco, pulled him close, and cried quietly with him. She stroked his hair gently, almost like a mother consoling her injured son. Marco felt a powerful connection to her, stronger than he had ever felt after sex. They sat together, hugging for a while, saying nothing but listening to each other breathe and feeling the beating of each other's heart.

"It's late," Cynthia finally said. "Let's go lie down together. We've had enough for one day."

They took off their clothes, got into bed, and lay motionless next to each other in the cool, still darkness.

Cynthia took Marco's hand and squeezed it. "You will be fine, Marco. You are a strong and courageous man."

Neither made any further advance on the other, but Marco felt so accepted, so relaxed, so understood. Sharing his distress with Cynthia seemed to purge him of the pain of his past experiences, making him feel lighter than air. They lay there a while in delicious silence. Eventually, they fell asleep in each other's arms, nothing erotic or sexual, just two people who cared for one another, spending the night together.

The next day, Marco awoke first. He looked at Cynthia lying peacefully beside him. He thought about his past with women he had known. Cynthia's caring and understanding in the face of his flaws and suffering had transformed him, teaching him, for the first time, what a real relationship was like.

Marco tenderly kissed Cynthia on the lips. She awoke. After her own minute of reverie, she said, "Marco, thank you for last night. It made me understand in a different way what you went through. It makes me appreciate you all the more. I feel so connected to you now." Marco smiled and brushed the hair away from her eyes. He felt exactly the same.

"Not a very good research subject, I guess."

They both laughed. But Cynthia winced and put her hand on her back as if in pain.

"Let's get up and go out to have some breakfast," Marco suggested.

"Okay, but before we go, I do have a favor to ask. My back has been killing me for the last few days. I think I strained it lifting a box of documents. Can you give me a rub down. Only a rub down. No sex."

Cynthia rolled on her stomach. Marco reached into his nightstand and took out some lotion he kept there exactly for this purpose. He applied it to her back and began kneading her muscles and relaxing them one by one. He started at the shoulders and slowly worked down the taper of her back to her round, shapely behind and then on to her thin, muscular legs.

As he worked his hands around her back, something unexpected happened. Spontaneously, he began to think about her beautiful breasts so near to his fingers, so easy to touch. As he rubbed, almost involuntarily, he began bringing his hands closer and closer to them with each movement. He thought about how sensuous it would be to massage them. He felt his penis begin to grow and harden. In a commanding, confident voice, he said, "Roll over, babe." She smiled and complied.

He began touching and rubbing her breasts. Then, still more aroused, he caressed her nipples with his tongue. Cynthia groaned ever so slightly. They kissed passionately. Marco's desire had returned. His anxiety about his ability to perform had evaporated like the dew at the first blush of the morning sun.

After making love, they lay together for a while. Then. turning to look at Marco, Cynthia spoke. "I have a rude question. You don't need to answer it if you don't want to."

"Okay, go ahead."

"How was sex with Semantha? When you were in my office, you didn't go into detail."

"It was nothing like what we just had together. I wouldn't even say you and I had sex. We expressed our deep emotional feelings for each other physically. It was beautiful, maybe cosmic is the right word."

Cynthia sat up and looked down at Marco. "And with Semantha?"

Marco also sat up and faced Cynthia. "With her, it was a carnal extravaganza magnified by the depraved circumstances in which it occurred. It was powerful and I felt gratified after it was over but in a perverted way. I thank whatever gods there may be that it was over before it began.

"Why do you ask?"

"I couldn't help but make the comparison between me and her, as strange as that may sound. What you told me relieves me of my nagging doubts."

"Nagging doubts? What were these doubts?" Marco furrowed his eyebrows and frowned.

"About how an ordinary person like me could ever match the sexual prowess of an exotic sorceress conjuring the seductive power of the Devil. About how sex could ever be as good with me as the otherworldly encounter you had with a person with one foot in the spirit world."

"And I doubted your motives."

"My motives, what do you mean by that?"

"I mean this: Whether, to you, our relationship was nothing more than your sexual conquest of a pushy female attorney. At one time, you know, I did have the power to hand your balls to you on a silver platter." Cynthia shook her head, "I was unsure where we were headed thinking about all this."

Marco gave Cynthia a long, tight hug, allowing that gesture to convey how much he understood. They laid back down and remained side by side for a while longer, immersed in their own thoughts, which each of them individually decided were premature to share.

IN THE COMING MONTHS, the relationship between Cynthia and Marco grew and deepened. They took trips to Miami, San Francisco, Boston, and other great cities. When they went to New York, it was the early spring. They picked a warm Sunday night for the obligatory visit to the Empire State observatory. Thankfully the observation deck was not very crowded. The sparkling lights of Manhattan glimmered behind Cynthia.

"I quit my job Friday, effective immediately," she told Marco. "I am now a free woman."

"Why? Thought you loved prosecutions."

"Well, as you so well know from experience, Dunland hates trying cases. He always tries to figure out some excuse to plea bargain. I was bored."

Marco nodded.

"But much more, every day when I went into that dreary old courthouse, it reminded me of the circumstances under which we met and that whole seamy situation in which you became embroiled. Rather than thinking about that unpleasant past, I want to concentrate on our wonderful right now and leave the past behind me. Behind both of us really."

She then paused and, peering directly into his eyes, said in a whisper, "Marco, I love you and have since that first night we spent together."

"I love you too, probably since I first saw you fuming in that coffee shop," Marco replied without hesitation.

"Marry me," Cynthia asked, looking a little anxious and expectant.

"In a heartbeat," Marco said with a beguiling smile.

After holding their gaze on each other's eyes for a long moment, they kissed passionately. A gentle zephyr caressed their cheeks. Both of them had found their hearts' desire.

Epilogue

A COUPLE OF MONTHS after the wedding, Frank and Marco headed out for another sail on *Provocateur*. It was a perfect day, sunny skies, a moderate southwest breeze powering the boat along at seven knots, and tame waves. The beautiful Chicago skyline provided a captivating backdrop. Plus Frank brought along a couple of bottles of Veuve Clicquot for this special day. After they were underway and settled in, he filled two large plastic flutes and put them in the drink holders.

"You know, Marco, this is the one-year anniversary of our encounter with *Blind Faith*."

"My God, didn't realize that. Seems like yesterday and an eternity ago all at once."

"So much has happened in the last year. It's a noteworthy anniversary."

"Here's to that year," Marco said. They took their glasses and touched them together.

As Marco and Frank sipped on the champagne, they recounted the lurid events which had taken Marco to the brink of disaster and back.

"Did these experiences change your ideas about mystical forces and mysterious causes, Marco?"

Marco diverted his attention from gazing at the skyline and turned his eyes to Frank.

"When we discussed this back at the time," Frank said, "you were more than a skeptic. If I recall accurately, you said something like there are no such forces or causes, only phenomena we have not yet fully quantified and analyzed."

"That is correct. I said that."

"But now that you have had this long brush with the otherworldly, I'm wondering if you think differently. So much remains unexplained. We still have no idea why the motor on this boat would not start, for example. That has not happened since despite being out in some extremely challenging situations." Marco recalled that dark, dank kitchen and his conversation with Semantha about Pappie's powers.

"Sorry, Frank. No change of mind. There was nothing otherworldly over in Michigan. Only a bunch of lunatics and sadists on parade."

"The cult leader too?"

"Ah, that eccentric old freak who got a stake in his heart? He just mesmerized those weirdos and whipped them into a frenzy about evil spirits," Marco said.

"Cummon Marco, you're being pretty myopic. He must've believed in what he was doing. If he didn't, he wouldn't have gotten anywhere, even with those strange people he got to join him."

"Believed?" Marco said, shaking his head. "Interesting word. You make his perversion sound almost noble."

"If not noble, at least he acted based on his convictions. I mean, obviously I don't know for sure, but I suspect he believed the Devil does exist, " Frank said.

"Fascinating to speculate about what in his background and experience could have led him to that unique form of insanity. We'll never know. Some researcher should do a study about how and why he landed there," Marco said.

"And you never actually saw him," Frank said.

"I saw what he created and met his so-called daughter. That's more than enough."

"What about her, where does she fit in?"

Semantha, Marco thought. What a blend of contradictions and perversions, all wrapped up in a deceptively angelic patina. She was, for sure, a tragic figure, cast about by forces sinister and benign, none of which she controlled. In spite of all she had put him through, his heart went out to her memory.

"She was only a luckless pawn in the old man's chess game," he said.

"Scary when you think about it," Frank said. "That old man's beliefs surely set off a chain of events that dragged her into a trap and almost did you in."

"No question beliefs have power. I confess, our encounter on Lake Michigan a year ago did lead to monumental changes in my life."

Marco turned away and thought for a moment. The alcohol was starting to loosen his tongue. "That's particularly alarming considering how beliefs about spiritual sorts of things are formed in the first place." Then, gesturing with his left hand, he continued like he was speaking to a classroom of new undergraduates.

"Human beings have always been pattern seekers. We look for patterns in events. When we think we have found a pattern we can't explain in ordinary terms, we tend to see if we can shape it into some sort of everlasting transcendence. That process comes out looking something like a search for a god or maybe, for this old cult leader, the Devil."

"I don't get your point, Marco."

"Beliefs are not reliable. There are no patterns, only chance occurrences, which sometimes randomly repeat themselves. That old man in Michigan was as delusional as our church fathers when he concluded that mystical, spiritual forces were at work creating these non-existent patterns. He's a perfect example of deranged thinking masquerading as reality."

"I see you haven't changed," Frank said.

Marco shook his head. "This is why we should stick with provable scientific fact. I go along with Nietzsche. He said smash the idols of otherworldly belief and search for meaning in stark, naked reality."

"That perspective ignores so much," Frank responded. "Think only about your own remarkable good luck. If all of that had not happened, you never would have met Cynthia."

"So true. And there's more. I haven't told anyone this. Please keep this to yourself." Marco placed two fingers on his lips. "The reason my data came out so well is because the accelerator abruptly supercharged and then immediately shut off when Saul caused the voltaic arc. Had it gone on even one nanosecond longer, right, it would have been just one more in a long string of inconclusive experiments. Oddly, I've gotten some notoriety in the scientific community for coming up with that innovation."

"More good luck," Frank said.

"It is, and not the first time in history that apparent genius turned out to be merely serendipity in disguise."

Frank laughed and poured some more champagne. "But I really don't get your dogged insistence on refusing to see that there could have been more at play than just measurable fact."

"Let me be clear, Frank. I would like to believe that there are mystical otherworldly forces, call it what you want, faith, religion, witchcraft, voodoo. Life would be more interesting in some ways, easier in others, right? But I just can't get there, especially based only on a couple of lucky events. Sorry."

"It's not just a little good luck. It's the intricate intersection of a mountain of apparently finite events. Our close encounter with that boat. You stumbling into that coven. Your fortunate escape. Meeting Cynthia. The unexpected appearance of the data you desperately needed. How the coven came into existence. Even the upbringing of that old man. The totality of everything which happened. All this coming together has got to be so much more than just random, unplanned coincidence."

"More than coincidence? Never. You see, what happened last summer was only a small slice of the eternity of random, arbitrary causes and effects. Like ping-pong balls bouncing off each other.

Same for everybody, me, you, everyone. All part of the never-ending series of chance happenings which make up human existence. That's how things actually work, Frank."

"It's distressing to hear you talk like that, Marco. You miss a lot of the joy of living by taking such a mechanistic view. Einstein, himself, made reference to a 'cosmic religious feeling' coming from his study of science. Think about that." Frank furled his eyebrows.

Marco smiled in a know-it-all sort of way. "Einstein was also a committed atheist. I'm not that extreme, but I am like him in one way. All I want to do is find the truth about things."

"Truth--talk about an elusive concept," Frank said, shrugging his shoulders. "One of my favorite poets, John Keats, said, 'Beauty is truth, truth beauty--that is all Ye know on Earth, and all ye need to know.' I always loved that line. Is that the sort of truth you are talking about?"

"Some physicists talk about the beauty they find in science and mathematics," Marco said as he took a long drink. "They go so far as to say that truthful equations are beautiful. Not exactly clear what they mean, but I believe they are talking about an aesthetic quality in how things work. That beauty is not incompatible with seeing everything in, as you put it, mechanistic terms. Whether beautiful or not, that is where reality lies. That's the truth I study."

"But think about it, there are many different sorts of truths, philosophical truths, mathematical truths, interpersonal truths, as you say, aesthetic truths."

Frank motioned for Marco to take the wheel while he opened the other bottle. After he filled their glasses, he continued.

"Some truths have their origins solely in emotional experiences or in art, for example, the beauty of a sunset on the Welsh coast or Beethoven's *Ode to Joy*. All these different sorts of truths combined make up the totality of the human experience. It is not possible to fully appreciate what it means to be alive without taking in all those divergent truths."

"Okay... but so what?"

"How can you say they all arise solely from simple random events? They do not, cannot. There must be qualities that fall outside of scientific cause and effect. Isn't that what you recognized when you got into that little spat with Chris and Jeannie? Remember, they wanted to discount the attraction you had for Semantha on the boat that day. Don't you recall?"

"Where is Jeannie anyway? She's missing out on the champagne. I know how much she likes it, especially the upper-end stuff." Marco chuckled and drank some more.

"She was going to come, but there was an emergency."

"At the time, I thought they were so impertinent, right." Marco was feeling the effects of the drink.

"Here's the point," Marco continued. "You know, no doubt we all have qualitative experiences of beauty, and when we have them, they seem somehow, perhaps mystically right. Could be that's what Keats meant when he equated truth and beauty."

Marco rubbed his chin as he thought about what to say next.

"In actuality, there's a more fundamental question, Frank, whether there's some sort of prime mover responsible for the flow of events we've been talking about, God, the Devil, truth, beauty, whatever you want to call it. Most spiritual belief systems try to discern one."

For a minute, Marco listened to the waves splashing against the bow. He wasn't sure he should say it but then, looking directly into Frank's eyes, he spoke: "I don't see any spiritual string-puller, either one profoundly good, or one hideously evil."

Frank raised his eyebrows as if incredulous. "If no spiritual force, what do you think makes everything happen?"

Marco shrugged his shoulders.

"Blind chance."

Marco stopped speaking. He felt he had irrefutably laid out his claim. He leaned back on the cockpit bench with his hands supporting his head. He looked to the sky.

"So, Marco," Frank asked, putting his flute in the cup holder. "Are you interested in my response? It sounds like you are way too certain of yourself to want to hear anything which contradicts what you believe, as obtuse as it may be."

"Cummon, Frank, don't be nasty about it. Sure, I want to hear what you have to say. You listened to me, right. Just don't expect me to jump on your spiritualist bandwagon as if I was some naive college freshman, ya know."

"Here's how I see it." Frank also stopped briefly as if to emphasize what he was about to say.

"Talk about being blind." He pointed his open hand at Marco. "You disregard as nothing the vast body of evidence all around supporting the existence of a creative, interventionist spirit. Instead, you stubbornly value only that which science can quantify or explain. And you do this despite mankind's total lack of capacity to experience anything beyond our remarkably puny, singularly finite sensory perceptions."

Marco turned away from Frank, looked at the skyline, and mulled over Frank's powerful statements. *No doubt he's great with his words, but could it be he is also right?* Here was a serious argument for the existence of another realm beyond the reach of scientific investigation and measurement. Possibly all that has happened in the last year, he thought, does demonstrate that there is something otherworldly somewhere in the ether. Could be arrogant to presume that only physical forces exist in the world. *After all*, he thought, *no one can prove scientifically that otherworldly forces do not exist any more than there is objective proof that they do.*

Without a doubt he had been unbelievably lucky to come through what he did and end up so well. *Is a spirit watching over me?* It would be hard to explain his astoundingly good fortune any other way. Too many ping-pong balls would need to bounce just right.

Marco spent the remainder of the voyage that beautiful day deep in thought, gazing intently at the sweet, azul water as *Provocateur* knifed gracefully through the gentle waves.

ON THE WAY HOME that night, Marco couldn't get Frank's words out of his mind. *These are complex, difficult questions,* he thought. It occurred to him that science can explain everything about how things happen, yet it ignores the why. Then, as he rounded the bend to his driveway, Marco was jolted from his musings by a disturbing sight. He thought he saw a dark figure standing in the bushes next to his front door. Whatever Marco saw quickly disappeared as soon as the headlights of his car turned in that direction. He wasn't sure, but he thought the figure had a beard shaped in two cones like Clem, the man on *Blind Faith* from exactly a year ago. Marco shuddered and a shiver ran down his spine. Whether ghost or real, Marco was terrified that a ping-pong ball may have just taken a dramatically sinister bounce. But he hoped against hope that what he thought he saw was nothing more than his imagination working overtime.

FIN

Thank You

Dear Reader,

I hoped you enjoyed your time with *A Boat Named Blind Faith*. I must let you know that writing about Marco and the changes he experienced was an immense challenge. I was so glad his attitudes toward women finally improved and that he came to realize what is really important in his life. But stay tuned because the saga is not quite over. He's got more to learn before he gets to his own happy ending. Right now, I am not sure he can get there. Partly, that depends on whether he can ever learn how to live with a strong-willed woman like Cynthia.

Since I published *A Boat Named Blind Faith,* I've gotten so many emails from readers expressing their views about Marco and how he could end up. Some thought he was a sympathetic character. Others didn't like him. I would really appreciate you telling me what you think. As an author, I love feedback. You can write to me at blindfaith1256@gmail.com and visit me on the web at BelmontHarborBooks.com.

Finally, I need to ask you a favor. If you are so inclined, I'd love your review of *A Boat Named Blind Faith* on the sales platform of your choice. What you think is so important to me, whether good or bad. Reviews are hard to come by these days. You, the reader, have the power to make or break a book through your review.

Thank you so much for reading *A Boat Named Blind Faith* and thereby spending a little time with me.

Yours in reading,

Norm Jeddeloh
Chicago, Illinois

Made in the USA
Monee, IL
10 January 2023

25022200R00142